THE
BEAST
OF CLAN
KINCAID

LILY BLACKWOOD

St. Martin's Paperbacks

This is a work of fiction. All of the characters, organizations, and events portrayed in this novel are either products of the author's imagination or are used fictitiously.

THE BEAST OF CLAN KINCAID

Copyright © 2016 by Lily Blackwood.
Excerpt from *The Rebel of Clan Kincaid* Copyright © 2016 by Lily Blackwood.

All rights reserved.

For information address St. Martin's Press, 175 Fifth Avenue, New York, NY 10010.

ISBN: 978-1-250-08473-6

Our books may be purchased in bulk for promotional, educational, or business use. Please contact your local bookseller or the Macmillan Corporate and Premium Sales Department at 1-800-221-7945, ext. 5442, or by e-mail at MacmillanSpecialMarkets@macmillan.com.

Printed in the United States of America

St. Martin's Paperbacks edition / June 2016

St. Martin's Paperbacks are published by St. Martin's Press, 175 Fifth Avenue, New York, NY 10010.

10 9 8 7 6 5 4 3 2 1

For Mom and Dad

G-O-O-D-J-O-B

Good Job! Good Job!

Acknowledgments

I feel so very lucky to be able to publish this big, exciting love story about two amazing, larger-than-life characters. I'm even luckier to be surrounded by family, friends and colleagues who are just as exceptional. Writing experts warn against the overuse of adjectives in one's prose, but I'm pretty certain that advice doesn't apply to the writing of acknowledgments . . .

To my agent, the sparkly-brilliant Kim Lionetti—thank you for being the first reader to fall in love with a tormented beast, with revenge burning in his heart, and the big-hearted heroine who saves him from all that hate. Thanks to everyone at Bookends Literary as well, for the feedback and suggestions and good-wishes.

And to my editor, the witty and astoundingly fabulous Elizabeth Poteet, thank you for your expert guidance in helping me bring Niall and Elspeth's story to life. I'm also thankful to everyone at St. Martin's Press for the stellar copy-editing, magnificent cover art (take another look at that arm!), meticulous production . . . and that super-fun RWA cocktail party!

Cindy Miles, Lark Howard, Mary Lindsey, Nicole Flockton, Shana Galen and Sophie Jordan. Beautiful, talented authors, one and all. Thanks for the pep talks, the lunches, the brainstorming, the cover conferences and road-trips. Your friendship means everything to me. To the amazing Monica McCarty, thank you for reading this book and offering your endorsement.

Lastly—but most importantly—words can't describe how much I value my family's support. When the world goes crazy, you are my anchor and I love you for it, with all my heart.

Chapter 1

Seventeen Years Before.

Flames arose outside the castle, reflecting off the stone walls of the tower room and the faces of the warriors crowded there. Some of the men cursed. Others prayed. Most remained silent. The clash of metal echoed in the night, along with the braying of distressed animals and screams.

Twelve-year-old Niall Braewick stood rigid, his hand clenched on the pommel of his sword. Being so young, he had never seen battle, but he was tall and strong for his age and had trained diligently with his weapons master. Tonight he would do whatever necessary to crush those who had betrayed his father's trust—and through trickery and deception, unleashed an unexpected attack against his *clann*.

His father, Raghnall, the Laird of Kincaid, turned from the window, his expression grave. Like his Norse ancestors he stood taller than most men and had fair hair—now threaded with silver—that fell to his shoulders. He wore no armor, only the tunic and *brat* he had worn to the day's festival, a gathering intended to foster unity with two neighboring clans. Yet once night had fallen, the Kincaid's invitation of hospitality had been betrayed in the vilest way.

Without warning, the war-chieftains Alwyn and Mac-Claren—the leaders of two smaller, once-faithful vassal clans to the more powerful Kincaids—had betrayed them, taking advantage of the laird's long-standing dispute with the king, David the Second, their ultimate goal to seize Kincaid lands.

When the laird spoke, his voice did not waver.

"There is no alternative," he said. "I must surrender."

The mere utterance of the word caused Niall's heart to stop beating. His father and his clan were renowned for their battle prowess. The histories of the Highlands were replete with tales of Kincaid valor, and their ancient and illustrious line often celebrated as the royalty of the north.

Surrender? His heart surged back to life, thudding proud and fierce in his chest.

Never!

Voices clamored all around him.

"No, my laird!" shouted the man beside him.

"We will fight—" another roared.

"Let us show the Alwyn and MacClaren clans the road to hell!"

"We can defeat them!" Niall shouted, raising his sword.

Yet Raghnall raised his hand—and all voices hushed.

"Perhaps that is so," he said, his eyes bright with hate and fire. His gaze met Niall's for a long searing moment, before sweeping away, over his men. "Perhaps we could defeat them. But not in time to save our clanspeople."

Their clanspeople. The scores of villagers who had been captured and penned inside a large barn, just within sight of the castle. Old folk. Children. Women and babes. Those who had been unable to get safely from their village of Inverhaven and inside the castle walls before the gates closed. Thankfully Niall's mother, the Lady Kincaid, was safe inside the stronghold with his brothers, eight-year-old Faelan and five-year-old Cull. However, the wives and children and mothers and fathers of many Kincaid warriors faced certain death if the laird did not comply with his enemies' demands.

"They are your families," his father said with a solemn nod. "They are my people."

His captain, Fionnlagh, a barrel-chested warrior with grizzled red beard and braids, stepped forward and answered quietly. "But you are our laird."

The Kincaid answered softly, but no less resolutely. "Which is why I must do this."

Fionnlagh shook his head and implored, palms upward, "But my lord—"

"It is *decided*," Raghnall bellowed. His voice echoed off the tower stones.

No one spoke. No one moved. Indeed, Niall felt certain no one dared breathe, including himself. He couldn't believe what he was hearing. His father would surrender. Niall's eyes blurred, stung with tears, but he blinked them away because warriors didn't cry.

The laird walked the line, pausing to peer into the face of each man. The ancient bronze brooch pinned to his plaid shone in the lamplight. The emerald eye of its wolf glimmered.

"Our clan has possessed these lands for centuries," he said. "This night will not see the end of the Clan Kincaid."

"Aye!" answered several men, their heads nodding. "*Never.*"

"*Tha . . . sinn . . . Kincaid,*" Raghnall said fiercely, turning back to walk before them again.

Niall's throat tightened, hearing the words. *We are Kincaid.*

The laird lifted one fist—and pounded it against his chest. "*Tha sinn bhràithrean.*"

We are brothers.
"Tha sinn seo talamh . . ."
We are this land.

His father recited the Kincaid vow of fealty—and Niall did as well, his heart swollen with pride.

The men joined in. Their voices unified and grew louder as they repeated ancient words learned from their fathers, who had learned them from their fathers before them.

When they were finished, a long silence held the room . . . until at last his father nodded to his captain. "Make the signal."

At the window Fionnlagh unfurled a swath of white linen so that it hung down the outside wall, and he secured it there with a stone.

A loud cheer arose in the night—followed by silence. Then came the rhythmic *thunking* of swords against wooden shields.

Thunk. Thunk. Thunk.

The ominous sound chilled Niall's blood. He feared, more deeply than he had ever feared anything before, that this night would change the course of his life forever.

Fionnlagh approached the laird, as did several others, and their heads bent in counsel. Niall caught just a few of the words spoken between them.

". . . ensure survival . . . of the clan . . ."

Thunk. Thunk. Thunk.

". . . not much time . . ."

His father nodded, with a solemn glance toward Niall.

The room became a jumble of movement, with some assisting his father in donning ceremonial garb, while others fastened Niall into an overly large quilted leather jack and strapped a dirk to his hip, and another to his leg. His father touched the Kincaid sword, displayed on its ornate wooden stand, and then nodded, at which time it was folded into a dark cloth and carried away. Fionnlagh brought three tow-headed boys into the room—one of them the captain's own son, Ian, a friend of Niall's. The other two boys were younger, and close to Faelan and Cull in age and size.

"Niall," said Fionnlagh, without meeting Niall's eyes. "Be a good lad, and give Ian your brooch."

Ian grinned at that. Of course he did. He did not *ken* what was happening. Neither did Niall, exactly, but he knew he didn't like it. Something felt wrong here. Something worse, even, than surrender.

"Why?" He clenched his hand over the circular badge, a hard bump beneath the vest he wore.

Thunk. Thunk. Thunk.

"Because you must." Fionnlagh moved closer, scowling. "Just do it, boy."

"No," Niall refused, and stepped back. "I won't."

His badge was special because of the emerald in the wolf's eye, just like his father's and his brothers'. It identified him as a son of the chief, and a descendant of two centuries of chiefs before him. One didn't just give that honor away.

Just then his brothers were brought into the room, sleepy-faced and confused, followed by his mother, her face pale with fear. Fionnlagh relieved Faelan and Cull of their brooches. Faelan complained of the loss to his mother. Young Cull was more interested in the warriors and their weapons. Niall watched as the badges were pinned on the other two boys who had been brought in moments before. Boys very similar to his brothers in age and appearance.

Now he understood. Ian was to take his place in the surrender. Ian would pretend to be him.

Thunk. Thunk. Thunk.

"Come, Niall," Fionnlagh urged sharply, his eyes intent beneath profuse eyebrows. "We haven't much time, now."

"No," Niall shouted, backing away. "I won't do it."

"You will," a deeper voice said, from behind. The Kincaid's shadow fell across Niall. "Because I command you to do so."

Large, calloused hands turned him by the shoulders and worked the badge from beneath his jack and his hand.

"I want to stay with you," Niall insisted, heartsick, feeling already half-torn away from everything he loved.

His father handed the badge to Fionnlagh. "You'll return when it's safe."

"In the morning?" he asked hopefully.

"Let us hope for that." The laird chuckled, deep in his throat, and looked at him long and hard. "But more likely, I'll be in the Alwyn's dungeon for a time. Not long, I vow." He nodded. "The courts will intervene and justice will be done. All will be as it should."

He rubbed his hand over Niall's head, ruffling his hair. The fear that banded Niall's heart loosened a fraction, because if his father smiled . . . then everything would be all right. Wouldn't it? He wanted that reassurance more than anything.

Raghnall squeezed his shoulder. "For now you must go with Deargh and keep your brothers safe."

He nodded toward a hulking, red-headed warrior who stood nearby—the same man he had chosen to train Niall in the skills of sword fighting and combat. Niall had known Deargh his whole life and held him in the highest respect.

Even so, his heart still vehemently rejected the idea of leaving. But he could not defy his father. He could not be anything less than dutiful and brave for a man he loved so deeply.

"Yes, laird," he answered, his voice thick.

"Go then." The Kincaid urged him in Deargh's direction.

Everything happened too fast. Deargh took hold of his arm and led him toward the door—

"My boy—" said a woman's voice. A blur of blue came from the corner of his eye, and soft arms came round him, squeezing him tight. The familiar scent of rosewater filled his nostrils.

"Mother!" He groaned, embarrassed to be treated like a child in front of the men.

But no one called out teasing words. Indeed, when Niall glanced over his shoulder he saw the smile had dropped from his father's lips, and that sadness filled his eyes. For that reason he did not squirm free when his mother kissed his forehead and clung to him a moment more before Deargh gently pried him away and led him toward the threshold, her tears still wet on his cheek. His brothers, after being kissed and cried over as well, followed him, nudged along by three more men who remained close behind.

Thunk. Thunk. Thu—

As they moved toward the center of the stronghold, stone walls silenced the sound.

With his brothers following close behind, Niall followed Deargh from the room and down the stairs, into the great hall that was crowded with clanspeople, around corners, through a heavy door, and down empty, narrower stairs into the shadows below the castle where he had never been allowed to explore. The air was colder here and he shivered, his nostrils filled with the scent of damp and earth. He glimpsed the dark cavern of a dungeon and a storeroom crowded with barrels, heaps of root vegetables and rows of earthenware crocks.

Perhaps . . . perhaps he had misunderstood and they would wait here until his father summoned them, when all was safe . . . hopefully, yes—*hopefully* tomorrow morning. That wouldn't be so bad. It wouldn't be like leaving.

However Deargh searched the floor, kicking aside dirt

and small stones and rushes to reveal a narrow indention, which he grasped and pulled, revealing a wooden panel that had been obscured and beneath it, a black hole of nothingness, the edge of which he sat upon.

He looked at Niall. "Follow me down."

Shoving off, he disappeared inside.

Niall did follow. They all did, only to be committed to true darkness when the last warrior did not join them, but instead, dropped the panel back into place. From above there came the sound of stones and dirt being returned into place so as to conceal their path of flight.

Niall's heartbeat increased. He was truly leaving his home. His mother and father. He didn't want to.

"All of you, follow me, now," Deargh's voice uttered from the dark. "You can't get lost, because there's only one way to go."

"I'm afraid," whispered Cull, pressing close against Niall's side.

Any other time he would have teased the little boy and told him to be a man, that real warriors didn't feel fear. Yet he too was afraid, so how could he tell the little boy not to be?

"Hold on to me," he answered, grasping his brother's small hand.

Sightless, Niall could only clench his teeth on his own apprehension and shuffle along the narrow crevice in the stone for what seemed an eternity, with Cull's face burrowed into his side, until at last their leader stopped and grunted, and with a fierce shove led them toward light. But only the faintest light, for they emerged just outside the castle through a concealed portal much like the first, onto a stony, uneven piece of ground enshrouded by mist. If his bearings were correct, they stood outside the northern wall.

"Wot was 'at?" said a voice in the darkness.

Deargh raised his hand and pressed a finger to his lips. Niall tensed, listening, and held tight to Cull.

"I dinna hear nothing," answered a gravelly voice.

Thunk, thunk, thunk.

The sound reverberated in the night, but duller and quieter on this side of the stone walls. Niall closed his eyes, and adjusted his grip on his sword, prepared to kill to protect his brothers if need be.

Suddenly a fervent clamor arose, voices shouting. The sound could only mean one thing. His father had emerged from the castle. The laird of Kincaid had made good on his intention to surrender.

Niall felt dizzied and sick.

A rush of footsteps sounded nearby, leather crunching on stone.

In the darkness, a voice said, "We doona want to miss this, lads."

"The fearsome Kincaid isn't so fearsome now, is he?" called another.

"The MacClaren will bring him to his knees."

The group of them laughed, their footsteps growing distant.

Niall exhaled through his nose, outraged. How dare those men laugh at his father, who had always been honorable and just in his dealings with all clans? How dare they set their *filthy* MacClaren feet on Kincaid lands. Hate twisted up from deep inside him and he lunged, sword raised—

Only to be snatched back, Deargh's hand in the neck of his vest.

"I'll kill them!" Niall hissed, struggling to be free. "All of them."

Faelan leapt forward. "Give me a sword. I'll help you!"

"Me as well!" said Cull, swooping out from under Deargh's arm.

"Quiet, all of you," the man growled, jerking Niall in place, as his companion warriors seized hold of his brothers. "We shall face them when the moment is right."

Deargh dragged him in the opposite direction, down the craggy incline until they and the others entered the forest. Over his shoulder, Niall peered up the hillside where wane moonlight illuminated the stone tower, above a swath of mist. *An Caisteal Niaul* . . . the castle in the clouds. His father had said he would return home soon, so why did this feel like good-bye? His brothers crowded close to his side.

"It's cold. I want to go back to the castle," said Cull, yanking on his sleeve.

"We will," Niall answered firmly.

"When?" the little boy pressed.

"Soon," he answered, but part of him doubted the words.

"I don't believe you," Faelan blurted, his face white in the night. "We're never going back."

"Never going back?" exclaimed Cull, halting, his eyes wide.

"That's not true—" Niall retorted, startled by the magnitude of fear that barreled up inside him at hearing the words spoken aloud.

"It *is* true, and you know it." Faelan glared back at him, stricken. "Why else would Mother have cried—?"

"*Silence*, all of you," commanded Deargh, suddenly standing amidst them, his large hands gripping their shoulders. "Do not speak again until I say otherwise. It is time for you to be men now, not boys. You must make your laird and lady mother proud. Do you understand?"

For so long Niall had wanted nothing more than to be a man, full grown. Now, he just wanted to be a boy, returned to his home. To his family. But they were all in danger now, and he must set an example for his brothers.

"Aye," he responded. "We do."

He strode past Deargh. His brothers followed in silence.

They walked for what seemed an age, venturing deeper and deeper into the forest, over stones and fallen, lichen-covered trunks. The air grew colder, and Niall drew his woolen plaid closer around his arms and shoulders, and helped Cull do the same as well, while Faelan scowled and refused any brotherly care. At last, Deargh signaled that they should stop. In the darkness, Niall perceived a half wall of stones, the remnants of an ancient structure.

"Rest," said Deargh, who stood watchfully, staring into the forest as did the other men, their hands never leaving their weapons.

Niall, however, could stand no longer. Och! How his legs ached, and his lungs burned. He slid down, his back against the wall. Cull slumped next to him, and within a few moments snored softly against his shoulder. On the other side, Faelan held himself apart, but over time inched closer until at last Niall grabbed the sleeve of his tunic and pulled him under his arm.

"We'll be warmer this way," he explained gruffly.

Faelan nodded. Soon he dozed as well.

Niall did not sleep. He missed his father and his mother. He missed his hound and his warm, soft bed. He stared into the mist, his heart tight and heavy, and wondered what had befallen his parents and his kinsmen.

A sound came from the trees. A rustle . . . and crack of wood.

The hair on the back of Niall's neck stood on end. The warriors silently drew their weapons. Niall shrugged out from between his brothers and stood, drawing his sword as well—

A figure hurtled out from the trees, stumbling to a halt before Deargh.

Niall recognized Angus, one of his father's men. Dark stains marred his hair, face and neck, and his yellow tunic. Stains Niall knew to be blood. He carried no weapon.

"Go," he said, gasping for breath. "*Now*. They are coming. They must not find you."

"What of our laird?" demanded Deargh.

"Our laird . . . is murdered." With a hand to Deargh's shoulder, Angus shoved past him and staggered, falling on his knees in front of Niall.

"Take . . . *this*." He pressed something circular and hard into his hands. "It is yours now."

Niall did not have to look down to know he held his father's brooch. His entire body went numb. Frozen. Through the fog clouding his mind, he heard the man speak again.

"You must survive. When you are grown, return. *Avenge* . . . the treachery done to your father. Your mother. Your clansmen. *Avenge them all*."

Those words. He did not want to hear them. His father dead? His . . . mother? It couldn't be true. His thoughts shattered. His mind couldn't comprehend.

A sound echoed through the small clearing . . . the sound of war drums and voices calling to one another.

Deargh looked to the other warriors. "You know what to do."

"Aye."

"Let us hurry."

"God bless and protect you all."

Deargh strode toward Niall. Seizing his arm, he dragged him toward the trees. Over his shoulder, Niall saw one of their protectors carrying Cull away, still sleeping, in the opposite direction. The third pulled Faelan into the shadows, as if to go elsewhere, toward the mountains—

Faelan called, "Niall—!"

The cry was cut off as if silenced by a hand.

"Don't answer," Deargh ordered. "They'll hear."

"My brothers," Niall gasped.

"We are safer apart." Deargh gripped the shoulders of his jack, his eyes wide and furious. "This way, if God wishes it, at least one of you may survive to see the morning. Tell me, boy, do you want to live or die?"

The drums grew closer. In his mind's eye he saw his father's face, intent and wise, looking back at him and he knew what he must do.

"I want to live," he answered.

Hours later as dawn broke across the distant sky, Niall sat on the narrow ledge of a stony hillside, wet and numb, his woolen brat wrapped around him like a shroud. At last, the rain had ceased. Deargh hunted nearby, having left him to attempt a small fire.

But he hadn't. Not yet. Instead, Niall stared at the brooch in his hand, and beneath it, his palm stained with his father's blood. For most of the night as they fled on foot, grief had tangled his thoughts, and the fear of not knowing his brothers' fate. Had he lost them as well as his parents?

Now, he sat still and quiet. A cold northern wind swept around him, tugging at his cowl, and filling his nostrils with the scent of rain and earth. His heartbeat, at last slowed, and his thoughts flowed crystal clear.

Lifting his head, he peered across the valley. There, in the distance, a stone tower emerged from the mist.

One day he would return. One day, he would have his vengeance.

His lips parted. *"Tha . . . sinn . . . Kincaids."*

Chapter 2

Autumn, 1387
Seventeen years hence . . .

Niall stood knee-deep in the frigid water, naked except for his plaid secured at his waist. Bending, he cupped his hands into the current and splashed his face. Straightening, he peered across the fast-moving river, swollen by days of heavy rain. Atop the stony hill above, he beheld a castle, barely visible through the trees and the morning mist.

An Caisteal Niaul. The castle in the clouds.

A vision from his dreams—one he'd almost convinced himself did not exist. Real at last.

For seventeen years he had traveled, and had grown older and stronger and wiser.

Now, he had returned to fulfill his destiny.

"What a wild stroke of luck," Deargh said quietly from where he stood behind him on the riverbank. "An invitation to visit the hearth of the very man you intend to kill."

"Luck?" Niall answered, with a slow shake of his head. A fire burned in his chest, fueled by hatred, but he had learned over the course of the years to tend its flames. How to harness strength and purpose from its heat, rather than to be consumed by it. "No, more like fate, I think. And don't forget, it's *my* damn hearth."

Deargh threw his head back, and laughed.

For weeks they had circled Inverhaven, making their way from one village to the next, doing their best not to draw attention to themselves as Niall sought, unsuccessfully, to discover the fate of Faelan and Cull, who he had long since conceded were both likely dead. Neither they nor the men who had sworn to protect them had appeared at the Greyfriars monastery in the Highland burgess of Elgin, five winters after the murders of their parents, as had been agreed upon the night they were separated.

His recent attempts to track them closer to the place that had once been their home had also failed. He had encountered only old bard songs about the murder of the Laird of Kincaid and his three sons, and ghost stories claiming they haunted the Highland countryside. What other explanation for their complete and utter disappearance could there be, besides death? Perhaps from Heaven, they now guided him . . . because two evenings before, a band of outlaws had chosen to terrorize the very inn where he and Deargh rested after having spent a fortnight outdoors. In no way amused at having their comfortable sleep interrupted, they had, in a moment's time, sent the thieves limping and bleeding into the night.

And at that moment, fate had smiled upon him, for a man had emerged from the shadows, introducing himself as Conall, the Chief MacClaren's war captain. He had informed them the MacClaren might have a need for men with their particular skills and had invited them to visit the castle at Inverhaven.

It was how he and Deargh had lived all this time—as mercenaries. *Ceathearne. Gallóglaigh.*

As a boy, Niall had served as Deargh's shield bearer, but before long he fought as well, becoming a fearsome warrior in his own right. At some point, their roles had changed. Now the aging Deargh acted more as his side warrior and counselor than his protector.

In time, Niall's skills were highly sought after by many a powerful leader. And so they had traveled and seen the world. At times, they had lived like paupers. At times, they had lived like kings. It had always been Niall's decision as to when they would return, and now that his decision had been made, after years of preparation and having obtained the assurances of necessary alliances, he would not turn back.

Now at Conall's invitation they had made their way here, encamping with their horses in the forest the night before, on the opposite side of the river from Inverhaven. Midmorning, they would find a boy in the village to carry word of their arrival to Conall, and await summons to present themselves to Laird MacClaren—one of the two men Niall knew to be responsible for the murder of his father.

And so it began.

Niall's heart beat steadily, at peace with the approaching conflict. All his life, he had anticipated and prepared for this moment. One way or another, he would prevail.

"How does it feel to be here?" asked Deargh.

Lines creased the corners of his eyes and he had some years before taken to wearing his thinning hair completely shorn, which only made him look more formidable, always a desirable trait in a mercenary.

Niall scooped up two handfuls of water and scrubbed his chest with a sliver of fragrant soap, which had been gifted to him at the inn by a fetching serving lass.

"It isn't home," he answered. "Not truly, not yet. But it will be, soon. What about you?"

That night seventeen years ago, Deargh had been a young man of twenty-nine, the same age as Niall now. A warrior to his core, he had left behind no wife or children, but his loyalty to his clan and his village had been strong and remained unbroken by the passage of time.

"It feels good." Deargh nodded and smiled, his bright gaze taking in the scene around them. "Very good. I can't wait to begin. To gather our clan. To take back our home. I only hope no one recognizes me. That is, not until I wish them to."

He gestured to his face and winked, his grin broadening with mischief.

Niall chuckled. "I don't think there's any danger of that."

It wasn't that time had aged his guardian badly. Rather, Deargh referred to the shadowy stains that covered half of his face, tattoos etched there over the years by Scottish and foreign hands. If one were to examine the symbols closely, they would find a history of their travels after they'd left Inverhaven.

"Are you hungry?" asked Deargh. "I snared two rabbits."

Niall nodded. "A moment more."

"Aye," answered Deargh. "Enjoy the solitude. It won't last for long."

He disappeared into the trees. Left alone, Niall simply stood, listening, but no, he wasn't alone. For years he'd been unable to recall his father's voice, but now a familiar rich timbre sounded all around him, woven into the deep rush of the river and the wind in the trees, full of pride and welcome. He belonged here and now that he'd returned, he would never leave.

There were so many questions yet to be answered. What happened the night his father and mother, and his kinsmen—including Ian and the other boys—were murdered? And his brothers as well. Who had found them, and when? What remained of the Kincaid clan? Would he find their remnants in the village, or had they scattered into the hillside or beyond?

Again, he looked toward the castle.

A movement caught his eye, near the base of the tower. From out of the mist appeared a woman, moving quickly along the footpath, young and lithe, with dark hair flowing over her shoulders. Despite the chill, she wore no mantle for warmth, only a simple dress of blue. His interest awakened. Even from this distance he recognized her loveliness. A pale, round face above a long neck and delicate shoulders.

Only she wasn't alone. A smaller child bounded past her—a boy in a tunic and trews, chasing a black puppy that streaked across the grass. Another woman followed, regal, tall and fair haired, and adorned in a long cloak thickly trimmed with fur.

Niall's muscles flexed with caution when other figures emerged from the mist behind the second woman—men at arms, some eight or nine of them, all dressed in a similar fashion, with ochre-colored plaids draped across their shoulders. Niall assessed the side arms each wore as best he could considering the distance. No doubt the men served the Chief MacClaren . . . although Conall, when he had met him at the village inn, had worn no such identifying color.

The taller blond woman called out to the young woman in blue, only he could not hear what she said for the distance and the loud rush of the water. The young woman halted, her shoulders visibly rigid. He could only assume she was a servant, and that she had displeased her mistress in some way. Whatever the matter, it was none of his concern, especially when his morning meal awaited.

He watched as the maid turned to accept her lady's address, and for one long moment he admired the way her hair cascaded down her shapely back, rich and shining.

Once inside the castle, he would look for her and see if she was as comely as she seemed from a distance.

Turning, he stepped out from the river and took up his tunic, shaking it free of leaves. He turned back for one last glance at the beauty in blue—

Just in time to see the blond woman strike her.

Elspeth gasped and lifted a hand to her stinging cheek. She had never—not in all her life—been struck in such a manner. Not by her parents. Not by either of her prior two stepmothers. Not by anyone.

Until now.

Elspeth's newest stepmother of a fortnight, Bridget—who was her same age, almost to a day—peered at her imperiously, with bright spots of color on her cheeks.

"Don't walk away from me when I'm talking to you," Bridget snapped. "Don't *pretend* as if you did not hear me. I will not abide such disrespect, do you understand?"

Elspeth stood frozen on the stone pathway. She had been doing exactly that, rushing away from Bridget as swiftly as her legs would carry her, pretending not to hear her calls, thinking that if she got far enough ahead they could avoid speaking to one another, because she wasn't ready yet. She wasn't ready to talk about what she'd seen.

For days, heavy rains had confined them to the castle and during that time Elspeth had been subjected to endless hours of Bridget's petty grievances. Elspeth realized her new stepmother was young and likely lonely and homesick, just as she would be one day soon as well when she married, but God spare her! The young woman's complaints were incessant.

One moment, Bridget was accusing Elspeth of undermining her authority with the servants, whom she criticized constantly. Next, she claimed Elspeth was vying to be her father's favorite, at Bridget's expense. And on, and on, and on, and now the MacClaren was ill and unable to mediate on either of their behalves.

All Elspeth had wanted was to escape the miserable confines of the castle walls and breathe and most of all, be alone—except for Catrin's company. The young girl's chattering and constant activity only annoyed Bridget. At just six years of age, her little half-sister still grieved the death of her mother—the second of Elspeth's three stepmothers—and had of late taken to dressing like a boy, Elspeth could only assume, in an attempt to gain their father's attention and approval. While the MacClaren loved his four daughters in his own way, he had never made a secret of his very deep disappointment in never having sired a son. She couldn't replace Cat's mother, but she and the child had always been fond of one another, and it was clear the little girl needed to be outside to run and play.

Elspeth looked over her shoulder to be certain the child had not witnessed the ugly sight of Bridget slapping her.

Only . . . she didn't see Cat, which worried her, because with the rains the river had risen high and the current would be dangerously strong—

"Answer me." Bridget leaned close, demanding all of her attention.

Bridget's personal retinue, a small company of warriors who had come with her to Inverhaven as part of her *tocher*, kept their distance, most of them looking off into the forest, their expressions distinctly uncomfortable.

All save for a red-haired warrior—Duncan—who stood just behind Bridget. He looked at Elspeth coldly, his demeanor very different than *before* when he'd been jovial and friendly.

Of course, things had changed since then because of what Elspeth had accidentally seen in the shadows of an alcove, in the castle's small pleasure garden, as she searched for Catrin that morning.

"Please, I must go and find Cat," said Elspeth between gritted teeth, her breath frosting the air.

She really *was* worried. She didn't hear Cat laughing or the puppy barking, only the roar of the river.

"Not until we're finished here," Bridget asserted, stepping closer and clasping her cloak at her neck. Several rings glimmered on her hand, studded with jewels. She was pretty, yes, but displeasure contorted her features into an ugly mask.

Elspeth did not shrink from her. "We *are* finished."

Dropping her hand from her still-stinging cheek, she turned and took several steps, and opened her mouth to call for Cat—

Bridget swung in front of her, blocking her way. The taller woman's chest rose and fell rapidly, her eyes bright and her nostrils flared.

"Please understand that what you saw . . ." Bridget cleared her throat. "What you saw taking place between Duncan and me meant nothing. Our embrace was . . . an innocent one. He was only comforting me because I was concerned about your father's health. Duncan is a dear friend, and has been for many years. He is my counselor. That is all. You understand, don't you?"

That wasn't true, and Elspeth knew it. The embrace she had observed had been one of unmistakable passion. *Unmistakable.* For one thing, both of Duncan's hands had been squeezing Bridget's bottom, as he lifted her off the ground against him. Not to mention all the groaning and gasping that had drawn her attention to that far corner of the garden in the first place.

Something told her that now wasn't the time to mention that.

She needed time to think about what to do. Should she inform her father of what she had seen? She didn't want to. She didn't want to hurt or, worse, to humiliate him—but how could she remain silent? She and Bridget stared at one another. The sound of the rushing river filled Elspeth's ears.

Cat, where are you?

"Yes, I understand," she said, wanting only to be free of Bridget and to assure herself that the child was safe. "May I go?"

"You're lying," Bridget accused, her eyes filling with tears. "You *don't* understand! You don't know what it's like to leave one's home and everything you've ever known—"

She choked on the words.

And just like that, Elspeth's heart did a turnabout, softening in sympathy. She did understand. She and Bridget had that in common. She too would have to marry soon, and leave behind her father and sisters and all she held dear.

Bridget's lip curled, transforming her face into one of cruelty. "—and be forced by duty to marry a *sick old man*."

Elspeth recoiled, her sympathy gone as quickly as it had come. A sick old man? Her father?

Fire blazed up from her heart. Vows of marriage were sacred and once sworn, to be treasured and upheld, not cast aside like rubbish in favor of a handsome face. The Laird MacClaren had welcomed Bridget into their clan like a queen. They all had. Yes, he had been ill of late, but he would soon recover and continue on as the formidable warrior and great leader to their clan that he had been since before her birth.

Elspeth blurted, "I can only imagine how the laird must feel to find himself married to a spoiled child, who impulsively seeks to satisfy her every trivial desire." Until this moment she hadn't replied harshly to Bridget, because she'd wanted to get along with her father's new wife, but the words rushed out in a tumble. "I know what I saw, and you can't tell me otherwise."

Her heart beat painfully fast. She hated the feeling of

being angry and losing control and, more than anything, she hated the infidelity she'd witnessed to whatever extent it had occurred. She wished she hadn't seen. She loved her father, and she wanted him to be happy. Only he wouldn't be. Not with this young, foolish woman. Not ever, and it made her sad.

"If you tell him," Bridget hissed. "I'll say you are lying."

"My father will believe me," Elspeth countered.

"He wishes you to marry soon." Bridget stepped closer, her eyes aflame. "He has told me this. I'm not without influence. I'll ensure your husband is *older* and *sicker* and *uglier* than mine."

"He couldn't be any *uglier* in spirit than you!" exclaimed Elspeth.

"Oh, you little—" Again, Bridget raised her hand high and swung down—

Only Elspeth caught her by the wrist and pushed Bridget away with such force her stepmother stumbled back against Duncan who had lunged closer, she supposed, to intercede if necessary. The faces of the warriors nearby turned to watch, but they did not move.

Elspeth glared at Bridget. "Don't ever strike me again. Do *you* understand?"

Again, she prayed Cat had not seen. Her concern for the child still foremost in her mind, Elspeth spun away and ran.

"Elspeth, wait," said Duncan.

"Come back," commanded Bridget.

But she did not. She fled over the grass, scouring the landscape for Cat. She crossed the empty meadow, descending toward the river and when she did not see her half-sister there she slowed and searched among the trees clustered near the riverbank.

"Cat!" she called, continuing on, looking this way and that.

At last Elspeth spied her at the river's edge . . . balancing on the stones, her arms outstretched and water rippling around her small, booted feet. The girl edged out farther, reaching for the puppy who had ventured onto a promontory stone and stood, wobbling and sliding, amidst a whorl of floating leaves.

"Cat, no," Elspeth shouted, leaping over a large tree root, fearful because of the strong current and the slipperiness of the stones. Cat could swim, but barely. If she fell in, the river would sweep her away. It would swallow her alive. "Don't move. I'll get him."

A log floated past, bumping against the stone upon which Cat stood—

The puppy crouched . . . and pounced onto it, paws grasping. The log rolled. The animal disappeared in a splash, then bobbed to the surface, to be swiftly carried away.

"No, don't!" Elspeth's fear heightened into terror because she knew what Cat would do. And she did. The child leapt—

Elspeth did as well, splashing knee deep into the frigid water, reaching—just missing the girl as she spun out of arm's reach, carried, arms flailing, away.

"Elspeth!" Cat cried, her eyes wide. "My puppy—"

Her small red head dipped under the water.

Elspeth dove after her. Shocked by the cold, her heartbeat staggered. After the first few strokes she could not even tell if her arms and legs moved as she wished. She glimpsed Cat's small hand raised—and strained to touch her fingers—

Only to be torn away.

The water. It dragged her—in what direction she did not know—so *fast*, churning, twisting her gown around her limbs, pitching her up—

Then sucking her down . . . down . . . down into darkness and a fear greater than she had ever known.

Its deafening roar filled her ears. She fought it. Tried to push out, but the river wouldn't let go.

Oh, Cat. No . . .

A sudden force seized her up, into the light.

Chapter 3

Elspeth coughed, expelling water from her nose and mouth, and gasped for air. A man—yes, most certainly a man of strength—dragged her toward shore, his hand fisted in the back of her gown, but she could not see him for the water and her hair streaming over her eyes.

Her feet grazed the river bottom and she stretched, trying to stand, but her boots filled full, dragging her down. She lost her footing and slipped under again. Her savior—whoever he was—wrenched her higher and closer against his body, all power and muscle, and carried her from the river, at last depositing her, palms down, on a flat expanse of stones.

Voices sounded close by, raised in alarm, and footsteps. Bridget and her retinue.

Elspeth crouched, still choking on each breath, alive and half-frozen—her thoughts frantic, her pulse racing because *Cat was still in the river*. If there was even a chance the child was still alive they had to go *now* and find her, to save her—

She opened her mouth, but only an unintelligible sound

emitted. Desperate for someone to understand, to help, she looked up at the man who had saved her.

A dark-haired stranger looked back at her, water streaming from his beard—

Over Cat, whom he held in his arms.

"My puppy!" the girl sobbed, straining over his shoulder to reach toward the river.

Elspeth's heart bounded with joy and relief.

"Cat," she croaked, leaping up and reaching for her sister.

The man's pale blue eyes looked into hers for one long, *startling* moment, before releasing the girl into her arms. Knowing the others approached, she turned from him, clutching Cat, eager to show them they had survived. Her legs, still weak and tangled in her drenched gown, faltered.

The stranger caught her from behind—fast against his chest, his arms coming around and under hers so she did not fall or drop the girl. He knelt, easing them gently to the ground.

"Thank you," Elspeth half-whispered, half-gasped, looking at Cat through tears, pressing a kiss to the girl's wet hair. It was a miracle and nothing less that both she and her sister were alive. She almost couldn't believe it was true that he had saved them both. Her heart nearly beat out of her chest with gratitude and joy. "Thank you."

Cat cried against her shoulder. "Puppy's gone."

"I know, sweet girl," Elspeth soothed. "I'm so sorry."

"Step away," thundered a voice, sharp with command.

The man's muscles tensed against her shoulders, and his arms tightened around them.

Elspeth's head snapped up. Duncan stormed toward them, his expression ferocious and his sword pointed in their direction.

Elspeth blinked in disbelief.

Bridget approached at a slower pace, surrounded by her warriors, all of whom had drawn swords and looked with outright distrust at the man behind her.

"*Now*," Duncan bellowed, lifting the sword higher, aiming its tip at the stranger.

Slowly . . . the man released her and stood. She heard the crunch of his feet on the stones as he backed away one step . . . two.

The loss of his warmth sent a chill down her spine.

Elspeth couldn't abide what she saw. Did they not realize what had occurred?

"This man saved our lives," Elspeth exclaimed. "And you think to threaten him?"

Duncan ignored her words. Instead he ventured closer, his jaw clenched, and his limbs poised for combat.

Bridget watched in silence, her gaze bright and interested.

Of course. Duncan made a show of bravery—of his *manhood*—for the Lady MacClaren. Disgust surged through Elspeth. If not for the two of them and the drama they had created, this might not have occurred at all. She would have found Catrin and her puppy sooner, before they went into the river.

Duncan scowled. "Aye, he saved your lives, but toward what end? Just look at him." His eyes narrowed on a point above her head. "Clearly, he is not one of us, but an *allmharach*—"

"A barbarian?" she repeated in disbelief. Her pulse pounding, she eased Catrin from her lap and stood between the two men. Water streamed from her hair and her gown, pattering on the stones.

Just look at him, Duncan had demanded. Yet even now, she could not summon a clear image of the man she defended. She recalled only the brilliance of his eyes, as they'd stared into hers. He had held her and Cat so gently.

He has risked his life against the overpowering current of the river, to save them. Why would he do so, if he intended them harm?

"Nay, he is not that," she concluded.

"Foolish girl, he is exactly that," Duncan spat with an arrogant jerk of his chin. "He has come down from the Dark Hills to pillage and thieve like his filthy brethren, who have already taken far too many of our livestock and horses—not to mention our women."

She, like every member of the MacClaren clan, knew of the half-naked, uncivilized warriors that reived along the edges of Inverhaven and outlying farms, absconding with animals and, yes, at least one young woman. But those attacks only came at night, and never this close to the castle. Certainly this man was not one of those criminals. Even if he was, she would not allow him to be mistreated.

"You know nothing about him," she countered, desperate to calm the confrontation. "Put away your sword and let us converse in a civilized manner." She shook her head. "What has happened to us that we can no longer offer a stranger hospitality?"

The fire in Duncan's eyes grew hotter. "Those old ways are gone. Now, in these northern lands, lawlessness rules where order and power does not. Do as I say, and hie with the child to the Lady MacClaren's side." He bared his teeth. "And let me deal with this savage, as I know is right."

"I will not," Elspeth cried.

Duncan lunged forward, and reached as if to seize her arm—

She jerked away, her back colliding into the chest of the stranger. Catrin wailed. Duncan snarled, and drawing back his arm, *thrust* his sword above her shoulder. Without thinking—she raised her hands to stop the blade—

Only to be seized by the waist and swept aside—

. . . *a blur of movement* . . .

. . . strong arms . . . flexing shoulders . . .

The sword clattered to the stones several steps away, cast there by the stranger who in a mere moment had disarmed Duncan.

All motion and sound seemed to stall. There was only the blood pounding in her ears, and the sight of Duncan's stunned and enraged face.

Then came the *hiss* of swords unsheathed as Bridget's men advanced. The stranger backed toward Elspeth—shielding her with his body.

"No!" another man's voice bellowed. "Stop."

Conall—her father's captain—appeared, dressed in a yellow, knee-length tunic and boots, his shoulder-length silver hair gleaming. A dozen more of her father's men followed and interspersed themselves among Bridget's, halting all forward movement. Breathing heavily, as if he had run all the way from the castle, Conall crossed the stones and bent to touch Catrin's cheek. The child leapt into his arms. He held her tight, murmuring a few soothing words, and rubbed a hand over the crown of her sodden head.

To Elspeth, he said, "I saw from the tower window, the two of you in the water, and arrived as quickly as I could." He exhaled. "Och, my poor heart beats so! I thought you had both certainly drowned."

"We did not," Elspeth answered, moving toward him, eager to explain. Conall's arrival did not necessarily guarantee peace. He and her father, much like Duncan, often made decisions directed at ending—and winning—a conflict, ignoring what they considered lesser matters of conscience or heart. "But only because this man saved us."

Conall's gaze settled on the man behind her.

"Aye, and so we thank him"—his voice increased from a gentle *burr,* into a thunderous boom, as he turned back toward Duncan and the others—"*by threatening him with a sword*?"

The muscles along Elspeth's shoulders relaxed a bit, realizing Conall did not consider the stranger an enemy. Cat wiggled, and he lowered her to stand on the stones. The child hurried to Elspeth and wrapped her arms around her waist.

After a long moment of extended glaring at the men, Conall shrugged and chuckled. "Not that I'm worried about this one. He can take care of himself—and all of you. You'll see. Aye, ye almost did, and you would have been mightily sorry!" Serious again, he said, "This man is a guest invited here by me, on behalf of the MacClaren. From this moment forward, you will treat him as such."

Relief coursed through Elspeth. A guest? New questions crowded her mind. Who *was* the man, and why had her father invited him here? Her gaze flickered aside, drawn by the towering figure, but morning sunlight shone in her eyes, obscuring all but the haziest outline of his features . . . the powerful burl of his shoulder . . . the masculine cut of his jaw.

"He made no such invitation known," gritted out Duncan, scowling, and bending to seize up his sword.

"You didn't give him a chance," Elspeth answered.

"Forgive Duncan's misunderstanding," Bridget gushed, moving forward and wearing a brilliant smile. "He is sometimes overzealous in ensuring my protection. But of course this man—our *guest's*—valor must be rewarded."

She removed a plaid from the shoulder of one of her men, and approached, her gaze never leaving the stranger as she moved past Elspeth and Catrin, without extending any measure of concern or comfort to them.

Turning to watch her stepmother, Elspeth, for the first time, truly took in the sight of the man who had saved her.

Her breath caught in her throat.

A barbarian. Yes, that word did describe his appearance.

He stood with every inch of his muscular body bare to her eyes, save for his hips, which were covered with a wet kilt that lay slick and dark against his powerful thighs. Tattoos decorated his skin, draping like armor over each of his shoulders, and down one arm. A beard, as black as kohl, covered the lower half of his face. He wore his hair much longer than the men of her clan, drawn back on either side in rough braids. It clung damply against his neck and chest, rising and falling as he breathed. He looked dangerous and fearsome—and beautiful. He was like nothing she had ever seen.

And thrillingly, he looked at *her* over Bridget's shoulder, his eyes the color of a frozen loch. Yet somehow their attention did not make her feel cold at all. Indeed, her cheeks flushed and she forgot all about her wet clothes and chilled skin.

"I am the Lady MacClaren," Bridget announced grandly, lifting the plaid toward his shoulders. "Allow me the honor of welcoming you to Inverhaven, and granting you this small comfort."

Did Elspeth imagine it, or was there something seductive in the tone of Bridget's voice—something possessive, as if she already claimed him for her own? Elspeth remembered what she'd seen that morning, her stepmother and Duncan in a tight clasp of passion. For a moment she imagined Bridget in the stranger's arms instead. A shard of misery struck straight through her heart.

Yet, at her offer of the plaid, the stranger lifted a staying hand. Bridget froze, the garment hanging down between them. Silence hovered everywhere, save for the rush of the river.

For the first time, he spoke. "I would have you offer it to your maidservant and the child."

His voice was like a warm fur blanket on a cold morning . . . rich, deep, and pleasing. Only his speech was not that of a barbarian. Rather, he spoke with the polished pronunciation of the king's envoys who sometimes visited the castle.

Bridget's eyes widened, bright as crystals, and she glanced at Elspeth, then back to him, an unkind smile curling the corner of her mouth. "Who is it that you mean, good sir? My . . . *maidservant,* you say?"

Elspeth flushed. He meant her, of course. He thought she was a servant, a mistake that wouldn't bother her at all if not for Bridget's sly taunt. She clenched her teeth down on an angry reply.

"*Her,*" the man answered, and with a lift of his bearded chin indicated Elspeth. "The one who went into the river to save the child." He paused . . . and when he spoke again, the tone of his voice had deepened. "The one whose cheek still bears the mark of your hand."

He sought to champion her. Elspeth melted just a little inside then. But relations were not good between her and Bridget, and his words would not improve them.

Bridget stood as still as a stone. Then, like a porcupine she bristled, her back and shoulders going straight. Exhaling, she stepped away and with a cold glare all around, thrust the plaid dismissively against Elspeth's shoulder as she moved past, toward the shore and the company of her men.

Elspeth clasped it there for a moment before wrapping the woolen cloth tight around Catrin. She offered the stranger a look of thanks.

Conall took Bridget's place at the side of the MacClaren's "guest," but glanced with concern at Elspeth's cheek.

To the stranger he said, "Welcome and thank you for what you have done here today. I apologize for this poor welcome. On behalf of the clan chief of the MacClarens, please accept his invitation to the castle where there is a fire, dry clothing, and a warm meal."

Bridget and her men left them, disappearing into the trees. The stranger watched until they were gone, at which time his stance relaxed and the hard gleam in his eyes lessened.

He replied to Conall, unsmiling. "I accept your offer of hospitality, but later, if you will. You remember Deargh. I want him present if we are to discuss arrangements."

The corners of his eyes bore few creases from age, and his torso and limbs were lean and taut. He was a young man. Younger than she'd first believed, and she wondered what his face looked like under his beard. Would he be handsome, or did the beard hide scars such as the ones she spied on his abdomen and shoulder?

Conall nodded. "At nightfall, for the evening meal, then. I and my laird will expect you. Bring your companion and your horses as well. And no need to swim this time." He gestured upriver, and chuckled. "Go by way of the bridge, just north of here. It will take you straight into the village, and you can follow the road to castle gate."

Catrin rushed to Conall's side and pulled him a few steps toward the river, woefully recounting the loss of her puppy.

The stranger looked at Elspeth again. A few steps, and he came to stand just inches from her, so close she felt the warmth radiate from his bare skin. She looked into his eyes and her pulse surged, beating faster.

"You are well, then?" he asked.

"Yes," she answered, breathless, struggling not to lower her gaze to the droplets that glistened on the bare skin of his shoulders and chest. "Very well."

"And the little one?"

"She is well also," Elspeth answered, looking up into his eyes. "Just sad about her puppy. Thank you for saving us. I will tell my father what you did."

"Your . . . father?" the stranger repeated in a low voice, his gaze fixed on her lips.

She nodded, blushing, for now he would learn that she was not, after all, a servant. Which unfortunately would likely end any flirtation between them, which was well and good because as Bridget had so *kindly* reminded her, her time for idly flirting was surely about to come to an end. Not that he was flirting with her, or she with him.

She nodded. "The MacClaren is my father."

The stranger stared back at her.

"Is he, then," he murmured.

There was something intimate in the tone of his voice that made her go weak at the knees. His gaze swept lower, over her body, over curves that she knew would be plainly revealed by her wet gown. Her cheeks flamed hot but she did not turn or shrink away. Rather his attention made her feel lovely and admired.

Conall answered, "Indeed. She is his *eldest* and much beloved daughter." His voice carried a gentle warning, no doubt intended to separate them. He neared, holding Catrin's hand. "The child is his daughter as well. Our clan chief will be most grateful for what you have done."

"No thanks are necessary," her father's guest answered, stepping away. "I am simply pleased they are both unharmed."

"Tonight then," said Conall.

"Aye," he said quietly. With a nod to Conall, he turned and strode toward the river and without hesitation, ventured thigh deep into the water before sinking in. Immediately, the current swept him downstream, but with a powerful turn of his arms he crossed toward the far shore.

Conall chuckled admiringly. "Oh, to be young again. Hurry now, we've been here far too long." Briskly, with a raised hand, he urged them away from the river, pausing a moment to remove the plaid from his shoulder and to tuck it around Elspeth's. "Let's get the both of you inside where it is warm before you fall ill. By now, your father must have heard what happened and he will be beside himself with worry."

As they walked his glance touched on Elspeth's cheek, and his lips took on a displeased slant.

"Bridget," he muttered darkly. "Tell me, what disagreement occurred between the two of you."

"I don't wish to talk about it," she answered quietly. Her emotions still welled too high and she hoped to summon some measure of calm and wisdom before deciding what to say to her father.

"Nonetheless," he asserted. "I know the MacClaren would not stand for any abuse. I will speak to him."

"Please, do not," she urged with a hand to his arm. "I will speak to him myself."

They passed into the trees, where the other MacClaren warriors lingered, talking among themselves, waiting to escort them to the castle. The men's faces were all familiar, as much her family as her own and they now looked at her and Cat with the same concern and care loving uncles and brothers might, in the aftermath of a harrowing event.

"God be thanked that the both of y' were saved," said one, his relief apparent in the hushed intensity of his voice and the paleness of his skin. He nodded jerkily at her and repeated, "God be thanked."

Another reached out to give Cat's head a playful rub. "When I saw y' in the river in the clutches of that giant, lass, I thought for sure one of those kelpies old Murdoch is always warning the bairns about had gotten hold of ye."

Old Murdoch being her father's bard.

"But the giant isn't a kelpie," exclaimed Cat, peering up through tearstained eyes. "Because he saved us rather than drowned us!"

"Aye, that I see," he answered. And more quietly, "A true miracle, that."

Elspeth glanced over her shoulder and saw the man emerge from the river, his dark hair streaming down his powerful back. He gripped the sagging, sodden kilt at his hips, and with a tug of his hand, yanked the garment free—

She caught only a momentary flash of his muscular buttocks before he was gone, into the trees.

She closed her eyes, suddenly feverish, and turned back toward the castle. Conall and the others proceeded, oblivious to what she'd just observed. It wasn't the first bare bottom she'd seen. After all, the Highlands could be mightily windy . . . but my, somehow, seeing his had made her feel differently. Flustered in the nicest possible way.

"Who is that man?" she asked him, slipping her hand into Cat's, so as to keep her close. "What is his name?"

"His name?" he repeated. "I'm not sure men like him have names, or perhaps it is best we simply don't know them." He paused . . . and shrugged. "But there were soldiers passing through the village where I encountered him. They knew him—or, knew *of* him, I might say. They had witnessed him in battle and were . . . remarkably impressed by his skill. They called him *béist*."

Elspeth's pulse increased.

"Beast!" she murmured.

Chapter 4

Conall nodded. "He is a mercenary, Elspeth. A *gallow-glass*. A professional warrior with no clan, and no loyalties, other than to serve whoever has the ability to pay him best."

"I see," she said, suffering a twinge of disappointment that he was only a soldier, and therefore would be deemed an unsuitable suitor, at least in the eyes of her father and their clan. Perhaps she suffered more than just a twinge.

Mercenaries were nothing new. Her father, like many clan leaders, hired them from time to time to defend their borders and their people—not only from the barbaric hill reivers, but more recently from the Alwyn, a rival clan chief whose lands bordered the MacClarens. Once an ally, he now seemed intent on provoking a confrontation.

But this man—the *béist*—was different than the others. Her intuition told her that. For one thing, he was undeniably *moighre*. Very handsome. At least the sort of handsome that made an impression on her. And according to Conall, other men considered him legendary for his fighting skills. Obviously he had power and strength—but Elspeth knew full well no warrior became legend on strength alone. There had to be intelligence as well, which she had heard distinctly in the words he spoke and observed in his blue eyes.

Conall pushed aside a wayward branch so that she and Cat could move past. "While I'm glad he was here to save the two of you, it is best you don't speak to him again."

Yes . . . Elspeth agreed, with regret. In truth, it was probably best that she not think of him again. What useful purpose would that serve?

And yet . . . as twilight fell, a nervous anticipation grew in the pit of her stomach. She felt intensely curious to see the man they called *béist* again, though she knew she shouldn't want to.

"And which gown will you wear this evening?" asked her maid, Ina, who stood willowy tall at Elspeth's trunk, her vibrant red hair hidden for the most part beneath a plain linen headscarf.

That was simple. She would wear the green dress if she were dressing for him.

"You choose," Elspeth answered, with a melancholy sigh, plucking at the sleeve of her chemise. "It matters not to me."

"The green, I think," Ina answered, reaching inside. "It will be warm and soft on this cold night, and it flatters your figure very nicely."

Elspeth suspected that to be true, from the admiring glances she received from the men of the castle when she wore it. The green gown was closely fitted, with delicate gold lacing in the front and back. Not that it mattered how she looked. She could be bald-headed and have a mouthful of rotten teeth, and it would make no difference at all. Soon she would be married to a man of her father's choosing, a man with holdings and influence. Someone who would swear to be an ally for her father and the MacClaren clan during times of prosperity and conflict. Her very generous dowry would ensure the interest of such a man.

Her husband wouldn't be a mercenary soldier, no matter how skilled or well-spoken he might be. Her stomach clenched with regret. Not that the *béist* was the man she wanted to marry, but wouldn't it be nice to decide for herself? Wouldn't it be nice to . . . fall in love?

Ina lay the gown on Elspeth's bed, and loosened its laces.

"I can dress myself tonight, Ina," said Elspeth. Ina was some ten years older than Elspeth, and happily married to a MacClaren stableman. "Spend your evening with Clach."

"I'll see him later," Ina answered, and taking Elspeth by the hands, urged her to stand. "I'm happy to be able to spend this time with you. After all, how many more times will we have like this together, before you leave Inverhaven to start your life with a new husband?"

"That is true," Elspeth answered softly. She raised her arms and Ina slipped the gown over her head.

Ina straightened the seams at her shoulders. "You seem very quiet tonight."

"It is nothing." Elspeth looked into her eyes. "Just that life is changing, and will change even more very soon."

The maid touched Elspeth's cheek, affectionately. "I have never heard you complain about your future."

"And I do not complain now." Elspeth shrugged. "It is my duty by birth to marry for my clan. I have been raised to it, and I understand the reasons why."

Ina's hands deftly tightened the laces at the front of the gown. "Are you . . . afraid?"

"Perhaps just a little. Only because I do not know what to expect."

"Perhaps you will already be acquainted with the man you wed," the maid said reassuringly.

"Perhaps he will be a stranger."

"Maybe he will be young and handsome." Ina grinned hopefully.

"Or old and *smelly*," Elspeth countered facetiously.

The older woman's features softened. "I hope he will be kind.

"What if he is . . . indifferent?" Elspeth raised her hands. "What if he has a *mistress*?"

Ina gasped. "What if he has *three eyes*?"

They both laughed.

"I think it is normal to feel the way you are feeling." Ina moved to the back, and finished the laces there.

"I *do* look forward to having a husband, and children. A family of my own." Elspeth nodded. A family, yes. She did want that. "I will do everything in my power to be happy and content."

"Unlike Bridget," Ina murmured.

Ah . . . yes, Bridget. Elspeth's stomach twisted in anxiety. Tonight, she had no other choice but to seek out her father and tell him privately about what she had seen take place between Lady MacClaren and Duncan. It gave her no pleasure, but what choice did she have? She couldn't just remain silent.

There'd been no opportunity to speak to the MacClaren alone this morning after they'd returned from the river. He'd been so relieved she and Cat were safe, and had listened carefully about how they had been saved by the mercenary, but all too quickly he had grown weary and had retired to his chambers. She hoped to find him alone for a few moments before the evening meal began, if he was well enough to attend.

"There," said Ina, stepping back to admire her. "You look lovely, which is only fitting given the occasion."

"What occasion is that?"

"Everyone belowstairs is talking about the man who saved you. He will be here tonight, will he not? You must take extra care to make him feel welcome."

Just remembering the way he had looked this morning—intense, drenched, and powerful, with the river rushing behind him—made her pulse pound with excitement. Such anticipation, when in truth, they probably wouldn't even be allowed to speak more than a few polite words. Conall had already warned her off speaking to him.

She sighed crossly. "I do believe it will be Father and Conall who entertain him. And Bridget."

"But certainly you will at least greet him, in a hospitable way."

Yes. She would at least be allowed that, before being sent to sit at the far end of the table, like a little child with her younger sisters.

She was glad Ina had chosen the green gown. No matter how fleeting her interaction with the mercenary, she wanted to look her best. Suddenly, it seemed very important that when she saw the man again tonight that she look very different than the wet and shivering, blue-lipped girl he had pulled from the river. She wanted to meet him as herself this time.

She wanted to meet him as a woman.

Ina retrieved a comb. "Now sit and I will fix your hair—"

"Oh, please! Let me!" declared another voice. It was Mairi, Elspeth's twelve-year-old half-sister.

As the eldest, Elspeth had been given her own private chamber just off the bower, the larger room where her younger half-sisters passed much of their time and slept each night. Mairi often joined her before the evening meal to help her dress or to fix her hair.

"Yes, come, Mairi," answered Elspeth. Looking at her maid, she raised her eyebrows teasingly. "*Clach.* We don't need you here. Now, go."

"If you insist." Ina handed the comb to the girl, a happy flush rising to her cheeks.

The thought of spending time with her husband clearly gave her pleasure, which made Elspeth glad for her, but wistful for the same experience.

When Ina had gone, Mairi smiled and gasped. "That is my favorite gown of yours!" She urged Elspeth to sit on a stool. "It's *perfect* against your skin and with your dark hair. It also makes your bosoms look *divine*. I hope I have bosoms like yours one day."

"*Mairi*." Elspeth laughed, though she was not at all shocked.

A thin rail of a child on the precipice of maturity, Mairi was fascinated by all things womanly and wasn't shy about voicing her thoughts and curiosities.

She skimmed her hands over Elspeth's unbound hair. "I think a circlet of braids, perhaps intertwined with some of that gold cording, and the rest left falling down your back? Do you agree?"

"Whatever you choose," answered Elspeth, with an encouraging wave of her hand.

Another girl entered just then, her hair as fair as Mairi's, dressed in a linen undertunic and woolen stockings, seventeen-year-old Derryth. "Elspeth, I need to borrow your red shoes. I can only find one of mine. I do believe Cat's puppy ate it."

Elspeth turned to her and said in a quiet voice, "Don't talk about Puppy so loudly, where Cat can hear. She is still very sad and you complaining about him will only upset her more."

Derryth breezed past her, her pale hair rippling behind her. "She's not here, so she can't hear what I say, now can she?"

"What do you mean, she's not here?" asked Elspeth.

"She's gone—belowstairs, I'm sure. I don't know." She

bent over Elspeth's trunk, and rummaged until she straightened again, holding two red leather shoes in her hands. "I can't watch her all the time."

Elspeth said, "You know she isn't supposed to just go wandering about without someone to watch her. She gets into trouble."

"You mean she gets into trouble with *Bridget*." Mairi made a face.

It had been a very difficult afternoon. At some point when no one was watching, Cat had cut all of her hair off so she now looked even more like a boy, which had infuriated Bridget.

"Yes, she gets in trouble with Bridget," Elspeth conceded. "Mairi, hurry, I need to find her. Just forget the gold cording, if you will."

"I wouldn't, if I were you," said Derryth in an I-know-something-you-don't-know tone. "You should look your very best tonight."

"Why do you say that?" Elspeth asked.

Derryth's face lit up, as it always did when she had all the attention in the room. "Because the maid who brought the linen a moment ago told me the kitchen had received instructions from Bridget that tonight's meal cannot be just a meal, but instead must be a feast. There are going to be special visitors."

"The man who saved you and Cat today," exclaimed Mairi.

"Not only the barbarian," Derryth coyly replied.

Elspeth frowned. "He's not a barbarian."

"That's not what I heard," she teased, leaning forward, before backing toward the door.

"Who told you otherwise?" Elspeth demanded.

"All the maids are talking about him. He was seen in the village this afternoon. They said he's terrifying, with tattoos and Devil-black hair all in braids that fall down his back. Yet for one so terrifying, they all seem very flustered and excited that he will be a guest here." Derryth shrugged—then *winked*. "But he is only a soldier. What I must tell you is that the maids also said Father has invited a number of potential suitors to pass the night."

"Suitors?" A trickle of alarm went down Elspeth's spine. In a blink, it felt as if the four walls of her room closed in. Why hadn't she been told?

Mairi excitedly squeezed her shoulder. "Perhaps your future husband is arriving even now." Yet it seemed as if her voice came from the end of a dark tunnel.

"And one never knows—perhaps even mine," declared Derryth excitedly, before disappearing again into the bower.

Elspeth shook off the feeling of unease. Of dread.

Suitors. She would have liked to have been informed. But she would accept her future bravely, and not hide in her room like a frightened child. She waited impatiently for Mairi to finish braiding and coiling her hair, with the gold cord and the threaded pearls that had once belonged to Elspeth's mother, and when she was done together they went belowstairs.

Voices sounded, loud and boisterous. The lively sound of a lute and a harp carried throughout. The great hall of the castle was indeed more crowded than on most nights, and yet she did not enter or look too closely at the faces there to see who might have been invited by her father to offer for her hand. She would know the answer to that question soon enough.

She bent toward her sister. "See if you can find Cat, and take her to the table. I need to speak to Father alone for a moment."

"About your suitors?" Mairi's brow creased. "Oh,

Elspeth, it's exciting to think of you marrying, but I don't want you to leave me. Not ever." The young girl took both of her hands and squeezed them tight.

"It's all very unsettling, isn't it?" said Elspeth, squeezing back. "For me as well. But I'm going to speak to him about something else."

"About what?" the girl asked, tilting her head upward.

"About *something*." Elspeth widened her eyes at the girl, and grinned, playfully letting Mairi know the subject was none of her concern.

"Oh, very well!" Mairi rolled her eyes, and ventured off into the throng. "I'll see to Cat."

Elspeth turned her attention to finding her father. Usually the MacClaren remained in a private room near the great hall, speaking to his counselors until almost time for the evening meal, at which time he would make his entrance with Bridget, and greet his men and his guests before joining the rest of his family at the head table.

She prayed he was alone now. Turning the corner, she found that he was. For a moment she stood on the threshold, still and silent, looking at him sitting in his chair, his gaze fixed on the fire instead of the scroll of parchment in his lap. So far away, and withdrawn to a place in his mind, as he had seemed so often of late.

Kermac MacClaren had once been young and strong and full of vigor. Elspeth remembered those times, though distantly, and often heard their history repeated in the songs sung by their old bard, Murdoch. Perhaps it was her own sentimental memories of the past, but after her mother's death his spirit seemed to have dimmed, and never fully revived as strong as before.

Affectionate and loving in one moment—and sharp and distant in the next—he wasn't always the easiest man to love, but she loved him anyway and worried over his happiness and what the MacClarens would do when inevitably he was gone, as there were no clear successors to his chieftaincy. No son or brother or nephew, and Conall, the warrior he had relied on for so long as war captain and council member, was just as old as he.

With his recent bouts of illness, the MacClaren clan council had out of caution pressed Kermac to name a successor, and yet he had stonily resisted, finding fault with every candidate set before him. She knew all this because she attended every meeting of the council. She also knew that his refusal had sent a ripple of unease through his people—and if Elspeth's intuition was right, discontent in the more ambitious men of the clan. Despite the smiles that continued to welcome her each day, and the outward displays of fealty everyone displayed toward her father and his family, she sensed that doubt, worry, and jealousy hovered like black shadows in every corner of the castle.

"Father," she said, entering the long and narrow room. Two large sconces burned at either end, in addition to a well-tended fire. Above them, a vaulted ceiling cleaved upward, supported by sturdy timber beams. Of all the rooms in the castle, it was her favorite, because she found it the most impressive for the history and beauty it displayed. At the same time, the room offered privacy and comfort, and reminded her of their old home—a smaller and simpler place where life had been so happy—at least in the memories of a little girl. Sadly, her mother had died not long after coming here, to this much finer castle and the wide, sweeping lands that had been awarded to her father by the same king he now despised.

"Daughter." With a huff of air from his lips, and visible effort, the MacClaren stood from his chair and reached for her, smiling out from a closely trimmed beard, his once brown hair now mostly taken over by gray. Tonight he wore a rich robe of dark blue, trimmed with fur, and a gold chain at his neck. Despite his age, he was still imposing and yes—handsome.

"You are feeling better?" she inquired.

"Yes, much," he answered heartily, though she could not help but take note of the dark shadows that underscored his eyes and that the hollows of his cheeks appeared to have deepened, nor could his smile mask the tension that surrounded him like a dark storm cloud.

Embracing her, he pressed a kiss on her forehead. "I'm glad you have come. There is something I have put off speaking to you about that can wait no longer." He gestured that she should take the armchair beside his, which she did, and they sat side by side.

"Might it have something to do with finding a husband for me?" she asked, her voice more strained than she would like.

His smile slanted sideways. "Aye, lass, so you have heard?"

"Word travels quickly through a castle."

He nodded slowly. "I should have spoken to you before now." His expression softened with tenderness. "It's just that this old man doesn't like the idea of his dearest daughter leaving him. You are so much like your mother. I have kept you here with me this long only out of selfishness, to comfort myself. Forgive me. I know you must want a husband and bairns of your own."

"I'll stay as long as you wish." Elspeth squeezed his arm. "And yet if it is time for me to marry, I will not refuse."

They were the words she knew she ought to say, and she meant them, though her heart was not without desires of its own. Unbidden, the memory of the mercenary came into her mind.

"That's my daughter, fair and dutiful." He reached and touched a tendril of her hair, the smile fading from his lips.

"You know that for some time the Alwyn has been escalating discord between our clans, and making assertions that much of what now belongs to the MacClarens was intended for him—"

Her temper sparked, and her spine went rigid. "Aye, based upon some old map we have not had the benefit of seeing for ourselves."

His eyes darkened. "I fear he will formally petition to have the property reapportioned—"

"No, Father," she insisted reassuringly, reaching to squeeze his hand. "The map, if it exists, is most certainly falsely put forth. A forgery or some such, to support a nonexistent claim. Secondly, too much time has passed. To ask for a reapportionment now would be a complete folly on his part."

The laird nodded. "It would be, yes—if he did not have such a powerful ally in Alexander Stewart."

Her heart grew heavy at hearing the Earl of Buchan's name, because it reminded her that her family and clan would not be allowed to simply live their lives. There would always be unwelcome interference from faraway Stirling or Scone or Edinburgh, in some form or fashion.

"Any alliance with Buchan is a pact with the devil," he responded bitterly. "His alliances change like the wind blows." He rubbed his creased forehead, as if soothing a sudden flare of agitation, and burst out with a rush of heated words, "Worse yet, I have learned that Buchan and the Alwyn have formalized an alliance, by way of a betrothal between the earl's ward and the Alwyn's son Hugh."

Elspeth's stomach clenched at the import of his words.

"That is indeed troubling," she murmured. Buchan—the youngest of Robert the Second's sons—held great sway over his father who had the power to dissolve clans or force them to renounce claim to their lands as punishment for rebellions or perceived slights.

Her father leaned forward in his seat. "And so, it seems the Alwyn has the devil on his side, and we find ourselves with very few guardian angels. We must do what we can to bolster our defenses, and our alliances, so that we can weather any challenges or attacks that may come upon our clan."

He nodded, and grinned, albeit a bit sadly. "As for the matter before us, for some time now I have been approached by men offering all sorts of promises in hopes of having you for their own—"

Not just her, but her *tocher*. Her father had promised her a generous dowry that included the old MacClaren properties and stronghold, where her family and their clan had lived before relocating to Inverhaven, after the crown rewarded her father with its extensive lands for his support in the regional tumult that had once divided their corner of the Highlands. Those had been different times.

He sighed. "They are all unworthy of you, at least according to the overly critical eyes of a loving father, but the time has come that I must think more with my mind, which is strong, and not my heart, which has always been weak where you are concerned." He looked at her a long moment. "However, I want it to be you who chooses from this . . . narrowed selection of suitors." He raised his hands, holding them close together. "I want you to be happy."

His words gave her some measure of solace. She would at least have some say. "May I ask whom you have invited?"

She was almost too afraid to hear the answer.

"Ah . . . that." He lifted a finger. "Even I do not know. Your stepmother, the Lord bless her, has put herself in charge of selecting the most promising candidates from those set forth by the council, and I agreed because she is a woman, like you, and would do a much better job at matchmaking than I."

At hearing this, a prickling sensation of alarm arose on the nape of her neck. *Bridget*?

"Like you, she is very astute in matters of diplomacy." He nodded, and eased back into his chair, oblivious to her concern. "There are only so many men in these *hielands* worthy of my daughter's hand, who would meet with the approval of the MacClaren council. I'm certain their names and faces will be familiar. Perhaps the Lady MacClaren will tell us when she arrives momentarily."

A loud burst of laughter came from the direction of the great hall. Shadows flickered on the wall as several of the laird's most trusted hearth warriors approached the door, as they did each night in preparation of escorting him and Bridget to dinner—which meant Bridget would be here any moment.

It was now or never, she realized, feeling anxious now, about speaking the words. "Father, there is also something I must speak to you about."

"What is it, child?"

Though it felt as if a large stone weighted her soul, she forced the words out. "It gives me no pleasure to tell you of this, but it is my duty as your daughter."

The laird's brows furrowed in concern and he leaned toward her. "Go on."

Elspeth swallowed hard and cleared her throat. "This morning, I witnessed something very troubling take place. Between the Lady MacClaren and her man, Duncan—"

The MacClaren nodded sharply, and held up a hand, as his face transformed into a scowl. "Yes. I know." He nodded. "She, too, came to me with this."

Elspeth's breath caught in her throat. "She . . . did?"

"Aye, lass." He shifted in his chair, as if uncomfortable. "She told me that this cur Duncan"—his lip curled—"had forced unwanted attentions on her this morning, and that she had fought him off."

That wasn't right. Elspeth had seen them. There had been no struggle. No imposition by Duncan. And yet she clenched her teeth tight and listened.

Her father closed his eyes, visibly seething. "She begged that I not kill him for the slight—as his family has long been respected in her clan, and that I instead remit him to her father for punishment. I . . . agreed, eventually. What is important is that he is gone, and he's not ever coming back, so you don't have to worry that he shall harm or dishonor your stepmother."

A shadow fell over them. Elspeth looked up and found Bridget staring at her. "You're discussing all the unpleasantness that occurred with Duncan." She lifted an eyebrow. "I told your father you had witnessed his shocking transgression against my person, and that you would testify against him if necessary, but the laird did not wish to distress you further, loving father that he is." She cast a sweet smile in the MacClaren's direction. "Come, my love, our guests will be arriving soon."

With a hand beneath his elbow, Elspeth helped her father stand and walked with him toward Bridget.

"I assume your father has informed you that your betrothed might very well be a guest here tonight?" she said, her pale hair shining in the candlelight.

"Indeed he has," Elspeth answered woodenly. "Can you tell me who has come? Whom you have chosen for me?"

Bridget laughed, deep in her throat. "And spoil the surprise?"

"What a wicked woman you are, to tease my daughter so," the laird chuckled in a lighthearted tone and escorted Bridget toward the door. She wrapped her arm into his, and glanced back over her shoulder at Elspeth, with a gaze that was both dark and punishing.

"It would seem that I am," she said.

Elspeth followed, dreading the moments to come, but reminding herself that her father had told her she would have a choice. She could rely on his assurances. He had never given her reason not to. Taking heart in this, she followed them to the great hall and entered the room behind them. A cheer went up at the laird's entrance, and the music of the minstrels spiraled into a triumphant and happy tune. Only *she* didn't feel happy. She followed them down the center aisle toward the dais.

Just then, Cat bounded out from the crowd, laughing and carrying a wooden sword, only to come face-to-face with her father and Bridget. Barefoot and dressed in a tunic and short trews, her roughly shorn hair only made her look more unkempt and wild.

Bridget stepped toward the girl. "Oh, you misbehaving child. Come here *now*."

The child backed away—bumping into a heavy wooden candelabra ablaze with lit candles.

The fixture teetered and *toppled*—but Conall lunged forward and caught it. Even so, several candles fell to the rushes, where others retrieved them, quickly stamping out the flames.

Cat disappeared into the crowd. Bridget turned to Elspeth, and closed her eyes, visibly seething. "Go get her, or I vow, *I will*."

Behind her, the laird wore a haggard expression, one of regret. Elspeth experienced a flare of annoyance that he did not simply tell Bridget to let the child be. After all, Catrin had simply been playing—like countless other children who were present, and had caused no harm until Bridget confronted her so unkindly. Elspeth brushed past her stepmother, following Cat's path as she wove in and out of their clanspeople. The child made her way toward the immense doors of the great hall, as if intent on escape.

"Cat, come here." She moved faster, nearly catching up

with her. Just then, the crowd parted and Cat halted and stepped back, bumping backward into Elspeth.

Because a man blocked her way, dressed in a floor-length cloak. A dark and imposing shadow in a room of faces, sound, and movement—

A gloved hand came up to push back the hood.

Startled, Elspeth gave a small gasp. She almost didn't recognize him, but it was the stranger. The *béist*.

He looked different now. He had shaved his beard and cut his hair, leaving his face, with its strong cheekbones and angular jaw, bare to her gaze. Cool blue eyes looked into hers.

"How fortunate for me," he murmured, with a tilt of his head. And yet somehow, in the din of the room, his voice was all she heard. "You're just who I was looking for."

Elspeth's cheeks flushed. She opened her mouth to reply—

But his gaze dropped to Cat.

"I have something for you, little one."

Cat peered up at him, uncharacteristically still and silent.

He crouched, and swept back one corner of his cloak—

To reveal Cat's puppy, cradled in his other arm.

Chapter 5

The stranger placed Puppy into Cat's open arms who, wide-eyed, seized the animal and gave a happy shriek of joy. The stranger's expression warmed, a smile turning the corner of his mouth. Elspeth all but melted, watching.

She knew she stared at him, and she knew she shouldn't, but she couldn't help herself. She felt compelled to examine him, to memorize his every feature—as if he might disappear in the next moment, a vision borne of her dreams.

Candlelight illuminated his skin, carving shadows beneath his cheekbones and reflecting off the silver in his blue eyes. His appearance was ethereal. Noble. Like an ancient *fae* warrior-king, come to mingle with lesser mortals.

He was not merely attractive. No. She had seen attractive men in her father's hall before. They spoke to her in softly teasing tones and looked at her with eyes warm with appreciation. Men from their clan and visitors alike. While she had enjoyed gazing upon their pleasing features and spending time in their company, this man . . .

This man was something *more*.

She could not even define what, precisely, made him so compelling. She only knew that every fragment of her being had taken notice of his smile. His stature. His bearing. It was as if the world had stopped moving. It was as if her heart for the first time had . . . *awakened.*

In a quiet, deep voice, he counseled Cat. "You must remember that animals are much better swimmers than we are. Almost always, they will save themselves from peril so please don't put yourself in danger again. Aye, little one?"

She doubted the child heard a bit of what the man said. She was too excited about the animal in her arms, which wiggled and licked her face.

Sounds filtered back into Elspeth's ears, voices and the minstrels' melody. The memory of the words her father had spoken to her of duty and clan alliances. Of her reality. She knew she must go. Her suitors, still unknown to her, waited to be greeted. This man was not one of them.

She exhaled evenly, and counseled herself to be satisfied with having witnessed such a wonderful moment, and to get on with the responsibilities of her life. She must thank him for bringing Cat's puppy, and again for saving their lives. Then she would take him to her father's table, and the laird would welcome him as he saw proper.

"Thank you," the little girl exclaimed. "Thank you for always and forever, sir."

The puppy barked and sprang free, scampering away.

"Puppy!" she called after him. "Puppy, you come back here."

She darted off, leaving Elspeth alone with the mercenary.

He stood, and as he did so his long cloak unfolded to swirl around his boots. Again, his gaze met hers.

"You're staring," he said, his smile fading.

"I don't mean to—" she answered, heat filling her

cheeks. "It's just that you look very different from when I saw you last."

"Oh?" He tilted his head and touched his ear, indicating the noise around them was too loud. He took one step toward her, all the while his silvery gaze held hers.

He might as well have embraced her, for the way her body reacted—with every inch of her skin going warm and her knees weakening.

"I almost didn't recognize you," she said. "With your beard gone."

His gaze moved over her face. "I'm certain I would have recognized you anywhere."

The words were a compliment, and how wonderful they made her feel. She flushed, and everything inside her—her heart and her soul—felt feather light and aglow.

As eldest daughter of the clan chief, she often received compliments. People said flattering things about her all the time, that she was lovely, intelligent, and hale—mostly, she knew, to curry favor with her father. She did not even take the words to heart, but . . . she hoped this man's words were sincere. She would like very much to be memorable in his mind.

But she couldn't just stand here like a starry-eyed maid, staring at him. He would notice her admiration and know she was smitten, and her pride would not allow that. Especially when she would soon be betrothed to another.

"I am Elspeth." She imposed an easy tone to her voice, hoping her cheeks were not as flushed as she feared. "I know my father wishes to meet you. May I take you to him?"

He nodded. "Thank you, yes."

"What is your name?" Aye, that she wished to know. A name would make him seem real—and not a mythical *béist*. A name would make him just a man.

He looked at her for a long moment.

Suddenly, a dark shadow moved between them—

A hulking figure that blocked her view of him. A strong arm banded around her back, leading her forcefully away.

"There you are, my lovely Elspeth," a man's voice wheezed.

Her vision focused on the shiny, pockmarked face of Keppoch Macpherson, just as her nose and throat seized closed against a witheringly strong stench—just one of the unfortunate traits for which he was known.

"Keppoch, a moment, please," she said. "I was just—speaking with someone."

She twisted, looking over her shoulder for the stranger, but he was gone. Vanished like a ghost.

Her heart sank, heavy as a stone.

Keppoch wasn't alone. A score of his men accompanied them, they with their long, damp hair and oily leather tunics. Like a dark wave, they pushed through the now silent gathering hall, making way for their chief, asserting his importance by displacing any who stood in his and Elspeth's way.

And indeed, Keppoch was an important man, the chief of a small but ferocious clan who presently swore fealty to another, larger clan to the west. Her father had, of late, sought to sway his allegiance in favor of the MacClarens. Such an alliance would bolster security along their weakest border where the Alwyns had taken to making costly incursions onto MacClaren lands, raiding farms and stealing livestock. Those raids, along with the ceaseless harassment from the Kincaid hill people, stretched the MacClaren's defenses thin.

A smile broke across Keppoch's face, revealing a row of yellowed, broken teeth. "Do me the honor of sitting beside me at your father's table tonight."

She stiffened at his words, recognizing by his cold tone

and unyielding grasp that they were not an invitation—but a command.

Lord spare her! Without a doubt Macpherson was one of the suitors Bridget had invited to pay court to her.

Once, several years ago, she had traveled with her father to the Macpherson stronghold. It stood stark and alone, a dark tower on a barren landscape, surrounded by a squalid village. The idea of spending the rest of her days there, forced to submit to such a slovenly creature, made her stomach turn.

Suddenly, another arm came round her waist. Strong and forceful, it wrested her free of Keppoch's hold. Spun round, she found herself face-to-face with the fine-featured countenance of Alan FitzDuff.

"My, my, my. Sweet Elspeth. A child no more, but a woman grown." His gaze swept over her face—before dropping straight to her breasts. "When did this remarkable transformation occur?"

His perfect smile stretched wider.

Curse Bridget!

Yes, FitzDuff was handsome and he boasted overflowing coffers and a fine castle. But the countryside was replete with stories of his ruthless womanizing. Indeed, it was an oft repeated jest that Alan FitzDuff was building a formidable Highland army, one bastard at a time.

Keppoch glared at FitzDuff, growling like an angry wolf.

FitzDuff stared coldly back, a smile of challenge on his lips.

From either side their men crowded closer, each entourage jostling the other in an attempt to claim dominance, pushing Elspeth more firmly between the two men.

Her heart beat painfully in her chest. She could hardly breathe.

These beasts were to be her suitors? *This* would be the manner in which she would be courted—and wed?

Anger flared up from inside. She wanted to plant an elbow in each of their sides—nay, perhaps even into each of their faces! She wanted to scream. The only thing that stopped her was an intense desire to preserve her dignity, for certainly the entire room looked on, including her young sisters.

Elspeth looked toward the dais where her father and Bridget looked back at her. The MacClaren wore a dismayed expression. In contrast, Bridget smiled serenely, as if all were well—and even lifted her goblet in salute!

Standing at her father's side, Conall scowled, his brows furrowed. Derryth and Mairi observed as well, their shocked faces proof enough that their excitement in the evening, and all their high expectations of romance, had been thoroughly dashed.

Rebellion rose up inside Elspeth. This would not do! She would not marry either of these men. Aye, she was a dutiful daughter, but she would not commit herself to outright misery for the sake of Bridget's amusement.

With a hard push she broke out from the melee and strode toward the dais, FitzDuff still clutching her sleeve and Keppoch muttering curses as he trailed behind.

Of course, she would not publicly rebuff either suitor. She would take more care than that, understanding as she was of the necessity of political alliances. But she must have some reassurance that her father did not support Bridget in these choices.

"Father—" she began.

"Macpherson!" the laird barked out, startling her. "Fitz-Duff."

He strode forward and grasped the arm of each man in greeting. "I and Lady MacClaren bid you welcome to our home."

Her father did not look at her.

She spoke again, albeit nervously. "Father, if I could speak with you privately for just one—"

"Daughter"—he interjected—"see that your special guests are comfortably seated, that their goblets remain filled. Also that they are sufficiently entertained and the recipients of your good graces all the evening long."

Elspeth stood stunned, her arms at her sides, realization filtering through her. Her father's abrupt manner denied her safe haven. His words forbade any complaint.

Certainly . . . certainly he could not be in agreement with Bridget's choices.

Seeing her hesitation, her father's face reddened and a dark scowl turned his lips.

She wasn't a fool. She would win no battles here, not with everyone watching. She must wait to speak to the laird in private. For now, she had no choice but to obey.

"Yes, laird," she said, her voice tight from the effort of speaking the words.

She lowered her head in acquiescence, and turned toward FitzDuff and Keppoch who both stared at her with such lustful expectation that revulsion stole her breath.

She should never have worn this dress. These men did not make her feel beautiful, but rather like a joint of meat to be snarled and fought over by hounds in the mud and filth of the castle's bailey.

The stranger had not made her feel this way.

The stranger. Her pulse jumped. How could she have forgotten him, for even a moment? No doubt he stood at the edge of the room, a witness to her humiliation. She turned back toward the dais.

"Laird," she said. "Another guest has also arrived who I know you will wish to welcome as well."

At this the MacClaren did cast a glare at Bridget, and he growled through clenched teeth. "Keppoch Macpherson.

Alan FitzDuff. I am brim with anticipation. Who might our next guest be?"

Bridget raised her eyebrows, peered down at the sparkling rings on her hand—and shrugged.

Elspeth answered, "It is the man who saved Catrin and me from the river today. The *gallóglaigh*."

Conall stepped off the dais, moving toward her.

"Where?" He searched the room. "I do not see him."

Elspeth turned with him, but found her view largely obstructed by the men who still stood thickly around her, Macpherson and FitzDuff, and their companions.

Suddenly, through the shadows and faces and wavering firelight, her gaze locked on his. He leaned in the shadows at the back of the room, his shoulder against one of the stone arcade columns.

"He is there beneath the unicorn tapestry. Do you see him?"

Conall struck into the crowd, shouldering through the men who still gathered behind their lords refusing to give up ground to the other. After the MacClaren's captain had passed, the two groups converged again, bumping chests and muttering challenges and slights.

A moment later, Conall returned, followed by a remarkable-looking, stone-faced man with every bit of his skin covered in tattoos. This man had a bull-like neck and enormous shoulders and appeared completely hewn of muscle. He eyed the warriors who cluttered the path and when one refused to give sufficient way, he reached out and planted his hand at the center of the man's chest like a battering ram, shoving him with such force the man's boots certainly left the ground.

At this, Conall caught her gaze—and winked above a satisfied smile.

Elspeth's heart beat in anticipation, because she knew for whom he cleared the way.

And indeed, a flurry of movement in the gallery above caught Elspeth's attention. Ladies leaned forward, murmuring excitedly among themselves, their breasts straining at their bodices as they watched someone.

It was the stranger, of course. Broad shouldered and self-assured, he followed the tattooed galloglass with the bearing of a conqueror.

"My lord," Conall called grandly, lifting his hand. "I wish to present to you—"

"*Béist!*"

Someone—a man—blurted the word in awe.

The outburst had come from one of Keppoch's warriors. Indeed, the man pushed through his companions toward his scowling chief and murmured fervently in his ear.

Elspeth could just make out the words he spoke.

"It is the *béist*—the *gallóglaigh* I told you of, who fights for Buchan. The one who fights like a demon from hell."

A shiver of excitement coursed down Elspeth's spine, followed by a rush of heat, over every inch of her skin. Such words were a high compliment coming from a member of Keppoch's personal guard, famed as they were not only for their skill with the sword but their brutal strength. But . . . the stranger had served Buchan?

She was not the only one who had overheard the man's explanation to Keppoch. Male voices repeated the words and they carried in a murmur to the farthest edges of the room. At that, the opposing factions that crowded the floor parted ways, providing a narrow but unencumbered path.

Elspeth stood in place, riveted by the unfolding scene. When Conall passed her, and then the tattooed warrior after him, each man pressed close by and in doing so forcefully separated her from her unwanted suitors who she had not even noticed remained at her sides.

"You're welcome, lass," murmured the tattooed man, a playful lilt in his voice.

Yet she forgot him in the next moment when her eyes met those of the *béist*. She thought he would simply pass her by, but when their arms touched, every so lightly as he passed, he paused and tilted his head toward hers.

"A troublesome night you are having, Elspeth," he murmured teasingly.

Obscured by the drape of his cloak, the back of his hand grazed the back of hers.

It was a secret touch. A forbidden touch. One that no one else could see, and it set her heart thudding hard and painfully in her chest and set every inch of her skin afire.

He was gone, moving past her as quickly as he had come.

Turning, she watched as Conall and the tattooed warrior stepped to the side, revealing her father waiting there. Along the dais, the laird's personal warriors and council stood, watching with keen interest.

The MacClaren smiled. "Welcome to Inverhaven. What an honor it is to have you here, in our home. Tell me, good sir, what is your name?"

The silence that followed seemed thunderous in the already absolute quiet of the room. But then he spoke.

"My name is Niall."

It had been important to Niall that he stand here—in this moment of all moments—unmasked.

To enter into their midst bare-of-face and to speak his own name . . . the name his mother and father had given him . . . the name by which he had been known when last he set foot upon these stones.

He would not sneak furtively like a rat. He would stand proud like a Kincaid and look the MacClaren and his warriors in the eyes so that they—his sworn enemies—would recall this moment later with clear understanding.

Soon enough they would know the truth of who he was and why he was here. And now that he was here, inside, they would not be able to stop him.

He would take everything from them, as they had taken everything from his family and his clan. And in that moment, he wanted them to realize, even as they took their last breath, that they had been given more honor in death than all the Kincaids who had been slain. He wanted them to know shame for it, in those last moments before they answered to God.

"Please join me," said the MacClaren, his eyes moving over Niall with sharp-eyed interest, marveling over his height and the thickness of his shoulders and arms, as one would a new and dangerous weapon being considered for one's armory.

Whatever he saw pleased him, because an even deeper admiration warmed his gaze.

Niall's soul snarled in response—but from deep inside his chest, where he had long ago locked away his fury so that it would not interfere with the calculated decisions of his mind.

"Sit beside me so that we may talk." The MacClaren gestured toward the long table and seated himself on the bench. "You saved the lives of my daughters today and for that your presence here must be celebrated."

"I will bring ale," said the Lady MacClaren, her eyes sparkling.

At the graceful signal of her hand, servants spilled from the kitchens holding steaming trenchers high above their heads. Behind them came young maids, bearing loaves of bread and bowls piled with lettuces and roasted vegetables.

Why, in that moment, his thoughts returned to the young woman, Elspeth, he did not know, but as he lowered himself to the bench beside her father, he turned his head, seeking her out. She stood just a few paces away, lovely, pale, and unsmiling, the rich curtain of her dark hair draped over her shoulder, pouring ale for her suitors and their companions. Clearly miserable.

But what did he care about her happiness? She was the daughter of his enemy, and none of his concern.

Conall urged Deargh to also sit, and the two took their places across the table from Niall and the laird with their backs to the room.

The MacClaren leaned toward him. "My apologies that my daughter cannot attend to you, as she should out of gratitude for your bravery today, but suitors have come to pay her court. Perhaps you know them, or of them, Keppoch Macpherson and Alan FitzDuff." He gestured toward one man and then the other.

"I do not," he answered, with a lift of his brows. "But it is no trouble that she is not here. I require no additional thanks."

He forced himself not to look again, but her image . . . her long hair . . . the curve of her cheek, returned to his mind as vividly as if he did look.

"Of course you do," said Lady MacClaren sweetly as she filled his cup. "And I am more than pleased to extend our hospitality and gratefulness to you, where Elspeth cannot."

He was no fool. If he heard the invitation in her voice, could not her husband?

Servants placed trenchers and bowls at the center of the table, generously heaped with boar and trout.

"So your name is not *béist* after all," the MacClaren jested, seemingly oblivious to his wife's flirtation. "It is Niall, you say?"

It was Deargh who answered, with a conversational lift of his hand. "Niall—yes. I thought it a good warrior's name. As good a name as any."

The MacClaren shifted in his seat.

"Interesting, that," he mused, looking away, his jaw drawn tight. "The previous lord of this castle had a son by that name."

Chapter 6

Niall's soul went cold. He had not expected such words to be spoken so soon. Nor had he expected that they would inflict such a powerful response within him.

"Did he?" said Niall, his hand closing on the goblet.

The MacClaren nodded, answering gruffly. "Long dead now, all of them."

Anger that Niall had believed well-controlled now simmered to the surface. It offended him that the MacClaren talked of his "murdered" self with such ease.

From across the table, Deargh cautioned him with a glance, and continued in an easy tone. "You have all heard of the famed King Niall of the Nine Hostages. No? It is an old tale in Ireland, where we spent several years before moving on, told around many a battlefield campfire." He grinned and looked around the table. "Except I would propose to you that it is I who have been held hostage since taking the lad as my shield bearer all those years ago."

The MacClaren laughed, as did Conall and Deargh— though Niall recognized the edge of artifice in his companion's voice.

"He was but a lad, you say?" the laird inquired, eyebrows raised.

"Aye, an orphan." Deargh nodded, his smile fading.

From his seat beside him, the MacClaren looked Niall up and down. "Tell me, where did you find this orphan, who turned out to be such a man?"

Deargh shrugged. "Aye, I hardly recall. Somewhere along the way."

The MacClaren looked to Niall. "You remember nothing of your family? Your clan? The name of your chief? Of the place where you were born?"

Niall's muscles tightened along his shoulders, tense with the effort of controlling his response, because in that same moment he happened to glance down and see something he had long ago forgotten—a series of marks carved into the wood of the table in the place where he sat. Marks he himself had carved, a young boy's prideful tally of the deer he had hunted and contributed to the Kincaid bounty. He focused on them, and remembered the reason he was here.

"I like to believe," he answered evenly. "That it would have been a place much like this."

The MacClaren tilted his head, and squinted. "I would say 'how sad' but it is the plight of so many in this life. And you have made good for yourself, have you not? See there, what those men said about you?" He lifted a hand toward the room. "I heard. Everyone in this hall heard. You are legendary."

Niall looked into the eyes of the man, who along with his neighbor to the south—the chief Alwyn—shared responsibility for his family's murder. He had hated the two men for so long, that his hate had become part of him. His thoughts. His blood. His every breath. For that reason, his pulse did not so much as waver when the laird's hand gripped his arm.

"Your father, whoever he was, would have been proud," the MacClaren said.

"Aye," said Deargh roughly, holding his goblet aloft. "No doubt he would have been."

Deargh looked at him, long and hard, a silent warning not to draw swords and slay the man now, whilst they were so thickly surrounded, before turning in his seat to listen to the harp player. Or at least pretending to do so.

Just then Niall's glance caught that of Elspeth's, who listened to their conversation. She looked at him, her eyes wide with sympathy . . . before having her attention drawn away by the man at her side—the one called FitzDuff, who did nothing but leer at her breasts, from what Niall observed.

Her sympathy for him raised his ire. Would she find his story so sad if she knew her father were responsible?

The MacClaren leaned closer. "After such an entrance, I will not humor myself into believing that I am the greatest or richest lord who has ever sought your services. Indeed, I may be hard pressed to afford you."

Lady MacClaren leaned over Niall's arm again, setting a plate—which had been filled at her direction by the servant assisting her—before him. In doing so she pressed her breast against his shoulder. "Certainly some satisfactory arrangement can be made."

Niall shifted forward and away. "These high lands were once my home, and Deargh's . . . before his own clan was broken up—"

"Broken up?" asked Conall. "Aye, it has been the fate of many. Which clan?"

"It is in the long ago past," answered Deargh, scowling. "I carry the memory in my heart, but do not speak of it."

Conall nodded. "Then we will not press you."

Niall said, "We have come to a time in our lives that, for now, this is where we wish to be."

"The wanderers come home." The MacClaren nodded. "Good. Good. If we can agree on terms, I and my clan would be pleased to have you—"

A child sprouted up between their elbows—the little girl Niall had saved with Elspeth, whom he had at first believed to be a boy. She peered up at her father from beneath a head of roughly shorn red hair. The puppy circled behind her, gnawing playfully at a leather leash.

"Papa, that ugly man touched Elspeth under the table," she said, scowling. "She slapped his hand away but he did it again."

Lady MacClaren lowered her husband's meal to the table before him and seized the girl's arm. "Catrin, don't wander during the meal. I instructed Derryth to watch you! Pah. I am not surprised by her disobedience any more than I am by yours. Come with me."

She led her—and the puppy—away. Niall again looked toward Elspeth. Seated between Keppoch and FitzDuff, her countenance revealed she struggled for composure.

"My daughter," said the MacClaren, in a quiet voice. "She is fair, is she not?"

"Aye," he answered. Any man laying eyes on her would surely answer the same or be called a liar. "She is that."

Elspeth scooted away from Keppoch, pushing his hand away from somewhere near her thigh. Yet when she turned from him, FitzDuff leaned over her in an obvious attempt to drop a pinch of bread down her bodice. Lifting her arm, she covered her breasts with the long drape of her sleeve and pretended to listen intently to the harp player's song.

Her breasts. *Jesu*, he'd be lying to say he hadn't noticed them as well, crowded so beautifully by the bodice of her green dress. They demanded a man's attention almost as equally as her dark, nettle-thick lashes and rosy mouth.

"Despicable men, the both of them," muttered the MacClaren. "But necessary alliances. Curse the way this world works, that I should be forced to give my daughter up to a man such as that."

Lady MacClaren returned without the child, something Niall only vaguely noticed because Elspeth held his attention completely.

Again, she shrank from FitzDuff, only to *again* be submitted to Keppoch's relentless attentions. The man leaned forward, jowls hanging, his eyes glazed—already drunk. He lifted a greasy hand under the premise of touching a tendril of hair that lay on her shoulder and in doing so heavily grazed her breast.

Filthy creature. Niall's muscles burned, prepared to react—to intervene.

Yet he did not. Because she was not his to defend.

Present alongside him were her father and a host of his warriors, all watching, all bound by honor to defend her before he should consider lifting a finger toward her protection.

"Don't touch her." FitzDuff struck Keppoch's hand away.

Keppoch snarled in outrage.

At hearing this, Deargh turned to watch—as did everyone else at the table. Numerous MacClaren warriors glanced at their lord, as if seeking some signal to act. The MacClaren growled, looking agonized . . . conflicted, and he clenched his hands into fists. He closed his eyes, and his lips parted—

But before any order could be given, Elspeth sprang from the bench, her expression murderous.

Niall's abdomen clenched, as he watched, waiting to see what she would do.

For several moments she stood rigid, before seizing up a pitcher from the table, her knuckles white on the handle. Niall feared—nay, hoped—she might crash the thing down on one of their heads. Preferably Keppoch's as he found him most offensive.

But she did not.

"We are out of ale," she announced, and turned away from them, a portrait of dignity. "I shall bring more."

A servant approached, offering to take the pitcher, but she continued on, storming toward the kitchen—a telling wave of ale sloshing over her hands.

As she passed her father's table, she glanced at the laird, her eyes ablaze with fire.

Niall's groin twisted with a sudden jolt of desire. *Jesu*, what a wild beauty she was. Every fragment of his being took notice, coming alive with awareness.

The tattoos on Deargh's temples wrinkled as he laughed. "Ah! Look! The lass is angry. I would be too." He waved a hand toward the two men left behind, watching her go. "Pigs, the both of them."

Keppoch and FitzDuff glared at him. His eyes narrowed—and he glared back.

Many who crowded the tables laughed, including Lady MacClaren, amused by her stepdaughter's torment. Not surprising after what he had observed from the river that morning. Despite the closeness of their ages, the two women were clearly not friends.

Niall watched Elspeth go, his eyes lingering on the curve of her back, over which her long hair cascaded in gleaming tendrils, beneath a narrow crown of braids entwined with gold cording and pearls.

She was only halfway to the door when a shout came from the back of the hall, joined by other voices raised in alarm.

Another guest had arrived—this one uninvited, as was apparent from the number of MacClaren warriors who imposed a wall of raised weapons and scowling faces around a striking young man with pale blond hair that hung to just below his square jaw, made all the more notable because he was completely garbed in black leather. Like Elspeth's two suitors he made his entrance along with a small company of companions who Niall could not help but notice, were younger and more attractive than the others.

Niall saw Elspeth freeze, her gaze fixed on the young man, and in that moment experienced a jolt of inexplicable jealousy.

"Magnus," growled the MacClaren, rising to his feet and leaving the dais.

Conall followed, but not before turning to Lady MacClaren. "The Alwyn's bastard? Did you invite him to pay court to Elspeth?"

She answered blithely. "You may think I am wicked— but I am not that wicked."

As soon as the two men were gone, the lady slid toward Niall and murmured conspiratorially. "I did not invite Magnus. He has nothing to offer. But I *might* have made it known, in a way that would reach the Alwyn's ears, that the others would be here." She bit her lip, and watched the unfolding drama with interest. "I thought perhaps the two clans could settle their differences by a marriage between Elspeth and his legitimate son, Hugh . . . but I have since heard he is betrothed."

She sighed in disappointment.

The MacClaren stormed toward Magnus, demanding, "Why have you come?"

Magnus wrested free of the MacClaren kinsmen that held him back. He stood proudly, muscles cording his bare arms, where they extended out from his leather vest. "For Elspeth, of course."

Elspeth gasped, and her face paled. Niall's mood darkened a shade more.

"Your laird wants nothing more than to destroy this clan," the MacClaren retorted. "He plots against us, and does everything to undermine our standing with the king.

Such aggressions cannot be overlooked. Any offer you make will be refused."

The young man's lip curled. "Keppoch Macpherson. Alan FitzDuff? I don't see how my suit would be considered any less welcome by the lady than theirs. Come now. I have brought my father's representative, who has authority to discuss terms." He gestured to a solemn-faced, older man who stood behind him, who held an official-looking leather case. "Elspeth?"

Niall watched, rapt. Annoyed. How did Elspeth feel about this young man?

"Go away, Magnus," she blurted, looking angry and miserable.

The tension that pulled between Niall's shoulders relaxed a bit. The room exploded into laughter, the loudest coming from Keppoch, who hurled a meaty bone at Magnus, which bounced off his chest.

"Yes, go away," Keppoch shouted, laughing dismissively.

All went silent. Magnus stood rigid, his cheeks darkening, his eyes fixed on Keppoch. He lunged—

"Stop!" The MacClaren stepped into his path, hands raised.

Yet Magnus's course was set and he collided with the laird, who stumbled backward, crashing against a table, which *tilted . . . and righted, but not before several* pitchers and bowls slid off and shattered, tossing and splashing their contents to the floor.

At his side, Lady MacClaren seized Niall's arm against her breast, and cried out.

Magnus froze, his expression one of fury tangled with intense regret.

"I—I did not mean to push you."

The chief's face darkened, and he shouted, "I would

marry her to the Devil himself before I allowed her to marry you. You tell your laird that, straight from me."

Elspeth rushed to her father's side, helping him to stand aright.

"Forgive me, I must tend to my husband," Lady Mac-Claren said to Niall, leaping from her seat, also moving in their direction.

Looking over her shoulder, Elspeth implored, "Please, Magnus, just go."

Magnus glowered between Elspeth and her father, and let out an angry sound. Turning, he stormed away, shoving aside any who stood in his path. His companions followed him.

Celebratory cheers and laughter arose from all about the room, and the lute and harp trilled into a cheerful song, which masked the lingering unpleasantness that clouded the atmosphere. Elspeth spoke pleadingly with her father, her expression one of concern and yet he responded sharply to her with words Niall did not hear because of the clamor of the room.

Her face paled, and slowly she returned to the table where Keppoch and FitzDuff and their unruly entourages waited, looking much like a woman condemned to execution.

Moments later, the MacClaren returned, a hand pressed against his side, as if he suffered some ache or pain, Conall accompanying him.

Lady MacClaren fluttered about him. "Are you hurt?"

"No," he growled. He exhaled raggedly, and sat with obvious discomfort, wincing.

"The pain. It has returned?" She pressed a goblet of ale into his hand.

"It never went away," he muttered. He exhaled, and summoned a forced smile. "Niall. Deargh. The MacClarens may not be able to pay you as richly as a king, but we can certainly give you a most entertaining night."

Lady MacClaren sat, frowning. "Entertaining indeed."

The laird added, "Partake in all the food and ale that you wish tonight. Sleep here at my hearth where it is warm and dry."

Niall answered, "Thank you for your offer of hospitality, but we prefer to maintain our own quarters. We shall seek them out in the village, or encamp again by the river."

He would not have anyone questioning his comings and goings. Besides, he would not sleep a wink in this place. He would lay awake until morning, examining every timber, every stone.

Remembering. Loving. Hating.

The MacClaren nodded. "Whatever you wish. Tomorrow we shall discuss all other matters between us, and see if we can come to some sort of agreement."

"That sounds very fine to me," said Deargh.

"Agreed," said Niall.

"Good," said the chief. "Until then I bid you, eat and drink. Introduce yourself to our beautiful ladies." He grinned and Lady MacClaren rolled her eyes. "Aye, look, the old bard has come. He will entertain us with song."

An old man entered the room, holding the arm of a young woman who led him to a place near the fire. He was obviously blind, which was an unfortunate relief to Niall because the man was the first person he had seen here that he recognized from his past. Deargh cast Niall a quick glance, his brows raised, indicating he recognized him as well.

It was Murdoch, his father's bard. But unlike the jovial man that he remembered from his youth, Murdoch had turned gray and frail.

The harp player strummed a few, haunting chords and

together they sang. For the first several lines, Niall could
not hear the words because of the continued talking and
laughter of those gathered about, but then the room became quiet.

> . . . *I look, I call and I listen in vain.*
> *I know I heard the voice again.*
> *You hear him in the tower, and then in the wood.*
> *You wish to join him . . . how I wish I could.*
> *Listen . . . again, the sound I hear.*
> *I do not worry, I do not fear.*
> *The Kincaid calls to them, one, two, three*
> *Three dead sons, all ghosts like me.*

Chapter 7

"What an intriguing song," said Deargh, his voice hollow.

The words echoed in Niall's mind. He closed his eyes, wishing he could not hear them.

"Oddly, it is my husband's favorite," the Lady Mac-Claren said with a sigh, looking bored. "I have heard that dusty old ghost story more times than I can count."

"We are all haunted by one thing or another, are we not?" the laird said, his voice distant.

What a peculiar thing to say. Was the song a sort of trophy of triumph past, or was the MacClaren more complicated than that? Could it be that the memory of the Kincaid clan deaths haunted him? That he had a conscience?

Niall did not want to know. He did not want to know this man. His hopes. His dreams. His fears. Because of this man's treachery, his father and mother's remains lay moldering in a grave somewhere, perhaps unconsecrated, and he would answer for it dearly.

A sudden movement caught his eye—Elspeth standing from her place at the table. With a gasp of outrage, she slapped Keppoch, and when FitzDuff laughed, she seized up a goblet of ale and doused his face. The firelight reflected off her hair, and bathed her skin so that it appeared golden.

Deargh, seeing this, lifted his hands and grinned. "Och. There we go. It's settled, I think. There will be no love match tonight."

Elspeth strode to stand directly before her father, bright spots of color staining her cheeks.

"I don't care what you do or say," she said in a low, tremulous tone. "Shave my head. Cut out my tongue." Her voice rose. "Drive a hot poker into both my eyes." She pointed forked fingers at the glittering orbs in question. "I'm not marrying either of those . . . those . . ." She grimaced, her composure all but shattered. "*Churls*."

Lady MacClaren chided. "We're being a bit dramatic, are we not, Elspeth?"

"*We* . . . are not!" Elspeth cried, her gaze hot and intense. "*We* do not exist. It is only I"—she pointed a finger at her chest—"who suffers, while *you*"—she pointed at Bridget—"are amused at my expense."

Niall watched, riveted, as her emotion unfolded in vivid color.

"Daughter—" her father warned. "Show respect to your stepmother."

"Respect?" Elspeth's eyes flared in anger. "What is that? I would not know as none has been accorded to me."

She whirled away on the heel of her slipper and stormed across the room, her gown whispering across the stones behind her. It took every ounce of his will not to launch up from his seat to go after her. To pursue her.

"I told you," Lady MacClaren sniffed, looking annoyed. "And I will say it again. She has grown headstrong. You have spoiled her."

"I will speak to her in the morning," the MacClaren said testily.

"Aye, tomorrow," she responded, haughtily. "For now, you must go and make amends with those she has so unforgivably offended."

The MacClaren stood, his eyes clouded and made his way down the table, where FitzDuff wiped his face with a square of linen and Keppoch stood with his men, receiving slaps on the back in apparent congratulations for having provoked such a response in the young lady.

Niall's attention shifted to the far end of the hall as Elspeth, in shadows, climbed the stairs—only to be stopped by a servant girl, who glanced over her shoulder before furtively leaning toward her mistress to say something, perhaps to deliver a message. Just as quickly, the servant left Elspeth, who remained there unmoving for several moments more, as if undecided about something.

At last, she turned and disappeared up the stairs.

Niall had no time to further ponder what he had seen, because the laird returned, his brows gathered.

"What a surprise," he muttered. "Both men have assured me they are even more determined now to have her as a wife than before."

"I don't believe it," exclaimed Lady MacClaren, with a dry laugh.

However, the laird did not look relieved or pleased—only bemused. Likewise, his announcement cast Niall's mood into darkness. Indeed, his soul growled angrily in response.

If anyone were to have Elspeth, it would be him.

The magnitude of his desire—of the realization that he *wanted* her—startled him, heating the blood in his veins. He could not deny that from the first moment he had seen her that morning, from across the river, she had captured his interest. In the hours since, she had remained an alluring promise that hovered in the back of his mind. Tonight, she had become something more. A prize to be claimed.

What better revenge could he have against the man who had murdered his family, than to take his eldest daughter to bed? To turn her against him. To marry her. Doing so would only further secure his claim to this castle and the stolen Kincaid lands, in the eyes of the king and the courts.

He would woo and persuade her. Remembering the fire in her eyes and the color high on her cheeks, his heart beat harder and desire twisted, tight and insistent, in the pit of his stomach. Elspeth was not just a beautiful woman, but a remarkable one. Seducing her, and making love to her—claiming her for his own, would be no hardship. Indeed, it was a challenge that made the vengeful fire in his soul burn hotter.

How strange that now that she was gone, all light seemed to have left the room.

Where before, he had found interest in observing his enemy in his surroundings, now all he perceived were flushed faces, overly loud laughter, shrill music, and spilled wine.

Suddenly he felt smothered by it all. These strangers . . . these *murderers*, living in his father's home, laughing and smiling as if nothing were amiss. It was as if the Kincaids and their history had been obliterated from all consciousness, save for a ghostly tale told only for the entertainment of a drunken crowd. His anger grew, searing his veins. He feared if he remained, he might do something he'd regret, and he could take no chances at that.

Standing, he offered his thanks to his host for the evening meal and entertainment, and bid them good night.

Deargh walked him to the doors. "I wish to linger a bit longer. You never know what one will hear when lips are loosened by drink."

"I will see you at the camp, then."

He left the light of the hall behind, and walked into the night. Outside, he crossed the bailey, which was lit by numerous fires, surrounded by MacClarens singing songs and conversing, and eventually he departed through the gate. A sturdy wind carried the scent of peat fires from the village, and tugged at his cloak, lifting it behind him. The cold air and longer nights heralded the arrival of autumn. He followed the winding path to the meadow below, where his horse waited at the stable. Once there, he passed through the circle of light cast by a solitary firepot blazing near the entrance.

To his consternation, he found his and Deargh's animals tied to posts outside, unattended by the stableboys who had promised earlier to secure them inside. The same stableboys whom he discerned some distance away, down the hillside nearer to the river, gathered around a fire, laughing and, from the sound of it, casting lots.

For a moment he considered summoning the lads for a tongue lashing for leaving his destrier—an immense, *costly,* and sure-footed stallion—unattended in a place where thievery could at any moment occur. But . . . he let them be, smiling despite himself at their boyish jests and vulgarities, carried to his ears on the night wind. He thought of his brothers, and remembered the way they had behaved in much the same manner.

Fitheach *harruphed* in greeting. Niall gave his nose a rub, and only then gave in to temptation.

He looked back at the castle, perched on the hillside above, surrounded by dark earth and stone, against a curtain of blue night sky, ablaze with thousands of stars. Villagers had built several small bonfires on the grounds below, which illuminated the high walls. Lamp light shone from a number of the tower windows, including one on the third floor where he had in childhood passed his nights, along with his two brothers, believing, in his boy's heart, that his happy and well-protected life would go on forever.

Where did she sleep, he wondered?

Just then he perceived a movement in the darkness—a cloaked figure hurrying from the castle toward the space behind the stable. A woman by the lightness of her movement, and the pale moon of her face.

He did not need to see her face to know it was Elspeth.

Elspeth rushed headlong into the darkness as fast as her feet would carry her, praying that no one had seen her leave, and if they had, that they would not question the story she had given the guards at the gate, that she was going to visit her old nursemaid, Fiona, in the village—which in truth she did often enough that they only nodded and watched her go on her way.

The servant girl who had approached her at the stairs had told her he waited in the area of the stables, near the cistern, but Elspeth did not see him. Until, suddenly, she did when he pushed back his hood and his blond hair shimmered in the shadows.

"Magnus," she hissed. "You should not be here—and I should not be meeting you. My father, if he knew, would never let me step foot unaccompanied from the castle again. Why did you come here tonight? Offering marriage! What were you thinking?"

He strode toward her. Just as always, it took her breath away just a little, seeing him like this. So tall and masculine. A full-grown man, when once he had been just a frail boy she'd taken under her wing out of sympathy because of his inability to speak, an affliction that invited scorn from his father and continued for years, until one day he suddenly spoke, surprising everyone.

But things had changed so much since then, for the both of them.

"If someone is going to marry you," he said. "It might as well be me."

She blinked at him. "What a romantic thing to say."

"We both know romance plays no part in this," answered Magnus.

Elspeth gathered her cloak tighter against the chill. "Your father sent you, didn't he? He wants my land. My *tocher*. Anything he can take from us."

"Nay, Elspeth, it is I who want your *tocher*," he said fiercely, gesturing with his hand. "Surely you understand, marriage is the only way I shall ever come to possess anything of my own. The Alwyn chieftaincy along with every *rood*, every *dabhach* of land, will go to Hugh, whether he is deserving or not."

A year younger than Magnus, Hugh was the Alwyn's only legitimate son—his designated male heir, or *ceann-cath*, formally agreed upon by the Alwyn clan council long ago, at the time of his birth.

"Hugh is not deserving," she answered softly.

Elspeth had always known, from the first time she encountered Hugh, that there was something wrong with him. As a boy he'd been relentlessly cruel to animals and other children, always without remorse. As an adult, she found him frightening. Not because he was fearsome as a warrior but because of his empty, black eyes and ever-present smirk. She had often wondered if he had a soul.

However, his father, the Alwyn, bestowed upon him every possible privilege and honor as if he were a prince—including, apparently, the recent betrothal to the earl of Buchan's ward.

Magnus, on the other hand, had proven himself not only a skilled warrior and leader among the Alwyn men, but an excellent strategian. The number of stingingly successful raids he'd inflicted on MacClaren holdings of late was proof enough of that. And yet, his father withheld all but the paltriest acknowledgments from him. It had always been so. The Alwyn had never officially recognized Magnus as his own.

"And yet you find me deserving, Elspeth—my dearest and most constant friend?" he demanded softly.

"Of course you are," she answered, stepping closer.

"Then marry me," he said urgently, catching her hands, pulling her near. "I know a priest who will marry us tonight."

She exhaled, and closed her eyes. "If I married you, you know as well as I that my lands would become your father's—and then Hugh's."

"No."

"Yes," she retorted softly, pulling away. "Eventually they would, in some way or another, as a way to dishonor my father. Your father would make sure of it."

"I assure you"—he held up his hands, as if offering peaceful terms—"your lands would remain separate from the Alwyn holdings."

"As if you'd be able to stop him." She wrapped her arms around her waist, as cold crept through her leather slippers, up from the ground. She sighed. "You must find another way to make a life for yourself. One that doesn't involve me. I hope you do, Magnus, because I truly want the best for you."

"I can't believe this," he said incredulously, looking up into the night sky. "You would choose that toad Keppoch before me? Or that lecher FitzDuff."

"No!" She shook her head, covering her ears because she did not want to hear those names, or even imagine those faces again. "I—I don't want to marry either of them. But neither does that mean I must marry you."

He turned back to her again, his face appearing carved of stone. "I know you are loyal to your father. Your clan. But you're a grown woman now, with a mind of your own. You see now, what he intends for you. If it is not Keppoch or FitzDuff, it will no doubt be someone of their ilk, chosen for their lands or influence, with no care for you. Consider your choices—and give your loyalty to me."

Elspeth stiffened, and poked her finger into his chest. "Perhaps that might have been possible before you stole forty head of cattle from our herd." She poked him again. "Or before you burned down the south granary. Aye, Magnus? Do you need more reasons why I could never take you as a husband? I will not marry without my father's consent, and he will never approve of you because of these things you have done."

He stared down at his chest where her finger remained lodged, his nostrils flared.

"Do I need to hear more reasons, you ask?" he answered sharply—then looking up, scowled. "No. I can remember them on my own, because I was there"—his voice rose and his eyes flared—"and I'd do it all again. I'd steal your cattle, and burn your granary, because those lands were intended for the Alwyns, *not* the MacClarens, and you know as well as anyone your father all but stole them from mine—"

"Even now, you take his side?" She rocked toward him, higher on her toes. "That makes you no better than Hugh."

His eyes widened, and he shook a finger in her face. "Now ye've provoked me, lass."

"Go home!" she shouted, and backed away from him. "Or jump in a *bogloch* for all I care."

He crossed his arms over his chest. "Not. Without. You."

She blinked at him. Opened her mouth to offer a retort. But snapped her teeth closed instead. Because she was finished. Tired. Disappointed. With everyone in her life! *Except perhaps Niall.*

"Well, then," she exclaimed, with an exasperated wave of her hands. "You can sleep here on these cold hard rocks and answer to my father's men in the morning, because you'll be waiting for me for a long time." She turned and took several steps toward the castle, calling back over her shoulder. "I'm going to bed."

She heard the hard stamp of Magnus's boots as he circled round to block her path.

"You're certain, then?" he demanded, walking backward, matching her pace, his face a featureless shadow in the night. Behind him, the castle walls shone, illuminated by the bonfires. "You won't marry me."

"Are you hard of hearing?" she cried, coming to a stop.

"There is nothing I can say or do to change your mind?" He tilted his head. "Last chance."

She answered, hands fisted on her hips. "Thank the lord above, because I'm done talking to you."

"Well then . . ." His voice softened, and he took one step back, his expression different now . . . somehow anticipatory. "I'm sorry, Elspeth."

Why the odd change in his manner? "Sorry about wh—"

Something dark closed over her. Rough cloth, imposed on her from behind her head by even rougher hands.

Shock rippled through her.

"Let me go!" She fought—but found her arms banded . . . her body turned . . . twisted . . . tightly wrapped in a heavy cloth.

She should have known he was not alone. That his companions were there in the shadows.

"Be still," Magnus ordered.

She screamed, outraged, but heard only the muffled sound in her own ears. Her only hope was that a stableboy or the blacksmith might be close enough to hear.

"Quiet!" he growled, clamping a hand across her nose.

She screamed again.

The hand shifted over her mouth.

Och! Now she could scarcely breathe. Despite writhing

and kicking as hard as she could, she felt herself seized by numerous arms.

"Careful now," he instructed.

They lifted her from the ground.

Her heart pounded so fiercely that pain cleaved her chest.

"No, no, no!" she shouted into . . . *whoever's* palm, desperate to convince them, one and all, to abandon whatever Magnus intended. Because she feared she *knew* what he intended. *I know a priest who will marry us tonight.*

Jostled . . . hoisted . . . heaved high, she was passed into the arms of another. Her fears confirmed, she felt the hard press of a saddle against her bottom and a man's body behind hers, holding her fast. She gasped for breath, turning her face, seeking enough air to scream.

"You know I would never harm you, Elspeth," said Magnus, close to her ear. "But if you insist on fighting me like this and fall on your head and die, it is no one's fault but your own."

Chapter 8

The animal tensed beneath them and bolted, Elspeth knew, toward the border.

She had snuck out of the castle, without leaving word of her true intentions with anyone. Would anyone even realize her absence until morning? That was too long. Once on Alwyn lands, secured inside their stronghold, there would be no saving her, not without a clan war.

It was up to her alone to escape. As the animal thudded over earth and stone, she held herself painfully alert, waiting for any pause or hesitation of motion in which she could spring free. But for what seemed like forever, they traveled on, she painfully clenched in Magnus's arms, gasping for breath as the jarring force of their travel over hill and vale threatened to loosen every tooth in her head.

"Take me home," she demanded for the thousandth time. Hurt, furious, and miserable, she had pled, begged, and railed ceaselessly until her voice was hoarse, not knowing if he could hear her, but making every effort all the same. "Take me home *now*."

At last the horse slowed.

She readied herself, knowing she must act quickly if given the chance. Whatever he intended would happen now. She had completely lost her bearings, but if she could escape him she could hide away in some furrow or crevice until first light and then stealthily find her way home. She wasn't afraid of Magnus. He wouldn't hurt her physically. Because of that, she felt no fear over attempting an escape.

Magnus dismounted. She felt his body gone behind her, and heard the hard stamp of his boots on the earth. He pulled her down. Tangled in cloth and darkness, she lost her footing and slumped against him, gasping.

"Are you all right, Elspeth?" he asked, holding her tight.

"No," she bellowed.

He was arrogant enough to chuckle.

Men's voices spoke in low tones around her.

"Take the horses. Secure them in the trees where they won't be seen."

"Take her that way, down the path, and you will see the light."

"Whatever it is you have planned," she cried, thrashing against his arms and the blanket, "it is a *terrible* plan, and it's not too late to stop. *Please*."

He did not answer. Instead, he hoisted her over his shoulder and carried her, near crushing her ribs as he climbed, up up up, she feeling each rise in elevation, as his boots crunched against stone and moss.

She kicked. He smacked her bottom.

"*Magnus!*"

"Then stop it," he commanded.

The others laughed heartily.

He placed her onto her feet and quickly freed her of the shroud. Cold air chilled her skin, and a strong wind caught her cloak. She wobbled, out of sorts and unsteady, trying to see through the darkness, and the wild tangle of her hair.

They stood atop a high *sìthean*, that much she'd already

surmised—but before she could bolt, he seized her hand and pulled her into a copse of trees, where in the distance a lantern flickered and a bald-pated man stood, wearing a cassock. Tree limbs creaked ominously.

She dug in her heels. "You cannot force me."

"Of course I can," he answered with a dry laugh. "It happens all the time."

"I can't believe you're laughing about this," she wailed.

"I think at least one of us should be happy on the night we are wed."

"I will *never* be happy," she blurted. "Not if it happens like this. Which means you will never be happy either."

He paused on the path, and turned toward her, grasping her by the upper arms.

"I know what troubles you," he said, suddenly serious.

"Yes, Magnus, *you*," she retorted.

He tilted his head, considering her thoughtfully. "You think because we have been friends for so long, like brother and sister, that being husband and wife will be strange. But you're wrong. You'll see. I will learn to love you, and you will learn to love me."

Squeezing her arms, and pulling her a few inches closer, he looked at her a long moment . . . and swallowed hard, as if gathering courage—

"Don't do it," she warned, eyes wide.

Seizing her close, he crushed his mouth to hers.

He tasted of ale—and *Magnus*—and everything wrong. She wrenched free, swinging her fist, and struck his jaw.

Stumbling back, she stared at him as he laughed ruefully and muttered a curse, all while rubbing his face. Her lips throbbed, offended by his unwanted kiss. His companions moved closer, as if to subdue her, but he waved them off.

"Don't touch her."

Elspeth stared at him. Things were changed between

them now . . . forever, and it made her sad. But she was too angry to cry over it.

"You shouldn't have done that," she said.

"*That* was a mighty wicked thump," he said, still rubbing. "But I am not surprised. I did teach you how to use your fists, if you recall."

Yes, to protect herself against Hugh, when they were young. Back when their clans had gathered together. He spoke of old times, and yet she did not know this tall, blond stranger anymore. He was no longer her childhood friend.

"It wasn't all that bad, was it?" he inquired teasingly.

She heard something else in his voice. Shame. A plea for forgiveness. He had transgressed, and he knew it, which gave her a glimmer of hope.

"Magnus—" she pled softly.

"You'll forgive me in time," he said with finality, straightening his shoulders. "So let us go now and get married."

Her stomach twisted at his words.

"This is *wrong*," she asserted, scooting backward.

He stepped toward her, and reached for her hand—

She seized her arm back, out of his reach.

He lunged—

But never touched her.

Because a shadow hurtled out of the night, slamming him to the ground.

Elspeth didn't know every detail of how it happened. She just knew that within moments, she was racing down the hillside, doing her best to keep up with Niall, who held her hand tight and pulled her along.

"Come on now." He paused, a step below her, his muscular legs braced wide on the uneven ground, looking back at her.

Her sleeve dangled, torn at the shoulder, and leaves and

twigs rustled and bobbed in her hair. Niall had blood on his face and sleeve—which she felt certain did not belong to him. The wind ruffled his hair. Even in the darkness, his blue eyes were bright and he wore an exhilarated sort of smile, as if he took satisfaction in a good fight.

Someone burst out of the trees behind them.

Startled, Elspeth scrambled closer to Niall. With one arm, he swept her behind him, shielding her with his body.

But it was only the priest, with the lantern swinging from his hand. He froze at seeing them and in a burst of movement, rushed past.

"Man of God!" he exclaimed shrilly. "Please don't hurt me. Peace be with you both."

He disappeared down the hill, until he was just a bobbing light in the dark.

Niall peered down at her, breathing hard and looking so handsome her heart turned over inside her chest. "This way. Best we hurry as well."

He offered his hand, open palmed.

"I'll try." She nodded, taking it, and with her other hand lifted the hem of her skirt. "But I seem to have lost my shoes somewhere along the way."

She was not tenderfooted by far, and often went barefoot, but the stones here were loose and sharp. He looked at her feet.

"We can't have that, now, can we?" he asked. "I will carry you."

"Ah, you needn't—" she protested.

Well, perhaps not *protested*, but the idea of him holding her seemed too much—

He dipped low, catching her up into his arms, and holding tight against his chest.

How nice.

The night sky spun high above as he thudded down the incline, deftly sidestepping outcroppings of stone, soft moss, and tufted ferns, carrying her as if she were no burden at all. She held fast, her arms around his neck, feeling the hard flex of his shoulder muscles beneath her palms as he twisted and moved. She remembered Fiona saying something once, that there was nothing more attractive than a competent man. At the time she'd been a young girl, without true understanding, but now she agreed.

She would remember this night forever. What a magnificent melee it had been. Bodies flying. Fists thudding. She'd even jumped on someone's back, and been thrown off, so she felt some pleasure in having done her part. What pleased her most was that Magnus and his men had been completely stunned and overwhelmed by Niall's sudden attack. Ha! They had deserved to be taken completely unaware, for what they had done. Magnus, she felt quite certain, had earned himself a broken nose.

At the bottom of the hill, hidden in the shadows, a horse awaited, an enormous black animal with wise, intelligent eyes and a disciplined stance. A battle destrier, most assuredly, finer than any she had ever seen. Niall set her down on a patch of moss, which was cool and soft under her aching feet. In the distance she heard voices. Shouts. Hooves, pounding on earth.

"They are coming," she exclaimed.

"Aye, let them." He chuckled—and she knew he meant it. For this man, fighting was not only livelihood, but apparently sport. He looked at her beneath the dark slash of his eyebrows. "Can you climb up?"

She did so, swiftly, thrusting her bare foot into the stirrup and swung astride the leather saddle, careful to secure her skirts about her bottom and her legs for comfort—and modesty—as she did when she rode her own pony.

In a breath, he was behind her, close and strong, his trew-covered thighs flexing against hers, bringing a blush high into her cheeks. She had never felt such excitement, such pleasure at being close to a man. Taking up the reins, he gigged the animal with his heels, and they started off into the dark at a rapid canter.

At his urging, the destrier moved faster, and faster still. And yet the terrain was neither flat nor clear of obstacles. The horse pivoted and lunged around the stones and leapt over a patch of sweet gale, sending up thunder from its hooves. She clenched the wide pommel and leaned forward, the muscles of her stomach and thighs clenching as she anticipated its next movement, half terrified she'd fly out of the saddle.

Niall's arm caged her tight across her ribs. "I have you."

And she was glad. She had never been on a horse so powerful, so mightily agile—in that way, a mirror of its master.

Her heart beat faster as shadowy figures hurtled toward them from either side—Magnus and his companions on their fast, strong-legged ponies.

Niall slowed his animal, speaking commands in a tongue she did not understand. The horse reared, as if in battle, and screamed magnificently before plunging forward and breaking through their ranks, sending the smaller animals spinning round in retreat. Voices shouted curses after them. She looked back, her hair flying over Niall's shoulder, and saw that Magnus and the others followed at a distance.

A moment later, when she looked again, she did not see them anymore.

They raced toward MacClaren territory. She did her best to hold herself forward in the saddle, to keep her body apart from his. She had never ridden on a horse thusly with a man, both of them astride and their bodies so intimately aligned. Oh, perhaps as a child, riding with some equally childish boy or with her father, but not as a woman with an awareness of a man, and never with a man such as Niall.

And yet when he pulled her tight against his chest, his hold firm and decisive, she gave into temptation . . . easing against him, her body taking on the rhythm of the horse, feeling so secure in his arms she almost dozed off to sleep. But she did not, because she did not want to miss a moment with Niall. In the past months, she had increasingly come to feel like a prisoner in her own life with no hope of ever seeing the light again. With him, she felt alive and free.

Eventually the night landscape became familiar and in the distance she saw the castle tower. She was almost home. Her time with him was nearly over. Would she think of this night later, when she was married to someone else? She knew she would.

Though it was after midnight, she wished the journey back had taken longer. That they hadn't returned so soon. Above, outside the castle walls, the bonfires still burned, though dimmer now. The music still played—but quieter. Voices still laughed and sang. Just fewer. No one had missed her at all. Anyone asking about her would have likely believed she had remained with Fiona for the night.

Niall guided the animal toward the base of the hill, where the footpath led to the castle, but he did not stop there. Instead, he continued on as if he would instead take the wider road used by riders and wagons, all the way to the gates. But she could not allow him to do that.

"You can let me down here," she said, straightening in the saddle, prepared to dismount immediately.

Yet Niall did not move his arm, which prevented her from going anywhere.

"I'll take you inside to your father and bear witness to what happened," he said, the deep tone of his voice sending a frisson of awareness down her spine. "It would be wrong of me to send you to face him alone."

"No," she answered, twisting in the saddle to look into his eyes—her heart beating wildly at finding their faces, their lips just inches apart. "Please, Niall, I don't want him to know what happened with Magnus."

Niall froze—nay, more aptly, *burned*, his every physical sense attuned to the woman between his legs, her pretty mouth speaking his name, so close to his that he felt her breath feather across his lips.

He hardly comprehended her words, for the pounding of his blood in his ears.

And elsewhere.

It was no simple thing, riding a horse with a winsome young woman, and Elspeth was . . . more than winsome. He had taken notice of *everything*. The way her bottom pressed against his groin. The way her waist felt against the curve of his arm. And God spare him. The weight of her breasts, each time their undersides brushed, warm and heavy, against his linen sleeve. Not to mention her hair. Her soft, honeysuckle-scented hair as it flew back on the night wind to caress his cheek, although she had done her best to secure it beneath her hood. Everything about her was sweet—and he was one dangerous breath away from being smitten.

Yet this was the MacClaren's eldest daughter and because of that, his seduction of her must be undertaken without the involvement of his conscience. In this—the claiming of his enemy's eldest daughter—he must proceed with the same calculated precision as he did in all things, and not to make a single misstep.

"Will you keep my confidence?" she asked, her hand squeezing his arm. "Please, Niall. I beg you. You must."

But . . . *Magnus*. What, exactly, was she asking him? Standing in the stirrup, he lifted his leg over and stepped down.

"Come here," he said, extending a hand to her. "I want to talk to you."

Not there in the saddle, where he could hardly think, with her being so close against him, his mind clouded by desire. She brought her leg over, and for the briefest moment he glimpsed her slender legs and ankles amidst the jumble of her skirts. She braced her hands on his shoulders and slid off the saddle.

Just like that, the temptation proved too great. His hands on her rib cage, he pulled her close—closer than he ought, as he lowered her to the ground. His blood hummed, from the simple act of touching her so, of feeling the crush of her breasts against his chest, her arms around his shoulders. His ardor roused, he knew in that moment that she would be a fantasy in bed.

Aye, in his bed. Furs. Tangled linen. Her mouth. Her skin. Her hair.

Now. Kiss her now.

Yet earthbound, she sidestepped him, quickly backing away, and turned to look at him expectantly. He remembered the request for secrecy that she had made.

"Your father must know about Magnus," he said. "That your virtue and your very life were threatened by him. Such a grievous assault against your person cannot go unanswered."

"My father doesn't even know I was gone," she answered urgently. "No one does. That must not change."

His heart flared with jealousy. Would Elspeth entertain the idea of marrying Magnus, if he courted her properly? If their fathers came to a peaceful agreement?

"Why is it that you want to protect him?" he asked darkly.

He wanted to know how she felt about the tall, blond warrior, a competent fighter who had slammed Niall to the ground, and rammed a fist against his jaw making him see stars that had nothing to do with those in the night sky above. He felt certain a bruise might be visible there, when not concealed by shadows.

She shook her head. "It is myself I protect. I have always enjoyed a certain freedom here. If my father knows I was taken, that will end. I will be confined to the castle, escorted everywhere by guards. If these are to be my last days of freedom before marrying, I wish to be free."

"And Magnus?"

She shrugged. "Things are already so tense between our clans. While I don't understand why he did what he did tonight, and I am very angry with him for it . . . he is a friend. Since childhood, Niall. I don't want him hurt. I don't want anyone to be harmed or to die, not for me. If my father finds out, I fear what he will do."

He looked at her a long moment, into her wide and pleading eyes, and reminded himself that everything must work toward *his* end, not hers. Perhaps sharing this secret with her now, would be to his benefit later.

"As you wish," he answered.

She gave a sigh of relief. "Thank you."

They looked at one another. *Jesu*, she was lovely, looking back at him from beneath those dark lashes, her skin illuminated in the night. His pulse quickened at the prospect of pulling her close. Of discovering the feel of her in his arms, the softness of her lips.

"I must go," she said, backing away. "Before someone finds me here."

He growled inwardly, watching her go—knowing it was too soon to do anything but. She turned, pulling the hood of her cloak over her hair, and climbed the path on steps created of earth, flat stones, and grass.

Niall bent and snatched up Fitheach's reins, prepared to return to the saddle and the solitude of his camp across the river.

Yet something made him turn back and watch her.

One moment he saw her shadow moving along the path—the next he did not. He stared hard into the darkness, but no. She was not there, on the path, as she should be.

Had she simply disappeared into shadows, or had she stopped along the way? Having seen her abducted once already this night, he could not simply ride away.

He dropped the reins and climbed the steps, his curiosity quickly transforming into concern. He peered into each curve and cranny—

Until he found her in the deeper shadows of an alcove.

Seeing him, she let out a small sound of surprise, and lifted a hand to her eyes, he knew, to strike away tears.

Something in his heart staggered.

"What is wrong?" he demanded. "Are you hurt?"

Could it be that she had been injured during the skirmish? He had seen no blood, or bruising and she had not spoken as if pained. What if in the blind state of attraction he felt for her, he had missed something?

"No," she answered, in a voice choked with emotion. "I just need a moment. I just . . ." She opened her hands. "I just realized I'm not ready to go back inside there."

She peered at him in the darkness, her eyes shining. "It's just that . . . for the first time, my home doesn't feel like home. Life has not always been perfect or happy, but I've always felt safe here. Protected."

How strange to hear her speak words that mirrored his own boyhood feelings for this place, his home. Also her home.

"Now, I do not," she whispered. "I do not know what life holds for me." She turned away from him, toward the stones. "I do not want to marry either one of those men, or anyone like them. And I don't trust my father not to force me to do so."

He stood in place, saying nothing.

She lowered her head, pressing her forehead against the stone. "You think my fears are foolish. I don't blame you. Not with all you have faced in your life, and accomplished."

He came to stand behind her . . . placing his hand at the center of her back. "No, not foolish."

He held his breath, not knowing if his touch would be welcome—waiting for her to shrug him off or twist away, out of his reach. He was not adept at offering comfort. He knew how to be brutal, to inflict pain and to kill. And yes, he knew how to seduce and make love, but not with a woman like this.

"Sometimes," she said quietly, turning to face him, her back to the stone wall, "I feel like running away and doing as you did, getting on a ship and sailing off to take my chances with the world."

Her solemn tone and demeanor did not indicate that she spoke impulsively. Instinct told him Elspeth was neither a foolish nor rash girl. But considering the walls closing in on her, he knew she must feel trapped.

"The world is a dangerous place," he warned. "It would destroy a woman like you. For that reason, your father would follow and find you, and bring you back. If he didn't, then I would."

He was startled when in the darkness her hands rested against his chest. His pulse went rampant and every inch of his body took notice of hers, so close to his.

"You would come for me?" she whispered.

He could resist no more.

With his hand, he cradled her chin and stared deeply into her eyes. "Just as I came for you tonight."

He bent, his mouth closing on her still open one.

She tensed—and gasped into his mouth, but did not pull away.

Soft lips. Sweet breath.

Desire. Want. Need.

His arm slid around her waist, and he seized her close.

Elspeth knew it was wrong, that he was forbidden to her. That she should refuse his kiss and push him away—

But any commands from her conscious mind grew silent as his head tilted, and his mouth moved on hers, sweetly demanding more. His hand, gentle and certain, cupped the underside of her jaw, making her feel fragile and treasured and precious.

His body closed warm and hard against hers, surrounding her. Enveloping her. She vaguely felt the cool stones of the wall behind her back. With each turn of his head, each ardent press of his mouth, each careful touch of his hand, she melted . . . surrendered a little more until her consciousness faded and she knew only a wild, delirious hunger.

The shadows around them blurred. Mouths widened. Tongues tasted. His hands, under her cloak, clenched her hips. Slid up her rib cage. Crushed into her hair. The only sounds in the darkness were their garments, rustling . . . sliding . . . as they grappled with each other. Embracing. Touching. A growl from deep in his throat. Her sighs. Nothing had ever felt like this. She had never felt more alive or light of being.

He was gone, suddenly, pushing away—leaving her dizzied and alone. She reached for the wall, steadying herself for fear she would fall.

"Hell," Niall uttered, deep in his throat, his eyes flaring with annoyance. "Come."

No. Why? she wanted to complain.

"Elspeth!" a voice bellowed.

Her father.

Chapter 9

Elspeth experienced a moment of terror before Niall reached and yanked her by the arm, out from the alcove, and up several steps—

The MacClaren met them there, followed by what appeared to be the entire population of the castle—including FitzDuff and Keppoch. Servants carried torches. Warriors carried swords. At the forefront of them all was a rusty-haired stableboy . . . holding her shoes.

Her heart seized in her chest, barely beating, dreading what would come next.

She glanced at Niall, but he looked straight forward, his jaw rigid, his lips unsmiling.

Lips she'd just been kissing.

"Go to your father," he commanded, under his breath.

She did so without question, rushing up the steps. The MacClaren's gaze moved over her, a thunderous storm, taking in, she knew, her torn sleeve, disarrayed hair and missing shoes. She prayed nothing more, for her lips still burned with Niall's kisses, and she feared passion still glazed her eyes. He seized her by the arms, and shook her.

"Who did this to you?" he demanded, before fiercely embracing her.

Bridget looked at Niall accusingly. "I think that's obvious."

Elspeth gasped. "No. He did not—I was taken. Abducted. He saved me."

The words spilled from her mouth before she could stop them, because in that moment all she cared about was protecting him.

"How did that happen?" Bridget demanded, eyes bright with suspicion. "Someone came into the tower, and took you? And yet your shoes were found beside the stables?"

"The lass is blameless," proclaimed a voice from the darkness behind Niall.

Deargh appeared there, breathing hard as he climbed the stairs. Though Niall stared at the man very hard, his expression gave nothing away.

Deargh went on. "She was tricked into meeting the villain. He took advantage of her good nature and kindness, luring her out of the castle with a false missive from her old nursemaid. Niall and I heard it all, and were able to react quickly enough to make pursuit."

He seemed to know what had occurred. Elspeth could only imagine that he and Niall had seen her leave the castle, and overheard what she told the guards about going to see Fiona. And then on their way to the river to encamp for the night . . . they'd observed her abduction? But for whatever reason, only Niall had followed, while Deargh waited behind. In the shadows.

At realizing that, Elspeth's cheeks filled with heat.

Had he seen them kissing?

Whatever the truth, it was clear he sought to place himself at the center of her rescue, so as to keep Niall out of her father's dungeon.

"It was a fierce fight, and we gravely outnumbered,"

Deargh boasted, clapping a hand onto Niall's shoulder. "Were we not, my friend?"

"Indeed," answered Niall. "There was also a priest."

"A forced marriage!" bellowed the laird, his expression enraged.

"But unsuccessful!" Elspeth blurted.

Deargh grinned boisterously. "Thank the good Lord above that we intervened in time. The maid's virtue is preserved."

"Who took you, lass?" Conall demanded. "Tell us who did this."

Everyone looked at her expectantly—but she feared telling the truth would bring about a violent confrontation, and that someone she loved would die, whether that be Magnus or her father or any other of her MacClaren clansmen.

"It was dark," said Niall. "I was not able to see their faces. Mistress MacClaren, were you able to tell who they were?"

"No," Elspeth whispered, hating the lie but fearing the consequence of the truth more.

"Nor I," added Deargh.

"It had to be Magnus," Bridget said. "Who else would it have been? He made his intentions clear tonight, only to be humiliated with a rejection. The Alwyn border is the closest. He must have thought he could take her there."

"I will kill him," the MacClaren seethed. "This offence will not go unanswered."

"No, Father, please," Elspeth begged. "Everything is well. I am safe and unharmed. If it was Magnus who abducted me, I am certain he would not have gone through with anything, after realizing I was so opposed—"

"You try to protect him—but he has dared too much this time," the laird thundered. "No doubt the Alwyn's bastard acted on the order of his father, for the sole purpose of humiliating me, of taking what is mine."

"More reason to see her swiftly wed," murmured Bridget. "Elspeth, come. Off to bed with you, where you belong."

Elspeth looked at Niall, but received no reciprocal farewell glance.

She allowed herself to be led away, but heard her father's voice behind her.

"Thank you, and I apologize that you have had to exert your energies, twice in as many days, toward the preservation of my daughter's safety. I swear to you, watching after my children is not at all the purpose for which we hired you."

Niall chuckled in response. "I am relieved that you do not expect me to continue on in the position of nursemaid. I much prefer a sword in hand to the company of a willful child."

Elspeth's heart constricted painfully in her chest, and her cheeks stung at the burst of amused male laughter that followed.

Elspeth heard nothing more. Wounded . . . and *infuriated* by his words, she hurried to the tower and, once in her room, barred the door against Bridget's continuing barrage of questions. In the dark, she discarded her ruined gown into the corner, and pulled on a night rail.

She did not know what would happen tomorrow. A clan war? Or a betrothal. One thing was certain. It had been a mistake to kiss Niall.

Nursemaid. Willful child! That he would say such things, after kissing her like that.

Perhaps for him, their kiss had only been a kiss. A momentary dalliance and nothing more, to be forgotten, as easily as it had occurred. So too must it be for her.

Crawling into bed, she pressed her fingertips to her lips—and willed herself to forget.

Deargh lifted a finger, and his shaggy brows gathered. "So then, I overhear the lass say that she is going to visit a . . . Fiona in the village, a former nursemaid I surmise, by the guard's reply, and yet when I follow a few moments later to go to the stable, I see she does not go toward the village, but the same direction as me." He pointed the finger at his head. "This makes me curious."

They sat beside the small hearth in Niall's quarters, a small one-roomed cottage located in a row of similar structures just inside the wall of the castle. The laird had insisted on them taking residence, as reward for saving his daughter a second time.

"You mean suspicious," Niall murmured, easing back in his chair.

"Aye, that. I got close enough to hear their voices and realize what was happening. But I saw you set off after them, and knew you would take the matter in hand." He shrugged. "You know I do not see so well in the dark anymore. So I waited."

"I am glad you did."

"As am I," he chuckled wickedly. "Because if the laird saw what I saw tonight, he'd have ordered you flogged, no matter how good you are with a sword."

Niall's thoughts returned to Elspeth, and her soft mouth against his. God, he had never experienced anything so sweet. So wildly pleasing. His body went to flames, just remembering.

"So . . ." Deargh leaned close. "It was good?"

"Aye, that it was," he answered, with a slow smile.

"Then I trust you have the matter in hand. As for the rest, I will send word tomorrow, by Alec, for the men to travel here. Three to four weeks? You are certain."

"I am."

Alec was one of five men, loyal to Niall, who presently camped in the forest, unseen, prepared to respond if needed, or in this case, to act as messenger to the larger company of men who awaited his summons. Men who had long fought beside him, and much like him, had lived too long without a home and who sought a permanent place. At his behest the five warriors had also spent time today searching the distant, dark hills for the surviving Kincaids. But without success.

Niall stood, and rubbed his fingers against the bridge of his nose. "We must not be overly confident, but I would say things are going very well."

"Very well, indeed." Grinning, Deargh stood and moved to the door. "That said, I am going to go enjoy my bed—which, don't think I did not notice is smaller than yours. And you have two chairs, where I have only a stool." He pointed at Niall. "I hold grudges, you know."

"Of that I am well aware."

Left alone, Niall turned back to the room, which he had only cursorily examined before. It was spacious and appointed with a bed, heaped with furs and blankets, a table, and two chairs. There was also a basin on a stand beside a narrow, shuttered window.

Very soon after his and Deargh's arrival, servants had arrived to build a fire and left a basket of bread, cheese, and ale.

He ate, and afterward, stripped naked and washed. After, he lay awake, unaccustomed to the comfort of a bed, of the sensation of linen against his bare skin. Though he should be exhausted, he could not help but think of her, of their kiss, and the way she had responded to his touch.

His heart beat strong and fast in anticipation for he knew with a certainty it would only be a few hours before he kissed her again.

* * *

Unfortunately, Elspeth did *not* forget Niall's kisses.

Indeed, they were the first thing she thought of when awakened the next morning by a hammering of fists on her door, and insistent female voices demanding to be let in.

"Go away!" she moaned into her pillow, exhausted, wanting only to return to the blissful unawareness of sleep.

The clamor did not cease. Knowing the relentlessness of her sisters, she pushed up from the bed and unbarred the door. Turning, she raced back to the bed and flung the blanket back over her head.

"Elspeth, come!"

"No, just tell me," she answered, sullenly. "Whatever it is."

If Magnus was being drawn and quartered in the bailey below, she did not wish to watch.

"You *must* see!"

"Look what the mercenaries have done."

Niall. Who considered her a willful child.

Her curiosity got the best of her. Taking the blanket with her, draped over her shoulders, she joined them at the window, which they pushed open. The scene beyond always took her breath away. The dramatic, sweeping expanse of green, interrupted to the north by high stone crags, and below, the wide, meandering river. But her attention dropped, drawn by the sound of thunder in the bailey below.

Cattle streamed through the open gate, twenty . . . thirty . . . nay, some forty head, lowing and mooing. A number of her father's men rode in with them, along with Deargh, and last of all, Niall. Wearing only a short tunic, and a plaid over his shoulder, his legs were bare and flexed powerfully on either side of his saddle. He sat tall atop his horse, his bearing masterful, his cheeks ruddy with color. Heat rose to her cheeks, when she remembering how passionately he had kissed her the night before.

But it had meant nothing.

"Good morning, sleepyhead." Ina entered the room carrying a bucket of water, which she poured into a wide basin for Elspeth's morning bath. After, she joined them at the window. "I saw them ride out this morning, before dawn. The tall, dark-haired one there . . . he is very handsome."

Elspeth sighed miserably, as Derryth teased.

"Ina! You are a happily married lady, and should not notice such things."

Ina glanced into the bailey once more. "Even the happiest married lady would notice a man like that."

The MacClaren men dismounted and gathered around Niall, laughing. Clasping hands. Celebrating. Several grasped up buckets from the well, and filling them, splashed Niall with water. Laughing, he removed his plaid from his shoulder, baring his tattooed skin. Securing the cloth at his waist, he lifted his arms and wrenched off his drenched tunic. Elspeth's mouth went dry, observing the flex of his muscles along his back and torso as he squeezed the water from the linen.

In that moment he looked up, and stilled, his gaze meeting hers.

"He has seen us!" Derryth exclaimed giddily. She leaned out the window, waving. "Well done! Well done!"

Elspeth withdrew, her heart racing, for in that brief moment she experienced the same flame-hot connection with him she had felt the night before, and feared if anyone saw her they would see her infatuation with Niall written plain on her face. At her bed, she pretended to straighten the linens.

Ina joined her. "Lady MacClaren asked me to tell you that your father wishes to see you downstairs."

Elspeth's throat constricted. "Of course he does."

More quietly, Ina said, "I also know he spent time behind a closed door with each of your suitors this morning."

Elspeth let out an aggrieved sigh.

Her maid plucked a twig from her hair. "I heard about your excitement in the night. Is it true, what they say? Was it Magnus?"

"I don't know who it was." Elspeth replied—then covered her face with her hands. "But yes."

"I won't tell," Ina said quietly, glancing at the girls who remained at the window. "Just as long as nothing of any concern took place."

Elspeth's cheeks flushed. "It did not."

At least, not with Magnus.

"Then get thee to the basin," Ina ordered, with a smile. "Wash, and then I will comb and braid your hair. You must look your finest if you are to inform your father and his council that you are refusing those men who have offered for you."

Elspeth gave a rueful laugh. "You know me too well."

Ina squeezed her shoulder affectionately.

Her sisters came away from the window, because apparently there was nothing more to see. They chattered and gave opinions as to what she should wear and how her hair should be plaited. Elspeth, for her part, sat silent, preparing herself for what would not be an easy audience with her father and the council.

Now, in the light of day, surrounded by her sisters and everything she loved so well, she knew she would never abandon her duty to her family and clan. She would not be the willful child Niall had so wrongly proclaimed her to be. But neither would she agree to marry someone she could not abide.

After Ina secured the final braid, Elspeth left them straightaway, silently exhorting herself to be brave. Downstairs she entered her father's council room, seeking no permission or announcement.

"No doubt the Alwyn is bewildered!" The MacClaren chuckled. "Wondering where a whole herd of cattle has gone."

Her heart clenched, seeing that Niall stood there, and Deargh, accepting accolades with a roomful of MacClaren warriors.

"Indeed, laird," answered one of the MacClaren men. "We acted with such efficiency and stealth, I do not think they have yet realized what has occurred."

"All thanks to this man," said another, gesturing toward Niall. "Aye, we all learned a few new tricks today."

Deargh looked at his companion proudly. Conall stood to the side, practically glowing in agreement.

Elspeth moved to stand beside the fire, listening in begrudging fascination, while pretending not to care. She wished she did not.

"Elspeth," said her father.

She pivoted toward him, holding her expression calm. Though she felt Niall's gaze fix on her, she did not allow hers to waver from the laird.

"You summoned me," she said.

"That I did," he answered, his features growing instantly solemn.

She knew also that she did not imagine the change in the council members who were present. All went quiet and pensive.

The MacClaren thanked the other men and led them to the threshold. She glanced aside at Niall, as he moved past, covertly examining the strong line of his nose, which bore the slightest arch, and the angular slant of his jaw. Regretfully, he remained an alluring mystery, with fascinating lines and details she could not help but seek to examine further and memorize.

Yet he did not deign to look her way, employing the

same air of disinterest she had employed a moment earlier, perhaps because his indifference was real, which was all for the best.

He disappeared from view, along with the others, which left her alone with her father and the members of his council, including Conall, who came toward her.

"Come and sit," he said, with obvious sympathy.

"Thank you," she answered in a steady voice. "But I prefer to stand."

Chapter 10

"Dear child," said Dunlop—one of the clan's longtime council members—his eyes twinkling kindly. "May I say it has been an honor to watch you grow into the beauty you are today."

Elspeth looked at him, her arms crossed over her chest, trying to keep a mulish expression from overtaking her face. She was fond of the man and had no wish to be outright disrespectful to him.

Before she was born Dunlop had been a formidable warrior of the clan, but now walked stooped with age. When she had been little he had always given her pretty stones he had found lying about. She still had them all in a pouch, which she kept in her box of childhood treasures underneath her bed.

"I hope you know we care about your happiness," said another, named Ennis, who years before had taught her many silly riddles, which she had in turn taught Catrin. "Each and every one of us, and we consider you as dear as a daughter. Especially those like me who have no children of our own." He touched a hand to his heart.

Ennis's only son had died two winters before of a fever.

Three more council members looked on, clearing their throats and shifting stances repeatedly. Tellingly, they did not meet her gaze.

Her father stood near the window, looking outward. Bridget sat in his chair, plucking unsatisfactory stitches from a small frame of needlework.

Elspeth wasn't a fool. Poor Dunlop and Ennis. They had been set forth by the others to carry out a most unpleasant task. She knew what came next.

Dunlop cleared his throat. "We hope you will be flattered to know that before departing this morning, both Keppoch Macpherson *and* Alan FitzDuff, made very generous offers for your hand. Separately of course."

He smiled up at her, chuckling faintly as if he had made some jest.

She did not smile back.

Ennis edged closer, clasping his hands together thoughtfully. "Either of these chiefs, along with their clans, would be a valuable ally to the MacClarens at a time when strong allies, who would bolster our authority, are needed most. But you know this, because you have faithfully attended these meetings of ours and understand the dangers of the world in which we live. You also know the threat from the Alwyn clan has become more serious. More grave. Which is certainly why Magnus attempted to force your hand last night, so as to legitimize their claims on what have become disputed lands. Including the lands upon which this castle sits . . . your family's home, and the heart of our clan. Of course, you know just as well as any of us, that we cannot allow that to happen."

Her father turned from the window. "What say you, my daughter? Which of these men would you choose as your husband?"

Although they were the exact words she'd expected to hear, she gritted her teeth, finding them utterly distasteful. But she must remain calm and dignified, and make the council and her father see rational sense. It was the only way she would win them to her side.

"I understand the danger to our clan," she said. "And can plainly see why you find value in these men as allies, but I respectfully decline to marry either of them."

"Think longer on this choice—" urged Dunlop, his hands raised in a gentle plea.

"Ponder all they offer for a few days more, child." Ennis nodded.

Though her heart beat a tumultuous thrum, she forced her countenance to remain placid. "I am no child, but a woman grown and I know my mind. I could have five hundred days to think on the two choices with which I have been presented, and I still would never choose Alan Fitz-Duff or Keppoch Macpherson to be my husband."

"Daughter—" the MacClaren hissed, in a warning voice.

The men of his council whispered among themselves, their faces grave and judging.

She had never defied her father. To do so now, before his council, sucked the air from her lungs and crushed her heart. She moved to stand before him, her composure close to fracturing—but not her resolve.

"I am prepared to do my duty. I am *not* unreasonable. I am agreeable to marrying, and marrying with haste." Looking at her father, she said, "You told me I would be able to choose—"

"So *choose*," he thundered, eyes wide.

"This is no choice," she shouted back with equal ire. "I will not accept it as such."

The words echoed in her ears ugly and shameful. Not because she did not mean them, or doubt she was entitled to say them but because she had shouted them and she had never before raised her voice to her father.

"Elspeth!" Bridget rebuked, looking shocked.

She stood her ground, unmoving. "I know my rights within the law. You cannot force me to marry either of those men against my will, and I tell you now, firmly resolved, that I will accept neither. I will not be swayed."

Her father's nostrils flared.

"Certainly there are other choices, and other clans," she suggested calmly. "Give me—give *us* just a bit more time to find a more suitable choice."

Elspeth's back ached from holding it so straight and proud. But she would not bow to their expectations until their expectations matched hers.

Niall's face flashed across her mind, blue eyed and handsome. Through mere will, she forced the vision away, knowing he was just as unsuitable as the others.

The chief's gaze faltered.

"Please . . . leave us," he said to his council. "I wish to speak to my daughter alone."

"I, too, would like to stay," said Bridget, standing from her chair.

Her father scowled in annoyance.

"It is my right," she said, standing and dropping the embroidery frame to the chair behind her. "As your wife and her stepmother."

He nodded, his lips pressed thin.

One by one, the council members left the room.

Her father turned to her. Rather than shouting out a lecture about her selfishness, as she expected, he looked at her with soft and loving eyes.

"Elspeth . . . certainly you know by now that I am ill."

She went cold, to her soul, not wanting to hear what he would say. "You will get better."

He shook his head. "I . . . will not."

Hearing the pain in his voice, Elspeth closed her eyes, feeling her own heart break. He all but told her he expected to die. But how soon?

Bridget looked at her as well, her demeanor calm, but . . . not unsympathetic.

"Don't say that," Elspeth whispered.

Yet she knew what he said was true. She had seen the signs for so long now, and they only became more apparent, rather than fading away. The wince of pain when he moved. The change in his body and his features as he grew frailer and weaker. Though she'd tried not to see it, the MacClaren was a dim image of his prior self.

Though he was maddening and blustery and controlling, she loved him, and loved him fiercely. She wanted to embrace him, to kiss his face and hold him close, but he had never been one for such affection. His love had always come from a distance, and that was all right. She knew it was strong and unwavering, just the same. The best gift she could give him now was respect.

He covered his mouth with his hand, and paced a few steps. "For this reason, I am being pressed to name a successor with more urgency than before. It is a difficult choice because as you know there are no clear candidates among the MacClarens. Good men are plentiful among our people, but a man who can be its leader to defend against our present dangers has yet to emerge. Until a choice can be made, I must do what I can to secure the future of this clan. And Elspeth, I must do so quickly, before I am unable and the choice is taken from my hands. The Alwyn, if he learns I am not long on this earth, will use my weakness and his royal favor against us to seize the very stones upon which we stand. We need the strongest possible allies, sworn to stand with us, else we will fall. You are not some pawn in this. You are my eldest daughter. A MacClaren warrior, just as certainly as any man. Though it is difficult and sometimes painful to our souls, we have a duty to do what is right."

Pride swelled her chest. What he said was true. What she had always believed. They were words she had needed to hear from his lips.

"I *will* do my duty," she answered. "No one loves our clan—our people—more than I. But—"

Bridget turned to them, speaking suddenly. "Perhaps there is another way."

The MacClaren looked at her, almost as if he had forgotten her presence.

"What is it?" he asked.

Elspeth dreaded what her stepmother would say, fearing whatever she suggested as a new resolution would commit her to an even deeper pit of wretchedness. After all, it had been she who invited Keppoch and FitzDuff to offer for Elspeth's hand.

Her young stepmother tilted her blond head. "I propose that we send word separately to FitzDuff and Keppoch, thanking them for their interest, and advising that Elspeth will make a decision very soon."

Yes. Elspeth was all in favor of that. But she remained unsure of whether she could breathe easier just yet, until she heard more.

Bridget went on. "The Cearcal will take place in less than a fortnight. Let us all attend."

She referred to an annual festival held each autumn, which Elspeth remembered attending with her mother and father as a child. Such memories! It had always been a time of excitement.

The "circle" referred to the encampments set up by the clans that attended, at all points around a circular valley, with an enormous bonfire at the center. It also referred to the inter-clan courting that took place, and the way men and women who had never been close enough to cross paths before had the opportunity to "circle" one another there.

On the last day of the festival, there were always a score of weddings, most among the common people, but sometimes there were dramatic surprises and stunning alliances forged among the powerful families of the north.

"The Cearcal," her father repeated, his gaze growing distant. "Our clan has not attended in years."

"It is not so far," said Bridget. "We could dispatch a messenger tomorrow to deliver news to all the northern clan chiefs—except for those we wish to exclude—that Elspeth intends to entertain and consider suitors there. If you make clear the extent of her *tocher*, and what you expect in exchange, I know you will draw many interested parties. There are many sons and nephews of powerful and influential chiefs and earls eager to start dynasties of their own, and like you, they don't want the interference of the crown. I know such travel will be tiring for you, but we could make the trip slowly so that you could be there to ensure Elspeth's decision is wise." She rested a hand on the chief's arm. "What say you, husband?"

He looked from his wife to Elspeth. "Would you agree to this?"

To answer now, outright, seemed so final and binding. But what more could she ask? She could imagine no better reprieve than this. At least at the Cearcal, she would have a broader choice of husbands than those with whom she'd previously been presented.

But no one to compare with Niall.

"Yes," she blurted. "I would agree."

"Then it is decided." He nodded, his gaze sharp. "I will inform the council."

A short time later Elspeth left the castle, inhaling deeply

of the cold morning air, needing time alone to think and renew her resolve, not as a young woman with romantic dreams—but as a MacClaren, whose vision and purpose must remain crystal clear. Not wishing to speak to anyone just yet, she took the wooded path she often walked with her sisters, which ran toward the river, purposefully avoiding the stone steps that would take her past the alcove where Niall had kissed her the night before. She would go to her favorite place beside the water, where she could sit in the crook of her favorite tree.

That she had won the immediate battle—surprisingly, with help from Bridget—offered little relief as far as the burden on her mind and heart. She would still be expected to choose a husband within a fortnight. Any wedding would take place very soon. The idea of being thrown into such an intimate situation, when she couldn't even imagine her husband's face, made it difficult to prepare herself.

One face did repeatedly come to mind. Niall's.

That had to stop, for obvious reasons.

She told herself he could *not* be as intriguing as her mind made him out to be. He was merely a superficial representation of all her girlish dreams, which she must now leave behind so that she could have an open heart and mind for a man with considerably more substance.

Oh, but his kisses.

All foolishness. Like many young women, she had made the mistake of being seduced by a handsome face and a strong body. It did not mean that *inside*, at his heart, he was anything she would admire in an enduring way, or ever come to love.

She simply had to stop thinking about him. Do her best to forget his kiss, and the way her body had come alive at his touch.

The way she conducted herself in the coming weeks,

and indeed for the rest of her life, would be testimony to her mettle as a woman. As a MacClaren.

A child's voice drew her attention in the clearing ahead. Through a break in the trees, she saw that it was Catrin, laughing and swinging a wooden sword, following the instruction of some unseen master, hidden by the trunk of a tree.

Catrin always made her feel better. She was such a happy child, when allowed to be so. Boisterous and full of energy and fun. She recalled with fondness a time when she had been that happy herself.

She moved closer, stepping quietly, wanting only to watch, not to interfere.

She recognized Niall immediately. The back of his dark, glossy head. His broad shoulders, beneath a linen tunic, and long, lean legs in brown woolen trews and leather boots. He held a long tree branch in his hand, as if it were a sword.

She weakened instantly at taking in the endearing scene. Just like that, all the attraction she'd felt for him the night before crashed over her, taking her breath away, leaving her feeling thrilled and defeated all at once.

"You must anticipate what your opponent will do, and react quickly," he instructed in his deep, resonant voice. The same one that had murmured her name in her ear the night before. The memory sent a frisson of pleasure down her spine.

"What does 'anticipate' mean?" Cat asked, laughing. She pressed her lips together, and tapped her sword against his.

"It means you must guess correctly what they are going to do before they do it." He assumed a fighting stance, albeit a gentle one. Even covered in wool, she saw the powerful flex of his legs. "If I am standing in this pose, with my sword already pointed down to the ground, after failing to strike you before . . . where do you suppose I shall move the blade next?"

"Back to me," the girl said brightly.

Elspeth covered her mouth, *sighing* . . . trying not to reveal her presence there. There was something poignant about what she observed. Catrin was so hungry for the MacClaren's attention. A father's love. And he so rarely gave it. Niall's manner seemed so easy with her. He would be a good father.

"And yet look how you are holding your sword," he noted gravely. "Would you be able to stop me from cutting off your nose and feeding it to the fish?"

Catrin giggled. "I should hold it here instead."

"That's right. So that when I—"

Slowly . . . he raised his sword . . .

Cat gave it a mighty *whack*.

"Very good," he announced, his voice warm with praise. "Now you know, you must always . . . what?"

"Anticipate!"

"Yes."

Catrin saw her then. "Look, Elspeth, Niall is teaching me how to fight."

Heat rose into Elspeth's face, and she took a step back. "Don't stop. I was just watching your lesson. I'll go on to the castle so I don't distract you."

Niall looked at her steadily, not smiling, his expression giving nothing away.

"Or . . ." he said. "You could take up a sword and join us."

"Yes!" shouted Cat, pointing her stick at Elspeth. "Join us."

She stood frozen for a long moment, indecisive over what to do.

But then the most reasonable answer occurred. The easiest way to forget him, to lose her fascination for him, would be to spend time in his company. To prove to herself that he was just a man, no different than any other.

And most important of all, she must let him know that what happened last night, in the shadows of that alcove, would never happen again.

Chapter 11

"It is a dangerous invitation you make," Elspeth said.

Niall watched, riveted by the sight of her as she moved toward them, lovely in a heathery purple gown, searching the ground. She bent, reaching for a straight-ish branch. In doing so, her breasts crowded against the round neckline of her bodice, full and tempting. His mouth went dry, and—

His loins stirred in his trews.

God help him, if she could arouse him like that, so innocently and without intention, he could only imagine his response if she were in his arms, willing and eager. When she stood again he quickly looked away, so she would not see his interest—nay, his hunger—written plain and clear on his face.

"A worthy sword, if ever there was one," he observed huskily.

She replied in a cool tone of exaggerated smugness— playful dramatics, he realized, intended for the child. "I can't believe neither of you claimed it for yourselves."

"My sword is better," shouted Cat, holding her wooden sword aloft.

Aye, her sword was indeed better than their bent, lichen covered branches. As it should be.

"I would take care if I were you," he said to Elspeth, tilting his head toward the girl. "Catrin is a cunning one."

"Cunning swordswomen *are* always the best." She extended her "weapon" and with a twirl of her wrist, gave it flourish. "The question is, Cat, are you more cunning than me?"

"Hi-*ya*!" The child lunged, swinging a sword at her sister's skirts.

"A surprise attack," exclaimed Elspeth, feinting back, bringing her branch around to defend her knees from attack.

And yet when she gently jabbed her weapon toward Cat, the child soundly deflected the attempt.

"Do you see, Niall?" Cat cried, turning to him and grinning triumphantly. "I anticipated."

"Aye, that you did," he answered through laughter. "But now is not the time for celebration. Watch out, she'll come sneaking up the back."

Elspeth poked the child in the bottom with the end of her sword. "Ha! Got you."

Cat ran behind Niall. "Cover my back!"

This left him face-to-face with Elspeth, who looked back at him, cheeks flushed, and a dazzling smile on her lips.

Yet her smile faded, and her eyes took on a darkly mischievous gleam.

She raised her sword—and lunged. *Whoosh*.

Requiring that he defend himself. *Smack*.

Stunned by her ferocity, Niall almost stumbled, backing away as she swung at him again with admirable form, whirling, her arms coming round, her weapon aimed square at his chest.

He intercepted her blade firmly with his own.

"You're good," he said, breathing hard. "You've had training."

Satisfaction warmed his cheeks as he stared into her battle-bright eyes.

"A little," she said between clenched white teeth.

He had an inkling that she *might* be displeased with him somehow. Perhaps angry even? Oddly, he found the possibility attractive. The only Elspeth he had observed before had been gentle and sweet-natured. This was a distinctly different and interesting side of her.

Proving him right, she lifted her sword and launched an aggressive assault, which he again repelled and countered, his heartbeat surging. Pushing toward her, his branch crossing firmly against hers, he crowded her against a tree where she glared at him, the sight of her tousled hair, flushed cheeks, and heaving breasts more intoxicating than any wine.

"I'm beginning to think I should fear for my life." He grinned, captivated . . . completely engaged in her and pleased that she should surprise him in this way.

"Perhaps you should," she answered, her gray eyes staring coldly into his.

But then her gaze shifted, moving beyond his shoulder.

"Cat," she called, her expression changing to one of alarm. "Where are you going? We're in the midst of a battle here."

"I'm *hungry*."

Looking over his shoulder, Niall saw the girl scamper out of view.

At the knowledge that they were alone, desire curled low in the pit his stomach, like an awakening dragon. Turning back to Elspeth—

She sidestepped him, a blush high on her cheeks.

"I should go," she said, moving in the same direction the child had gone.

"Elspeth?"

Was she angry because he had kissed her the night before?

"I wouldn't want you to have to play nursemaid," she said huffily.

Or there was that.

He caught her by the wrist, and pulled her around. She stared up at him, eyes flashing.

"You are angry with me, for saying that?"

"Of course not," she asked, yanking her arm free and stepping behind a tree trunk, where he could not see her. "It let me know the truth of how you feel."

He dropped his branch and followed to find her standing against a backdrop of lichen, her eyes closed, breathing deeply through her nose, still clenching her improvised sword.

He touched his hand to her upper arm.

Her eyes flew open. "Don't touch me."

Again, she pushed past him. This time he caught her by the back of her skirt, just above her bottom, and hauled her back against him. With a small cry of outrage, she twisted around, leveling the branch at his head. He ducked— and her sword smashed into the trunk behind him.

He exhaled, eyes wide and focused on her as she stepped back, arms raised, clenching her weapon, poised and ready.

"My life is not some child's game," she said. "And I am not a toy for you or anyone else to play with."

In that moment he realized he had never seen anything more beautiful than Elspeth, holding her weapon high, in her purple gown, prepared to knock his head off.

"You think it was true? Those things I said?" he demanded in a low voice, closing the distance between them.

"If they weren't, you wouldn't have said them," she replied smartly.

"What is it you want?" Towering above her, he intentionally tried to intimidate her.

Yet she did not back down. "I don't want anything at all from you."

"I don't believe you," he said. "I think you want me to kiss you again."

Her eyes flared wide and her cheeks flushed more deeply.

"Of course I don't," she retorted. "If you kissed me again, I would have no choice but to tell my father."

She whirled, and moved toward the path, her every step away from him filling his head with rising thunder.

"Please do tell him." He started after her, moving fast. Because now *he* was angry. Perhaps because in that minute, he believed her. "I would be more than happy to tell him how eagerly you kissed me back."

"Oh!" She pivoted on her heel, swinging the branch.

He caught it with his bare hand—and stared into her wide, tear-filled eyes.

Seeing this, every bit of anger, every vestige of resolve, fell away.

With a yank, he pulled the stick from her grasp and threw it to the ground.

In one step, he caught her face with both hands, and crushed his lips onto hers.

She moaned into his mouth, going up on her toes . . . swaying against him . . . her hands clenched in his tunic. And he was instantly returned to paradise, a paradise made all the more exquisite because just a moment before he had feared, as he had feared nothing else in his life, he would never touch her again. He pulled her close, lifting her into his arms, off the ground, breathing her in, tasting her, backing her against a tree . . .

Her fingers speared through his hair, clasping his head tight as his lips moved to her cheek . . . her eyes . . . her nose . . . the fragrant place behind her ear. Along her throat, as she arched, clenching his arms, to press his mouth against the pillowy upper swell of her breast.

"No," she cried in a thick voice—

And wrenched away. Arms empty, he stared at her, his body raging and feeling half out of his mind with need for her.

"I am to be married within a fortnight," she gasped, her expression stricken. "If you care for me at all, this can't happen again."

Turning, she fled, disappearing through the trees.

The next morning, after an early morning ride with six of the MacClaren's favored warriors, Niall and Deargh stepped into the great hall, having received summons from Conall that the laird and his council wished to see him after the morning meal.

Niall was instantly besieged by two small assailants, one that immediately wrapped its arms around his leg while the other gnawed at his boot strap. He pried Cat loose, and lifting her high, tossed her up in the air. The girl let out a happy squeal, her arms and legs spread wide. Chuckling, he caught her, and returned her to the ground. He liked the little girl, but shuttered off the immediate thought that sprang to his mind—that one day soon he would likely make her an orphan.

"Again!" she pleaded, throwing herself against him. Her puppy yapped excitedly, now chewing on her trouser leg.

"No, dear," said a handsome woman wearing a head scarf and apron, whom Niall assumed to be the child's nursemaid. "Back to the table. You and that animal. Finish your porridge like I told y', before Lady MacClaren returns and sees what mischief you're up to."

She smiled at Niall fleetingly, but winked saucily at Deargh. "Sit yourselves down near the fire. I'll instruct the kitchen t' serve ye as well."

"Someone you met last night?" chuckled Niall, when she was gone.

Deargh had again remained in the great hall late into the night, listening to any conversations of interest, and as always, paying court to whichever lady, or ladies, struck his liking Niall had again retired to the solitude of his quarters, which he much preferred to revelry—especially when Elspeth had not attended the evening meal.

Deargh responded beneath his breath. "I met quite a few intriguing MacClaren ladies after you left. You on the other hand . . ." He directed his gaze to the little girl at the distant table, who grinned bright cheeked at Niall over an earthenware bowl. "Have claimed the heart of the wrong sister."

Niall winked at Catrin, who giggled back.

Last night he had lain awake for hours, committing every detail of the castle's defenses to mind, as well as the strengths and weaknesses of the MacClaren warriors who protected it, as he had observed during the afternoon's weaponry practice. However, in the end, his thoughts had settled on Elspeth, and the manner in which they had parted. Her stunned, tear-filled eyes. The color in her cheeks. Her insistence that he must never kiss her again.

And yet after such a magnificent attraction had ignited between them, he was only more determined to do just that. Aye, he would have Elspeth MacClaren in his bed. As his wife.

Lowering himself to the bench, Niall raised his eyebrows. "There's still time."

His companion sat beside him and leaned close, keeping their conversation private as other warriors entered the hall. "Not much, I vow. Best hurry, if you wish to have her. I suspect the MacClaren is sicker than anyone knows and that he will try to do his duty to the clan and see her usefully wed before he has no say in that decision. Hopefully not to one of those eejits who offered for her. That would be a damnable waste of a fine woman."

Niall's chest tightened in response. If it were up to him, neither Keppoch nor FitzDuff would ever look at her again . . . or so much as touch the edge of her sleeve.

"I won't allow that to happen," Niall answered, accepting a filled goblet from a servant.

But he would take his time with Elspeth, to the degree he could. Her father and her clan already made demands on her. Despite the impatience that roiled his blood, he must not do the same. To attempt to force her affection would only make her flee. He must take greater care than that. He must be gentle—and ruthlessly so. She must come to see him as her safe place, so that when she chose him it would be by her own decision. Once her loyalty belonged to him, he would use her to break her father.

His blood hummed with the desire to see her again. Where was she now? Would he see her, or would she keep to her chambers abovestairs?

Servants arrived with their morning meal. Surrounded on all sides by MacClaren warriors, he and Deargh ate their fill, after which time Conall appeared at the doorway and gestured for the two of them to join him. They followed him down a corridor, and even though he knew what to expect his heart darkened when he saw the MacClaren inside, ensconced in the same room where his father had once held council, surrounded by five astute-looking men in robes, all conversing with some fervency.

When he and Deargh entered the room, all fell silent, and stood. The MacClaren came to his feet last, his lips pressed thin with the effort it took to rise from his chair.

"Good morning," he said in a gravelly voice. "Please come inside."

They did so, and Conall shut the door. The room looked much the same as it had when the Kincaids had held the castle, with tapestries and screens, and scrolls and maps set about. Before Niall sat, he glimpsed the Lady Mac-Claren in the corner behind him, only halfway concealed by one such screen, watching him over a needlepoint frame.

Introductions were made all around, before everyone sat again, in chairs around a long table near the window, save for Conall who remained standing, his arms crossed over his chest.

"There is something we must discuss, Niall and Deargh, before we proceed. Something that yesterday I decided not to make note of, for reasons of my own. But the subject . . . the *concern* continues to arise here within the council, and must be addressed. We hope you will not take offense."

"What is that?" asked Niall, lowering his chin in assent.

He had been waiting for one particular discussion, and believed this to be it.

"The night you arrived, the man in Keppoch's company, who recognized you . . . while he spoke to your skills and indeed, your legend, which is the reason we have invited you here, he also said something else."

"That we fought for Alexander Stewart, the earl of Buchan," Niall answered, with a nod. "Yes, it is true. Is that of particular concern to you? If so, tell me why."

"The MacClaren clan once supported Buchan as well—" Conall answered, with a lift of his hand.

"But no longer," interjected the MacClaren gruffly. "Even before his father became king, he . . . instigated conflict among the clans, to serve his own greed for land and power. Particularly of concern, is that the Alwyn clan, the same clan that harries our borders, has of late threatened to seek a reapportionment of lands that were granted to us by his father's predecessor, David the Second, shortly before his death. I fear they court Buchan's favor, in hopes that by his influence, that egregious deed will be carried out."

"What lands?" Deargh uttered, speaking the same words that clamored in Niall's mind. "*These* . . . lands?" His nostrils flared.

"Indeed." The laird scowled.

Damn. Buchan? It was a complication he had not expected, and his mind worked to fashion a solution that on the surface served the MacClaren, but secretly, himself as well.

Standing, he addressed the MacClaren directly. "We are well aware of Buchan's methods, lawful and otherwise. And I will tell you . . . you have every cause to be concerned. Murmurings in Edinburgh say the king will name him Justiciar of the North, if that entitlement has not been granted already."

"Justiciar of the North?" The MacClaren leaned forward in his chair, his nostrils flaring.

The room filled with the voices of the council.

"Say this is not true."

"Disaster!"

"This will only embolden the Alwyn!"

Niall waited until they grew quiet before speaking again. "I am not here to tell you what to do. But neither do I boast when I tell you Buchan holds me in high respect, as his former personal guard, and with me, the hundred or more wintering mercenaries I can summon to my side, loyal to *me*—not to Buchan—to protect your lands." He looked into the eyes of the council men. "I make no guarantees, but I suspect if you were thusly fortified, and my name set forth as supporting your defense, Buchan would not act against you in support of the Alwyn."

The MacClaren's cheeks flushed, but he held silent. Niall recognized the face of a man trying to decide whether to believe something that sounded too good to be true, a valuable instinct the laird might wish to pay heed to, but not for the reasons before him.

"Why did you come here, allowing us to believe you were a common mercenary?" Conall said, his eyes wide with suspicion—and admiration.

"Because in truth, that is all I am," Niall said. "Now that I have left Buchan's service."

"On the best of terms, if you are curious," Deargh inserted, with a tilt of his head. "There is no malice between them, which would only work to your benefit in having Niall and the army he can raise, here in your service. Hear my words, Buchan will not wish to enter into any conflict with this man, who sits before you now."

The MacClaren pressed his hands flat against the table. "I shall have to speak to my council. A hundred men? I must be honest. I do not know if we can provide sufficiently for such a force."

Niall dipped his chin in acknowledgment. "Of course. You could always bolster your present forces with less. I will await your decision."

But he suspected, from the hopeful, relieved expressions of the council members, an invitation for a hundred men would be forthcoming.

Conall looked at him evenly. "Have you any questions for us, before we meet privately to discuss your proposal?"

Niall returned to his chair, and seated himself. "Other than the Alwyn clan, have you any other threats against your people or property?" Specifically, he wanted to know where his surviving Kincaid clansmen had gone after their laird was killed. "I have heard mention of wild barbarians from the Dark Hills?"

The MacClaren was silent for a long moment. "We are

not the first clan to possess these lands. The Kincaids were here before us. After David the Second displaced that clan, we absorbed some into our own clan, in that they took to the furthest edges of these lands, and for the most part kept to themselves. Others . . . the most lawless and rebellious of them . . . migrated to the Dark Hills."

It took all of Niall's strength to conceal the rage that awakened inside him at hearing the laird's passionless account, utterly devoid of any details about his personal involvement in seeing the Kincaid clan all but destroyed.

"Aye, a fractious lot they be," added Conall. "They come in the night, and harry us with endless petty bedevilments."

Fractious? Aye, he would take much pleasure in teaching the MacClarens the true meaning of the word. When the time was right.

The laird scowled. "I don't believe Donald MacClaren would appreciate your calling his daughter's abduction a petty bedevilment."

Ennis, one of the council members, leaned forward. "We've never found her or the fiend who took her."

"Most believe the savage killed her," said another, named Dunlop, with an aggrieved shake of his head.

"Perhaps it is that she does not wish to be found," suggested a female voice from behind Niall—one he instantly recognized as Elspeth's. "Perhaps she has no desire at all to return home."

Chapter 12

Niall turned, his gaze searching for and finding her. Behind the same scarlet screen that only partially concealed her stepmother, he perceived a slender figure reclining on a padded bench strewn with pillows.

His skin flushed with pleasure at realizing she had been there behind him all along. He was not a boastful man, but took pride in the accomplishments he had made during his lifetime—the greatest of which was yet to come. It pleased him that she should know more about him. That he might now be more esteemed in her eyes.

"What do you mean, Donald MacClaren's daughter would not want to be found?" demanded Dunlop. Turning to Ennis, who sat beside him, he repeated, "What *does* she mean?"

Behind the screen, Elspeth shrugged. "All I'm saying is that she may prefer the Kincaid savage who stole her away, to the tyrant her father betrothed her to marry." Her voice dipped. "Certainly I'm not the only one who heard she went willingly."

Lady MacClaren lowered her frame to her lap, and

peered imperiously toward her stepdaughter. "Elspeth, now is not the time to share gossipy details overheard from the lips of servants."

Niall returned his attention to the men at the table and observed the MacClaren's jaw twitch in annoyance, he could only suppose, at the prospect of a disobedient daughter.

"We are done here, now, I think," muttered the laird, who then paused to cough into a linen cloth. "If you and Deargh will leave us now, I and my council will come to a decision."

Niall followed Deargh from the room.

Conall followed. "I will come and find you shortly. Don't go far."

Recalling the MacClaren's demeanor when they had left the room, he suspected Deargh's earlier judgment was right. The laird was ill—more ill than anyone realized. If the MacClaren realized this, he would rush to marry his daughter as best he could, while he still remained in full control of his clan and his council.

The way she'd spoken to her father and his council with such ease . . . his admiration for her grew. And yet she had seemed a thousand miles away behind the screen, and had not in any way addressed him directly.

Suddenly he felt separated from her by more than just a screen. Doubt weighted his thoughts. He had been arrogant to think he had time. To simply assume the power of their attraction would bring them together.

Niall paced a few steps, ignoring Deargh's inquiring gaze. Of course, he would reclaim his birthright, with or without Elspeth, but in his mind she had become the jewel in the crown of his revenge. He loved a good challenge, and this one set his blood afire. He *would* have her, one way or another.

"I know what you're seething about," growled Deargh,

beside him. "But forget her for now. We have a much larger problem. *Buchan*? Damn it. We need to talk."

Niall shook his head in impatience. "There is nothing to talk about. Nothing changes. Buchan has no idea I am son of the Kincaid, and even when he does, he won't raise arms against me."

"And if he does?"

Niall's eyes narrowed. "I will deal with him then."

Men's voices sounded behind them as members of the council emerged from the corridor. Some returned to the great hall, while others made their way to the bailey. Conall crossed the room toward them.

"It is decided," he said, smiling. "The council is in unanimous agreement. Summon your hundred."

Niall's chest expanded in triumph—and no small amount of relief. His seizure of the castle and surrounding lands would go relatively unchallenged with his force in place.

Deargh nodded. "Very good."

"How long until they arrive, do you think?" the captain asked.

"A fortnight," Niall answered, looking toward Deargh, who nodded in affirmation. "A little longer, perhaps. They will travel with horses, livestock, and supplies, so we must account for that."

"Just after we return from the Cearcal. That is more than sufficient." Conall crossed his arms over his chest. "It gives us time to prepare. The MacClaren wishes to build new structures in which to house them, and a barn as well, I suppose. We must also prepare our MacClaren men and families. Some won't take kindly to outsiders coming in such large numbers."

"Understandable," answered Niall. "Remind them the arrangement is temporary and will remain in place only until the Alwyn threat is resolved. And be assured, as well, that this is a well-disciplined force that will answer to me. Your people should not fear for their safety or property. We will discuss all this more in detail later, but I suggest that once my men have arrived, we station your men at the castle and in the village, while my mercenaries will make a show of patrolling the borders, where they will be most visible."

It was a false plan. By the time his men arrived, he intended to have gained the trust of all involved, allowing him to place forces within the castle itself, as well as without.

Conall nodded. "A sound strategy, I think, as it provides a comfortable degree of separation."

As the three of them made their way to the doors, Elspeth emerged from the corridor, wearing a vivid saffron-colored gown. Her hair had been twisted into a smooth coil at her nape, which drew his eye to her graceful neck and delicate shoulders.

She paused, her gaze grazing heavily against his, until the Lady MacClaren appeared behind her.

"The task simply cannot be put off any longer," her stepmother announced. "I will summon your sisters to assist. The upstairs maids, if necessary. Everyone must live and breathe with a needle in hand until your household linens are complete."

Elspeth closed her eyes in obvious unhappiness.

Yet the Lady MacClaren continued on with her henpecking, urging Elspeth up the stairs. "Don't sigh at me. What if you are married at the Cearcal? Your things must be ready. We wouldn't want you to linger here any longer than need be, when you could be off starting your new life elsewhere, now would we?"

Conall shook his head, muttering under his breath. Niall knew he was not mistaken in detecting an insincere, even cruel undertone to the woman's voice. Even now, when he

looked at the Lady MacClaren, all he could think of was
the bright hand mark on Elspeth's cheek, erased now by
time—but never from his mind. Though he could not
intercede on Elspeth's behalf now without drawing attention to himself and his motives, he took satisfaction in
knowing that Bridget, like her husband, would soon have
no authority in this castle.

After that the afternoon passed quickly, with barely a
moment's time to think of Elspeth. There was a careful re-
view and inventory of the armory, the promised visit to
the blacksmith, where he and Deargh examined newly
hewn weaponry. Afterward, they rode out to see the Mac-
Claren's flock of sturdy ponies and as night fell, returned
to the castle, in time for the evening meal.

The first thing he saw upon entering the room, was
Elspeth's straight, proud back.

Elspeth knew the moment Niall came into the hall. It was
as if her every instinct—or perhaps it was her soul—
took notice. Glancing over her shoulder, her eyes met his
blue ones, and a thrum of excitement awakened in the pit
of her stomach. Which was why, when her father summoned Niall to sit at his table, she quietly removed herself to sit, with her half-sisters, a table away—her back to
him, so she would not be tempted to look upon him again.
Though she could not help but notice with no small amount
of consternation that Derryth stared and smiled at him
quite openly.

"The mercenary is even more handsome when he is
near," she said.

"I had not noticed," answered Elspeth.

Mairi looked at Derryth. "Maybe you could marry him."

A sick feeling settled into the pit of Elspeth's stomach.
Such a thing was certainly possible. Derryth was not the

eldest, and her *tocher* not as generous. She would not be expected to marry as prestigiously as Elspeth. And Niall had elevated himself in the opinion of everyone that morning, when he had revealed his ability to command a small army. He was certainly a good enough husband for the laird's second daughter.

She prayed her sister was not serious. If such an arrangement came about, she feared she would not survive it.

"Look, he's smiling at me," said Derryth, blushing.

Mairi rolled her eyes. "He's smiling at Catrin because she put that lettuce up her nose."

Derryth glanced down to her side, her expression mortified.

"Catrin," she hissed. "You stop that right now."

The sound of his laughter, intermingled with Deargh and the others, came from behind. Elspeth steeled herself against the urge to turn and look at him. And yet somehow, not seeing him only made her more attuned to his presence. Against her wishes her ears listened, craving, and taking pleasure in the sound of his voice. Admiring the deep, smooth tones in which he spoke. The slight accent he had acquired from traveling abroad.

It was the same voice that had murmured her name in her ear this afternoon. It took all her concentration to remain composed and to appear disinterested, when inside, her thoughts and emotions spiraled into disarray, returning time and time again to the memory of their forbidden kisses in the forest . . . and the way he had touched her so boldly, setting her body on fire. And she burned still.

After the meal, circumstance found them together beside the fire in the company of others. When their elbows touched, she nearly gasped in reaction. Knowing she could remain no longer, she went directly to her father and said her good night.

Conall passed her on the threshold and gently caught her arm. "I could not help but notice you seem to avoid the mercenary, Niall. Is something wrong?"

She shrugged. "It is nothing. As you yourself told me, he serves his own purposes, and I have seen enough to know that is true. But in truth it is nothing more than I simply wish to spend time with my sisters, rather than listen to men talk of patrols and horses and weapons."

He nodded, but did not bother to conceal a knowing look. Which was fine and good. Let him believe she disliked Niall.

At least she had succeeded in convincing someone, if not her own heart.

Niall lost interest in his MacClaren companions the moment Elspeth left the room. She had held herself cool and distant, and he found himself at a damnable loss as to how to get closer to her. His blood agitated, and his mood gone dark, he lingered a while longer, feigning interest in his companions' jests and stories, until he could bear their voices no more. It had been a long day, spent in the company of his enemies, and he had much to think about. As had been his practice on previous nights, he left the great hall early and alone.

But he did not return to his quarters. Instead, he collected his mount from the stable and rode in the night, taking a path that led him to a steep incline at the foot of a towering crag. When the ground became too steep, he left his horse tied to a tree and continued on foot, placing his hands against stones that he and his brothers had touched years before. Aye, they had come here together often, and played, just themselves and with an unruly hoard of village boys. But even those were not the best times.

The best times were when he had come here with his father, at night, just as it was now, with only the light of the night fires to illuminate the walls of the castle below.

He climbed quickly, until his thighs burned, and soon reached the top. There, with a bracing wind on his skin, catching his hair and his cloak, he strode toward the Laird's Perch, or at least that was what the Kincaids called it, a natural formation in the stone, nestled into the side of the crag, shaped like a throne. His father had brought him here, along this high ridge, and they had spent hours side by side, looking over the castle, the village, and their lands. This was where the Kincaid told him stories of their Norse ancestors and how they had arrived on the shores of Scotia and conquered, but most importantly, intermarried and settled here, and built a proud history that they as lairds, must defend at all costs.

But seeing something ahead . . . Niall slowed. A faint glow of light emanated upward from the perch. His mood fell. He had come here to be alone with his thoughts. To remember. To ruminate over all he had heard and seen tonight. It annoyed him that he could not find solitude in this, *his* sacred place. He glowered for a moment, seething on the spot, and almost turned to depart, but curiosity drew him near to the edge in careful, silent steps, where for a moment, he stopped breathing.

It was *her*.

Elspeth sat at the center of the perch, wrapped in a cloak, with a small lantern at her side. She leaned forward, looking across the valley, where below, the windows of the castle glowed with light, and bonfires dotted the darkness. Her hair, no longer bound in the careful style she had worn earlier in the hall, rippled out over the shadowy expanse like a banner. She looked beautiful and mysterious and . . . perfect. A gust of wind blew her hair across her eyes. She smoothed it away, against her shoulder, and in doing so, turned her head toward him.

She gasped, startled. The lantern's glow illuminated her wide eyes, and she stood.

"I did not mean to intrude," he said.

And yet he did not step back. Now that he was here, with her . . . alone, he would not retreat.

Another strong gust of wind swept along the ridge, sweeping her cloak back, momentarily revealing the blue gown she wore beneath, and the alluring curve of her hips and waist.

Claim her.

"May I sit?" He stepped closer.

She swayed, almost as if she would flee. But she did not. Nor did she tell him no.

"There appears to be room enough for us both," he added, in an easy tone.

"Yes," she whispered.

Her dark-lashed eyes widened as he stepped down onto the narrow path and made his way toward her, his heart beating harder as the distance between them closed.

Out of nowhere, like a blaze of fire across his mind, his instincts warned him to tread cautiously.

Why?

He knew the answer. It was because Elspeth . . .

Elspeth—with her innocent eyes and enchanting manner—was different. She was the sort of woman a man lost sleep over. The sort of woman that enslaved a man's heart. She was the sort of woman a man would throw himself on a sword to defend and keep. Which made her just as dangerous to him as she was desirable. If he allowed himself to feel too greatly for her—

Ridiculous thoughts. Why was he having them?

Because he was here, in this place that meant everything to him, his damn heart torn open in grief and remembrance. He would risk nothing in his quest to retake Inverhaven.

She was just a woman. His enemy's daughter. A forbidden prize to be claimed.

He must stop thinking and feeling—and *act*.

When he was close enough to touch her, she quickly sat on the far side of the lantern, leaving the space on the other side for him, too far away for his liking.

But as he sat, he lifted the lantern by the handle and, lowering himself beside her, set the metal cage on the other side of his booted feet, leaving the two of them shadowed in deeper darkness, side by side, close but not touching. The muscles along either side of his abdomen tightened, spearing into his groin, as his male body took notice of her delicate person, so pleasingly different than his own.

He turned his face to look at her. She looked back at him, her gaze cautious.

"I . . . am sorry I made you unhappy in the forest. That I kissed you when you did not wish to be kissed, so that you wanted to kill me with your mighty stick." He chuckled, low in his throat—a rueful sound. "That you . . . dislike me now, and feel you must now avoid me."

Taciturn by nature, Niall had never been good at conversation with ladies, but then, he supposed he had never really seen the need to try very hard, because they seemed to like him well enough without words. In this way, he found himself very much out of his element with Elspeth.

She still did not speak, but she listened, her eyes fixed on his mouth.

"I used the words I used . . . that I did not wish to be your nursemaid, to put distance between us. I feared if your father and the others looked at my face, they would know. That I had been kissing you. While I do not fear for myself, I would not want you to be punished for my transgression."

They sat together in silence for a long moment, both looking out over the valley until she spoke again.

"It's beautiful here, isn't it?" she asked.

"Indeed."

As it had been for him and his father, when they had come here.

Oh, but he liked the sound of her voice.

Chapter 13

Elspeth knew she should stand, and go, and leave him and not look back. But in the next moment, her lips were moving, and she was speaking the truth. "You did not make me unhappy."

Niall's blue eyes stared intently into hers.

"I don't dislike you," she added. "I . . . I like you too much."

He moved closer, shifting beside her, turning . . . casting her corner of earth into deeper darkness. His hand cupped her face, and he tenderly stroked her jaw with his thumb. Her heart leapt at his touch.

"Then what do you want?" he said, his voice vibrating low in his throat, his breath brushing her lips, making her ache for more.

"I want you to kiss me again," she whispered.

He bent his head close. But she lifted her hand, and pressed her fingertips against his handsome lips.

"Don't," she said, but softly.

"How can I not?" he murmured. He kissed her fingertips. At the same time, his hand came up and his fingers delved between hers, as his mouth pressed past onto hers, hungry and claiming.

"Niall . . ."

"Just a kiss," he answered, kissing her again . . . and again, rendering her drunk and weak and wanting. "I won't demand more. Just this."

His words said one thing, but his urgency, and his body said another, as did hers. His boots crushed against the earth as he embraced her within the sanctuary of his powerful arms, and pulled her legs . . . her bottom closer against him, so that the length of her body more closely touched.

He guided her hand to the top of his thigh, where through his trews she felt the power of his muscles flex as he leaned more heavily toward her. Her heart beat wild in her chest, as each foray of his mouth and tongue became deeper and more passionate until she felt certain each kiss claimed a part of her soul she feared she would never get back.

Gasping, she pulled away, breaking free of his arms and pushing at him with flattened palms. "That was more than just a kiss."

She smiled ruefully. He did not smile in return.

"Because it means something more to both of us," he said, breathing hard, staring back at her with dark eyes.

"Perhaps that is true but I am not at liberty to decide." She stood, feeling as if her heart tore in two. "Please, Niall, I must go," she insisted. "This has only proven what is true. I cannot be alone with you again."

He stood as well. Because of the breadth of his shoulders, and the stance of his booted feet, he all but blocked the narrow path. She passed close beside him, so close she felt the heat radiating from his body, tangled up with the scent of wood smoke and leather.

He caught her arm, with his open palm, just above the

elbow. Startled, she stopped. His cloak snapped in the wind, curling about her, and they stood in what was almost an embrace.

"You're forgetting something," he said.

Bending low, he took up the lantern and passed it into her hand. Its light cast his angular jaw and his lips into light and shadow.

"Good night, Niall," she murmured, and pressed past, her body burning to be touched by him again, her heart filled with an ache she had never suffered before.

When she had gone several paces, she glanced back and saw him watching her, his expression hidden by the night.

He strode forward, and seized hold of her again, murmuring as he bent, "As long as this is good-bye, I'll dare to kiss you again."

And he did so, turning her face up to meet his kiss, openmouthed and commanding. Pleasure consumed her, and she moaned into his mouth, feeling her hips and shoulders pressed back against the stone ledge. His arms came beneath her cloak and hands boldly stroked over her gown, smoothing over her hips and breasts and back. Consciousness blurred, and she gave herself up to desire.

He released her abruptly.

"Go," he growled. "Before I make love to you here on the ground."

She didn't want to leave, but as the cold air struck her skin, her senses returned, and she knew she must listen to his warning.

Pulling up her hood, she proceeded down the dark trail, suspecting he followed at a distance, a truth she confirmed near the base of the hillside, after she passed a magnificent horse tied to a tree, and glanced back to see him, in moonlight, approach the animal with an extended, open hand.

Extinguishing the lantern, she continued, moving along the edge of the village and up the road to slip past the castle guards by hurrying through the gates amidst a cluster of chattering servant girls who carried fresh buckets of water from the cistern and blocks of peat. A scant moment later, she slipped up the stairs, where once in her room, she set the lantern down and threw off her cloak. Hurrying to the window, a blush still burning her skin, she pushed open the shutters to look toward the river, thinking to catch a glimpse of him in the moonlight.

She sighed, disappointed, seeing nothing but the night.

Two nights later, Elspeth sat at Fiona's table, eating honey cakes, her favorite treat since childhood. Her old nurse-maid always made them when she visited.

"Things will all work out for the best," said Fiona, with a smile. The lantern's light glimmered off her silver hair. "I truly believe that."

Elspeth nodded, taking comfort from another bite.

The past two days had been torturous. In that time, she had seen Niall from a distance . . . in the courtyard, half-naked and training ferociously with her father's men. Riding off in the company of Deargh and her MacClaren clansmen. He seemed to garner more respect and accolades each day, and she often saw him in counsel with Conall and her father. He partook each night in the evening meal, in the great hall, sitting at her father's side, but he had avoided her completely, offering only a jerk of his chin and a politely worded greeting, and nothing more. Her father had even teased about her apparent dislike of the man.

Niall was only doing what she'd asked him to do. So why did it hurt so badly?

Tonight she had sent word to her father and Bridget that she would be supping in the village with Fiona, where she could enjoy a night of peace and conversation, without her nerves in tangles. But Fiona had sensed something was wrong, and soon the words spilled from Elspeth's mouth.

Fiona looked across the table at her sympathetically. "Perhaps that is why you have such strong feelings for this Niall. They are true feelings, but . . . exaggerated, because of the dread you feel over your coming nuptials to someone else. Right now, your future husband is just a man with no face. What young woman would not feel unsettled, and torn?"

Heat rose into Elspeth's cheeks. "I should not have kissed him."

Kissed. The description seemed an insufficient description for what happened each time hers and Niall's lips touched.

"Do not chastise yourself over that. A kiss is just a kiss." Fiona winked at her. "Kisses are nice and young people should enjoy them often. I know I did, with more than one young swain." She wagged a finger. "Just so there is nothing more."

"Have no fear of that," Elspeth assured her, mortified by the bold turn of the conversation, with a woman who had tended for her since birth. Still, she trusted Fiona completely with her secrets. Fiona would tell no one what they discussed.

"Whether you merely kiss him"—Fiona winked at her again—"or if there is *more* between you, you misunderstand the warning I seek to give you."

"And what warning is that?" asked Elspeth.

Fiona reached and squeezed a knobby fingered hand over hers. "Be cautious, my dear girl. Guard your heart. If your feelings are true, and Niall's as well, spending too much time together could be . . . dangerous. Your new husband, if he does not capture your heart in equal measure, may find it impossible to compete with the memory of another man. It could bring unhappiness into your marriage, where none would have been there otherwise."

"We need not worry about any of that," Elspeth

answered. "I have made clear my wish that our flirtation
go no further, and I believe he will respect me in that. I am
resolved. I *will* forget him. Soon."

"Of course you will," said Fiona reassuringly.

"It is late." Elspeth stood. "I must go."

She pulled her plaid around her shoulders. She had
worn only a simple linen *lèine* tonight.

Fiona moved, as if to stand. "I will walk you there."

Elspeth gently pressed her back down. "I won't allow
it. I saw those ankles. Tomorrow I am sending my father's
physician to have a look at you."

"It is just normal for an old woman, such as I," Fiona
protested.

"Perhaps, but I will feel better for him confirming that
is so."

She bent down and planted a kiss to Fiona's cheek.

"I will return in a few days."

"Yes, do. Because soon you will be gone, and I won't
see you anymore."

"Why don't you come with me?"

Fiona shook her head. "I am old. I could never leave this
place now. It is my home."

"I understand. That does not mean I will not be very
sad not to be able to see you whenever I wish."

She already was sad. Her life was moving too fast
toward an uncertain change. She felt as if a storm was rising around her, and she had no anchor to hold on to.

Leaving Fiona's simple home, she closed the door
behind her and set off along the path toward the castle. It
was night, and Fiona's neighbors in the village were outside, sitting on stools around fires, talking and laughing.
Many called out greetings as she passed, and she stopped
here and there to exchange pleasantries and to admire
children.

Once home, she would avoid the great hall, and the possibility that Niall was there, and go straight to bed, though she dreaded sleep inasmuch as each passing night took her one day closer to the Cearcal. Crossing through the gates, she found a bailey crowded with young villagers, dancing around a small bonfire. The wind carried the scent of smoke and ale. She pulled her plaid over her head, so as not to be pulled into a dance—which she enjoyed on some nights—and sidled past in the shadows.

Curiosity drew her glance down the narrow lane that led toward Niall's quarters, though she knew not which belonged to him.

A movement caught her eye, a figure hurrying toward a shadowed door and pushing it inward. For a brief moment, firelight from within revealed a woman's profile.

A servant, bringing food or tending to a fire?

No, Elspeth realized, seeing a glimmer of her hair as the woman pushed down her hood, just before closing the door.

The woman she'd seen going into the cottage was Bridget.

Niall sank naked into the steaming hot water, and in that moment, felt bliss. He had arrived a short time ago, to servants filling a large wooden tub, and they had quickly left him alone to enjoy the bath. He knew not who had given the order, but he appreciated it all the same.

Because . . . what a miserable day it had been.

He had spent far too long with the MacClaren and Conall, and their warriors. It was fatiguing hiding his true feelings, and spending hours in the company of men he despised and intended to conquer—and very likely slay. He resolved that once this thing was done, he would involve himself with intrigue no more. It was not in his nature.

Later, he had met his secret forest warriors beneath a darkening sky, and been told they had been unable to find any trace of the Kincaids in the hills beyond Inverhaven. Being skilled trackers, their report had stunned him—and disheartened him greatly. Aye, regardless, he would conquer the MacClaren and seize this place with or without a Kincaid force, but he wanted more than anything for them to fight by his side. Though he felt certain many Kincaids lived in the village and in the nearby farmlands, it would be a tricky endeavor to inform them of his presence among them. Did their loyalties remain firmly Kincaid? Would they take up arms and stand beside him? He could not be certain. Neither could he risk word of his true identity and intentions reaching the MacClaren's ears too soon. For now, he had instructed Deargh, who enjoyed flirtations with numerous ladies in Inverhaven, to discreetly seek out their clanspeople, so that when the time came, the announcement could be made.

And yet those challenges were not the only blights on his mood.

He cupped his hands, and splashed his face, wishing he could wash Elspeth's memory away. Her skin beneath his fingertips. Her kiss. Her smile. Ironically, it was not his failed seduction—as part of his plot against her father—that troubled him so greatly.

It was that as much as he wished to deny it . . . he wanted her.

He, Niall, wanted Elspeth.

Having lived his life thus far solely concerned only for himself, it was an unsettling feeling to discover that after all these years he cared for another person. That another person occupied his thoughts. It wasn't that he'd never wanted to cherish a woman—to claim one for his own. It was just that his life as a mercenary had never allowed for anything but the most fleeting and self-serving of affairs. For the first time, his heart signaled revolt, wanting something more.

He rested his arms on the wooden edge of the tub, leaning his head back and closing his eyes.

Just as Elspeth had made it clear that she wanted nothing at all.

The door opened, without a knock of warning, and he came alert. Looking, his gaze narrowed on the intruder and his muscles tensed.

A woman hovered in the doorway, her head covered in a cloak.

For a brief moment, he thought it was Elspeth, hoped it was—but then, when she pushed away her hood he saw it was not.

Bridget came toward him, smiling. "Do you like your gift?"

"Very much, thank you."

It was not the first time he had been visited thusly by a lady of the castle, to be served during a bath. Indeed, it was considered a good and proper practice, although normally said ladies arrived accompanied by servants, for propriety's sake. He would venture to guess Bridget's husband did not know she was here, alone with him.

She removed her cloak and tossed it to his bed. She wore only a thin white kirtle. Her unbound breasts moved provocatively beneath. Proceeding toward him, she lifted a cloth from the table, and dipped it in the water.

"May I?" she offered seductively, her lips curving into a smile.

Chapter 14

"If you wish," he answered, his soul darkening.

After all, he owed no particular loyalty to the Mac-Claren—or to Elspeth. And Bridget was beautiful, in a different sort of way than the young woman who haunted his dreams. Perhaps he should welcome this opportunity to rid her from his mind.

She rubbed the cloth over his shoulders and across his chest, leaning forward so close that the warm mist bathed her breasts. Allowing the cloth to sink into the tub, she spread her hands over his shoulders and down his arms.

"Your muscles are so hard, and tight." Her fingers traced his tattoos, and moved down over his chest and stomach, lower with each teasing stroke. "I know how to ease your tensions."

He closed his eyes, feeling the first stirrings of desire . . . but not for her.

Damn him to hell, he wanted someone else here. He wanted someone else's hands on his skin offering him pleasure. Until he forgot Elspeth, no one else would do.

He seized Bridget's wrist—just as her fingertips grazed his sex.

"Thank you," he said, opening his eyes. "But that is enough."

He heard the breath catch in her throat, and she gave a little laugh. "No one has to know."

"I appreciate that," he said coldly. "But I am very tired, and wish to be alone."

She stared back at him, her eyes glassy with arousal, her lips parted in disbelief.

"Another time then?" she said hopefully.

After drying her hands on a cloth she reached for her cloak.

"Perhaps." Truly. Perhaps. Seducing the MacClaren's wife would be just as cruel as seducing his daughter, but tonight he had no taste for it.

He suspected he never would.

When she was gone, he left the bath and dried himself. Dropping the damp linen on a chair, he pulled on knee-length *braies*, rolling them at his hips. Normally he slept naked but if Bridget were to suddenly return at least his manhood would be somewhat secured.

Crossing the earthen floor, he climbed beneath the furs and stared up at the shadows dancing with the firelight on the rafters above. The fire crackled on the hearth. He laid his arm over his eyes, praying he would not only sleep, but not dream again of Elspeth.

His breathing slowed.

Until a sound came from across the room. The door, again.

Why had he not thought to secure the bar? Annoyed, he lifted up onto his elbow to look, expecting to see Bridget or possibly Deargh—

But it was Elspeth, dressed in a simple linen sheath, a

plaid covering her shoulders and her hair. His heart stopped beating in his chest.

"It is true then," she said in a whisper, her face pale.

He sat up quickly, pushing back the furs.

"What is true?" he asked, standing.

Her gaze descended over his body—his chest, abdomen, and hips—as he moved toward her. A blush rose into her cheeks—and yet her gaze accused. She even appeared to tremble.

"I saw her leave," she blurted, her hands curling into fists at her sides.

He knew instantly what she believed . . . how it must look, with Bridget sneaking away from his quarters and her coming in to find him there in bed.

What he didn't know, was how she felt about it.

He approached her, slowly.

"Did you, then?" he said in a dispassionate voice, intended to provoke her.

With an angry cry, she flew at him, her fists striking his chest. His face. *Hard*.

He had never been more well pleased.

He caught her wrists—seizing her up against his chest and carrying her to the bed as she writhed like a furious cat—and he tossed her down. She moved quickly to escape him, but he captured her easily there atop the furs, pinning her wrists and halting the thrashing of her legs with his thigh.

He looked down into her beautiful, outraged face.

"*You* are jealous," he declared.

She struggled, wrenching her arms, and twisting. She felt so good beneath him, lithe and womanly all at once. A dangerous pleasure tightened his loins.

"Nay, not jealous," she spat. "You betray my father with her and for that I hate you."

He admired the fire in her, finding it enthralling. At the

same time, he took pleasure in the differences in their bodies, his size and strength—and her femininity. He over-powered her every attempt to strike him or throw him off, but gently, with an intent toward seduction.

"That's not it," he said, his hands moving, binding her still . . . but lowering his head to nuzzle the tantalizing skin of her neck . . . kissing her there, and savoring her fragrance.

"*Niall*," she gasped, squirming, warm and soft against him. His body reacted, his sex going hard against her thigh. "Please stop."

"Confess it," he growled low, in her ear, grinning. "You were jealous over me."

"Let me go." Her body remained rigid.

"Not until you say it," he murmured.

She turned her face away from him, and closed her eyes.

"I won't," she exclaimed softly. "I can't."

His eyes hungrily memorized her delicate profile, which now reflected more hurt than anger. He understood her refusal. She had her pride just as he did, which made certain confessions difficult. But he would be nothing less than ruthless in drawing her out from behind the high bastion of her pride, and making her his own.

"You think I kissed you . . . toyed with you, and then made love to her," he said in a quiet voice.

"Kisses are *only* kisses." She pushed against him, straining her muscles to be free. "You mean *nothing* to me."

"That's not true," he dared answer, an edge of arrogance in his voice. "You only say that because you think I betrayed you—"

"—you *did betray me*," she choked out.

The torment in her voice satisfied him, to his soul. It all but confirmed she had been as miserable as he. Tenderly, he grazed his thumb along her cheek.

"How could I ever betray you," he answered gruffly,

"when from the first moment, there has only been you?" He exhaled through his nose. "I see you . . . everywhere. Every time I close my eyes. Even when I sleep."

Elspeth remained rigid, but she listened. He knew she did.

"She came here, yes," he said. "But I sent her away, because she's not you."

He used the words as a weapon, yes, but they were true—so true that speaking them made him feel like he walked naked onto a crowded and bloody battlefield, blindfolded, with no weapon in hand.

Beneath him, she stared up, her gleaming dark hair spread out across the fur, her breasts rising and falling, crushed by the neckline of her lèine.

The tension in her body slowly . . . eased . . . and she went soft.

"*Niall.*" She shifted against him, innocently, he had no doubt, but in doing so, she brought his sex more intimately between her thighs.

He clenched his teeth as heat rippled through his body, the power of his need causing his vision to blur. *Slow down*, he commanded himself. *Slow down, else you'll frighten her away.*

"Don't move that way, lass," he warned. "You don't know what it does to me."

She sighed. "What do you think it does to me?"

Her words surprised him, and he laughed, but then . . . the smile fell from his lips because he felt more for her than he ought to feel.

"I've been so miserable," she whispered, her cheeks flushed and her lips parted, a temptress peering up at him. Gently, she pulled free from his hold, and touched her hands to either side of his face. "I don't want to be miserable anymore."

Firelight bathed her face half golden, half in shadows.

In this moment, surrounded by darkness and completely alone, with their bodies so intimately matched, he forgot about revenge and saw only Elspeth. Not because of blind desire, which he could control, but because she was the first woman to calm his raging soul and in this moment he needed to make love to her like he needed his next breath.

He lowered his head, kissing her, gently at first, but then, as his heartbeat ramped higher, pressing his mouth hard to hers, slanted and open, only to pull back, grazing . . . teasing . . . until she let out a sigh and lifted her head from the furs, kissing him back.

"I tried to forget you," she whispered against his lips, her hands touching the bare skin of his torso.

"I tried to let you forget me, but I cannot."

He kissed her again—more fervently, a drumbeat of warning even now sounding in his head, telling him he must lock his heart securely away before going any further. Caring for her too deeply would be a dangerous thing. Despite this, all he felt was the need to claim her, and keep her. To make her his woman.

Pulling back, wanting to *see* her, he delved his fingers through her silken hair, cradling her delicate skull. Her hands came up between them, smoothing over his naked chest, and higher, to clasp his shoulders.

"You're so beautiful," she said breathlessly. "I have never seen any man more so. Not just you, on the outside, but your heart. Every time I look in your eyes, I see a good man. An honorable man."

Her observation shook him to his core. He had his reasons for seeking revenge against her father. Honorable reasons, yes. But one day soon she would see the darkness in him, and recognize him as the vengeful beast he was. No doubt she would hate him for it, and this magnificent attraction between them would cease to exist.

Desperate to have her while he could, he pressed his face to her neck, inhaling, tasting her soft skin, moving lower to the edge of her bodice where her breasts crowded the linen. A ragged gasp burst from her lips. Her body moved beneath him, her hands touched his skin, equally eager in their exploration.

"I have dreamt about touching you like this," he murmured reverently.

"As have I," she whispered, her cheeks vivid with sensual fever.

He bit her lower lip, sucking it between his. She moaned, bringing her arms around his back, pulling him closer, his bare chest crushing against her breasts. Ravenous, his mouth opened on hers, deeply claiming her with lips and tongue.

"Like this." He closed a hand over her breast, caging it within his hand, and then stroked slowly, savoring the fullness and the sensation of her aroused nipple grazing his palm through the linen.

"Yes," she sighed. Again, her hips moved, her dark eyelashes feathering down against her cheeks.

His sex was painfully hard and ready, but she was innocent, and he would not take her carelessly. His mouth dry with desire, he hooked his fingertips into the collar of her lèine and gently tugged, exposing one *perfect*, pink tipped breast.

"It is you who are beautiful, Elspeth."

She made a frantic sound, and wrapped her hand around his wrist, but she did not push him away.

His desire rose, rampant in his veins. Impatient to see all of her, he shifted off enough to grasp the hem of her shift and seized the garment up, bunching it near her shoulder, baring the full length of her body to his gaze. She shifted, clenching her legs together, but did not shrink from his gaze. God, she was more than he even believed.

A fantasy come to life. His hand moved over her golden skin, caressing her breasts, her smooth stomach and the curve of her hips and soft thighs, to settle possessively on the shadowy place in between.

He bent to kiss her mouth.

"Let me touch you," he commanded softly, stroking her there.

She closed her eyes, and arched, gasping out his name. Her legs parted. Another stroke . . . and her thighs squeezed. He touched her more intimately, combining slow-building pressure and rhythm to give her pleasure. She moaned, and her hips moved until he knew she sought something more.

Enveloping her in his arms, he reached down to urge her knees apart. Looking into her enraptured face, he lowered his hips between hers, groaning, his cock only separated from her body by the linen he wore.

Her hands moved over his back, smoothing over his muscles, clenching there.

All he could think was that he needed to be closer. He hooked his thumb inside the waist of his garment, yanking them down—

". . . wait," she murmured, breathing hard.

"I can't," he rasped, kissing her face, finding her lips.

She kissed him back ardently—then twisted her face from his, her entire body going rigid. Her hand seized his against his hip.

"Niall, stop."

He froze, the words and her sudden stillness filtering through. He breathed heavily against her cheek. "Elspeth?"

"I can't," she choked.

He blinked, dazed . . . confused. Had he . . . taken things too far? Had he misread her willingness, blinded by his own passion?

"I can't," she repeated, exhaling. "I want to, but I can't."

He bit his lower lip, almost hard enough to draw blood, and pressed his face against her cheek. "All right."

He had never forced a woman, and would not force Elspeth now, no matter how badly he wanted her.

"Please don't be angry," she pled softly.

"At you," he murmured, kissing her temple, "I could never be."

And yet his body ached for completion. He rolled off her, onto his back, and covered his face with his hands, willing his body to calm.

In the darkness beside him, Elspeth pulled her garment down, covering herself. "I'm sorry."

He heard the dejection in her voice, and turned, raising up onto one elbow and touched her face, a fierce surge of protectiveness rising in his chest.

"You mustn't be." Lowering down, he kissed her nose. "I should have kept my head. I should not have allowed things to go so far."

She shook her head, and took hold of his hand. "I have no regrets."

"Then nor can I."

"I don't want to go," she said. "But . . ."

"But I know that you must."

He stood, his body still in agony, and crossed the room, where he pulled on a tunic and went to the door. A glance over his shoulder showed Elspeth arranging her plaid on her shoulder. She joined him at the door, where he looked down into her eyes. She leaned close, curling her hand in the front of his tunic.

He would not force her to make promises. But neither would he make any of his own.

"I feel like I should explain," she said quietly.

But he did not need to hear more of alliances and arranged marriages and how little time he had left in which to claim her.

He shook his head. "I know who you are, Elspeth. And I know who I am not. You need not explain to me why you should not be here. Why we cannot be together."

He also knew that the only way to ensure she returned to him, was to let her go.

"Niall—" she whispered.

His finger beneath her chin, he tilted her face up and kissed her. She breathed into his mouth, and he opened his wider, tasting her deeply with his tongue. Instantly, he wanted more. His hands went to her waist, pulling her against him. Her arms around his neck, they kissed again, against the door, shrouded in shadows.

Until releasing her, he stepped back and murmured, "I make no demands on you. But I am here, and you may come to me if you wish."

Without waiting to hear what she might reply, he pulled her plaid high, to cover her hair and face and then opened the door and peered out. "Come, this way."

Outside, he led her down the lane, back toward the gate, where together they slipped into the still crowded bailey, not touching one another, but moving shoulder to shoulder with others who milled about, drinking ale and laughing.

As they moved toward the castle, Conall appeared out of the darkness.

Niall kept his manner easy as the man came toward them.

"Elspeth, there you are. Your father had sent me to walk you back from Fiona's."

"Niall was kind enough to give me escort."

Conall looked between the two of them, perhaps . . . a bit suspiciously.

Niall nudged her toward Conall.

"Kind?" he said in an ill-tempered tone. "No. I'm not kind at all. I just don't want to be galloping across the countryside to save her from peril again. The lass wanders alone too much at night. Her father should keep her confined to the castle until she is wed."

Conall's face broke into a smile, and he laughed. "Aye, you are right about that. Good night then, I will see her home from here."

He led her away from Niall, toward the castle.

"How is Fiona?" he heard Conall ask her.

"Well and happy," Elspeth replied. "But I should like to send father's physician to examine her tomorrow."

"That can certainly be arranged," he answered.

Elspeth glanced over her shoulder at him. He did not break a smile.

But he *did* wink.

Chapter 15

Three mornings later, shrieks awakened Elspeth.

In the moment before awakening, she feared that she had somehow been found out, and that everyone in the castle knew what she had done—and almost done—with Niall in his quarters. Things she'd just been dreaming about, in a drowsy-warm, half sort of sleep.

Her eyes flew open to see all three of her half-sisters jump on her bed, wearing excited smiles.

"Get up Elspeth. Have you forgotten what day it is?" Mairi exclaimed. "We are going to the Crystal Spring to bathe in the waters."

"So we will all be *fertile!* exuded Derryth, with a mischievous gleam in her eye.

Cat sprang up. "What does fertile mean?"

"It means healthy." Derryth threw Elspeth a wink. "Robust!"

"No it doesn't," Mairi answered knowingly. "Not exactly."

"Shhhhh!" Elspeth shushed.

Aye, it was a tradition they partook in once a year, a day

of fun they all looked forward to. A daring plunge into the frigid waters of the Crystal Spring, which local legend told would make a woman fertile.

"You especially, Elspeth," said Derryth. "Because you will be wed very soon and will want babies as soon as possible."

Did she want babies as soon as possible? She did not know how she felt about that, and didn't really want to think about it anymore. If she did, Niall's face would spring to mind, and the fantasy of a life with him, and she must not wish for such unattainable things.

It had been three days since the night in his bed, and she had existed in the most bewildering state of distraction ever since. She could think of little else but his kiss and his deep voice in her ear. His lean body and his tattoos, and the way he had felt so heavy and warm and powerful against her bare skin. Not to mention the things they had done in the shadows of his room, for which she still could summon not one bit of regret.

Since then, they had crossed paths numerous times, and had pointedly ignored each other, at best exchanging cool greetings—but also the most thrilling, *secret*, burning glances and once, a daring touch of hands that her father, if he would have turned a second sooner, would have seen. But frustratingly there had been no opportunity for even a single private word. It was torture, not only being separated from him, but knowing in only a few days she would be traveling to the Cearcal Festival, which would take her away from him forever.

Fiona had been right. She feared if she opened her heart to him any more than she already had, that she would never find happiness as wife to another man.

And she knew better than to venture to his quarters again. She *knew* without a doubt where that would lead, and she no longer trusted herself to resist. In her waking hours, her conscience did constant battle, one moment arguing that she should seek happiness in Niall's arms while she could, but . . . what of her husband, whoever he might be? She had always promised herself that she would save herself for marriage, and that powerful voice always won the argument in the end.

Aye, their attraction was wildly intense, but in truth she had known him but for a brief span of days. Did she *love* him—or was she only infatuated? Her instincts told her he was a good and honorable man, but how could she know for certain? She couldn't. For that reason, she knew she must hold fast to her honor, rather than surrender her virtue to a man who was in truth, still very much a stranger.

Oh, but how would she ever forget him? She didn't want to.

Perhaps a frigid plunge was just what she needed.

She arose and dressed in a short chemise, a *lèine*, and a dark blue woolen overdress, and with her sisters and maids left the castle without seeing Niall, or any of the other chosen warriors who regularly followed him off each day to ride the borders to engage the Alwyns whenever possible so as to show that the MacClarens would not quietly accept the aggressions that had been directed toward them.

Stableboys waited in the bailey with their ponies. Several wagons already moved out of the gate, full of ladies from the village and the castle—old women and young women alike. Ina was there, laughing, crowded shoulder to shoulder with all the maids from the castle. Fiona cheerfully led her wagon full of more mature ladies in song. Other wagons laden with tents and linens and baskets of food trundled behind.

To Elspeth's surprise, Bridget appeared atop the fine white palfrey, which had been a gift from the MacClaren on the day of their wedding. Their stepmother had previously scoffed when informed of the tradition and legend, saying she had no intention of joining them and subjecting herself to the misery of the cold.

"So you have decided to come after all?" Elspeth inquired pleasantly.

"I have," Bridget answered. "Your father has insisted upon it. Can you believe he still hopes for a boy, after so many years of disappointment?"

Derryth snorted. Mairi rolled her eyes.

Was it any surprise that they galloped off ahead, leaving her behind?

Niall and Deargh had ridden since dawn with Conall and a number of other MacClaren warriors, along the border between the MacClaren and Alwyn lands.

He had ridden this particular path before, but it had been many years. Although by appearances, he was simply doing the duty of a paid soldier, protecting his lord's border, he needed to know how the MacClarens and Alwyns had divided up the Kincaid lands, those many years ago. It was important that when the time came that he knew specifically who he was killing over what.

A sound carried to his ears on the wind. But Conall, beside him, was in the midst of describing a nearby farm, and though he paused his horse to listen, he did not hear it again.

"Our greatest challenge of late is the Alwyn's recent claim that this portion of land that we have traveled this morning, to include Inverhaven and the castle, belongs to him based on some interpretation of an old map that no one has ever laid eyes upon."

Deargh raised his eyebrows, playing false. "When was this map supposedly created?"

"Some seventeen winters ago, before the lands were

granted to the MacClarens by the crown. He alleges he was promised one thing, for his support of the king in the regional conflict here against the Kincaids, and then given a lesser portion, whether through subterfuge or simple mistake. We do not yet know the extent of his allegation."

The sound came again.

"Do you hear that?" said Niall, interrupting.

The wind seemed to carry . . . the sound of voices shouting.

"It comes from the direction of the farm." Conall jerked his reins. "This way."

He raced down the hillside, and they followed, over a sweeping plain before coming into view of a barn and a thatch-roofed cottage. Five riders on horseback circled round, their horses loaded with sacks of grain and flapping chickens and whatever else they'd taken. A farmer and his wife challenged them on foot, jabbing hoes and hurling rocks but doing little to fend off the attack.

Niall recognized one of the men, by his pale hair and stature in the saddle, as Magnus.

Yet the five were outnumbered. As soon as they saw the approaching riders, they threw much of what they carried to the ground and launched their mounts into flight.

The MacClaren men seemed to see this as a victory, shouting taunts after them, and dismounting to do what they could to assist the farmer and is wife in collecting whatever the raiders had left behind, strewn across the earth.

It wasn't enough for Niall. He dug his heels into Fitheach's side. He *raced* . . . *thundered* . . . caught up with Magnus, pulling alongside him. Seized him by the shoulders, and wrenched him from his saddle, throwing him to the ground!

Magnus's companions galloped on, leaving him behind.

"Get his horse," Niall commanded, and Deargh raced past.

Magnus leapt to his feet, his sleeve torn, and glared.

"*You*!" he shouted.

Closer, he could be seen to be wearing two faded black eyes, a gift from Niall on the night of Elspeth's abduction. This brought Niall an immeasurable degree of satisfaction.

"Aye, it is me. Did you not learn your lesson with the cattle?" Niall circled him, turning in the saddle, relishing this moment of dominance over the other man for the simple fact that he had tried to marry Elspeth, which made him a competitor. "Every time you or one of yours takes something that does not belong to you, I will come and take it back, and you will forfeit something equally dear of your own."

"Aye, what a fine horse we have now," boasted Deargh, returning, leading the animal by its reins. "The children of the village shall enjoy riding him, I think."

"Who *are* you?" Magnus strode closer, eyes flashing with challenge. "You fight for the MacClaren? You protect his lands?"

"As if they were my own," Niall growled. "And hear this, I'll come for yours next."

Deargh laughed. "That he will. Wait and see."

They rode away, pulling Magnus's animal along behind them.

Conall met them halfway, delighted at seeing that they returned with a prize. At the barn, the men gathered round.

When they had dismounted, Deargh gestured to the animal. "Should we give the horse to the farmer, in payment for his trouble?"

Niall rubbed his hand along the animal's neck, begrudgingly admiring Magnus's possession, along with its finely worked saddle. "It is a very good horse."

"We shall take it back to the village." Conall nodded. "It gives Magnus less reason to return here to harry them."

Niall agreed. "I would leave several of the men here for

the night, perhaps even two. Deargh and I are going to continue on, if that is all right with you."

Conall waved them off with a smile. "I will see the two of you at the castle then, before night." He pointed. "Ride there, along the ridge. It will bring you to the river, which you can follow back to Inverhaven."

The farmer's wife sent them on their way with a bundle of bread and cheese, and a cold jug of ale, which she had drawn up from a large basket in the well.

Eventually they arrived at a stony riverbank where they had their meal. Afterward, Deargh lay back into a tall bed of grass.

"All this riding has made me tired. I think I'll close my eyes for a short bit."

Niall stood, not tired, but restless. "I'm going to walk a bit and look about. You never know when one might cross paths with a Kincaid."

"I hope you do," Deargh answered, covering his eyes with his arm. "We're running out of time."

Niall walked upriver, needing time alone to think. To sort his thoughts. Time passed, bringing closer the day when his company of warriors would arrive to support him in reclaiming his birthright—and closer to the day when Elspeth would travel to the Cearcal to choose a husband.

His heart had not warmed toward the MacClaren or his men. His need for revenge was justified, and he remained resolute about taking back what belonged to him and his clan. If he wanted Elspeth as well . . . he must move and move quickly, before she was gone, and it was too late.

He did want her. Fiercely.

But though the attraction charged between them, hotter than before, she had not returned to his bed and he was left with the problem of how to proceed. To claim her as prize, which he felt must occur before he revealed his true identity, he must either present himself to her father as a clear choice for her hand, which would be a most difficult prospect without a known clan to support him, and no ownership of lands. Aye, he had previously served powerful patrons, and more than one might be willing to voice their support of him, and even gift him with some measure of land. However, such an endeavor, and all of its formalities, would take too much time.

His only other choice was to plot a more intentional seduction, with the intention of boldly demanding her hand from the MacClaren and the council, once it was done . . . which would require humiliating Elspeth to a certain degree. He had no wish to subject her to shame, but knew it must be done, not simply to punish her father, but for a greater cause, to more firmly secure his claim.

He sat on a large stone, watching the river meander by, trying to work out in his mind, how he could betray her, and protect her all at once. His head a snarl of thoughts, he removed his boots and tunic, and naked, eased into the river, allowing the cold water to clear his mind. He swam upstream, pushing against the current, exerting his muscles . . . a catharsis of sorts . . . and followed the sound of rippling water.

He discovered a wide, calm pool and waterfall, which he swam toward, until his feet found purchase on the stones below.

Though not a large waterfall, the force of the downward flow inflicted sufficient pressure on his muscles so as to be pleasurable. He bent and stretched his neck, moving so that the water struck the center of his back, and thundered in his ears.

Out of the corner of his eye a movement drew his attention. Riders.

Muscles clenching, he ducked backward under the curtain of water, and found a place beneath an outcropping of stone. Hidden by water and shadows he peered out as best he could, water streaming over his face and skin.

He need not have been alarmed. The riders were all women, and there were quite a number of them. No doubt they had come to wash or bathe.

He had no wish to remain here, unseen and watching. Peering out toward the direction from whence he had come, he estimated the distance across the pool and prepared to swim along the bottom to escape unseen.

But then Elspeth rode into view, and he decided he might not leave so quickly after all.

It had taken them nearly an hour to arrive at the spring. As her father always did, he had sent a number of the older men of the clan to hold watch. That band of hoary old fellows set up a simple camp a short distance away, chuckling as the women rode past them and calling out bawdy jests.

"Be sure tae gie yerself wet, heed tae toe!"

"Come back this way dry, and we willnae let ye pass. Yer guidman wants bairns, and bairns he shall have!"

Arriving riverside, where a curtain of trees concealed them from outside view, Catrin leapt to the ground and ran to the water, swiping it with her hand.

"It's cold!" she cried, spinning around. "We'll catch our death and die."

"Not in this river," said one of the women with a wise smile.

"Because it will make us fertile!" shouted Catrin.

All the ladies laughed. "Aye, child. That is right."

Maidservants quickly set up three circular tents, threw blankets about, and started several small fires.

"In with you all!" shouted Fiona, waving a swath of linen like a flag. "Every one of you."

Laughing in rueful tones, the young women of marriageable and childbearing age removed the warmer, outer layer of their garments. Dressed in chemises they ventured in. Soon the air was filled with the sound of screams and shrieks. The older women of the clan stood on the bank, laughing and urging them on.

"It's too cold!" cried Mairi.

"It is *miserable*," agreed Derryth, her teeth chattering.

"It is not so bad," said Elspeth, laughing. "But you must keep moving."

"All the way!" a maid shouted from one of the tents. "Remember, you must dunk your heads! It doesn't work unless you do."

Most remained at the stony edges of the river, gingerly easing themselves further. Bridget ventured in only to her ankles, looking peevish and annoyed.

A few of them ventured into deeper waters, including Elspeth.

"Those girls, do you see them," shouted Fiona, to all the rest. "They shall bear many bairns for sure. Strong, healthy weans."

"Aye," shouted another. "And if you swim all the way across to touch the waterfall, they say you get a handsome husband too." Behind her hand, she added, "If you're already married to an ogre, you can hold out hope for your second husband."

The air filled with more laughter.

"That's unfair!" shouted one young woman, who from the crestfallen look on her face, took the whole thing very seriously. "Some of us can't swim."

As Elspeth neared the waterfall, she felt a surge of colder water, pushing against her. She turned, treading water, her chemise afloat at her waist. She waved to those who remained on shore.

"I'm here! There shall be a handsome husband for me."

She thought of Niall then, and how he had made her feel so beautiful and wanted, and wished for a moment that she could marry him instead of a stranger. That he would remain here forever, and become a part of the MacClaren clan. It was a girl's fantasy she knew, not one her father would ever share, but she allowed herself to have it. She would be beset by reality soon enough.

All the women on the shore cheered. The following calm was broken by a water battle, with everyone splashing each other—especially those older women who stood dry and warm on the bank. Many ran from the river, squealing of the cold, disappearing into the tents where they would dry their hair by the fire and drink warm cider.

At the waterfall, Elspeth sought out the stepping stones she knew were there, and lifted her arms, allowing the water to pour over her . . . to wash away her fears and cares. It pulled at her chemise, and flattened her hair.

Large hands touched her waist—

Seizing her inward. She *screamed*—

A hand—and then *a mouth* covered her lips.

In the wavering shadows, with water streaming all around, she looked into Niall's blue eyes—and she laughed. He laughed too, a deep, rumbling sound that sent a shiver of pleasure though her.

"I was swimming here, and then there you were. How fortuitous for me," he murmured.

He held her tight against him, pulling her legs around his waist, and holding her there, his hands beneath her thighs.

Even chilled as she was, she blushed at his boldness.

Feeling just as bold, she wrapped her arms around his neck, holding him tight as he kissed her again . . . this time not laughing, his mouth urgent and demanding, taking her breath away. He was warm and strong in her arms, and she never wanted to let him go.

"I have missed you."

"I have missed you too. And I wish I could keep you here with me longer," he said, moving his face near her ear. He bit her earlobe. "But here they come."

Before she could respond, he pushed her away, through the curtain of water and back into the pool. Delighted and thrilled by what had just occurred, Elspeth laughed again.

Another young woman swam past her, breathing hard as she swam. "Elspeth, you have inspired me to be brave as well. I want a handsome husband too."

Elspeth's eyes widened, and she called out a warning. "Don't go under as I did. It's very dark, and frightening. And the stones are sharp. I may have even cut my foot."

"I'll be careful." She took a breath and ducked under.

Elspeth covered her mouth, waiting for a scream.

Yet it was she who let out a sudden shriek—as fingers *pinched* her bottom under the water.

Looking down through the clear water, she glimpsed Niall's tattooed back and his long legs kicking past. Then he was gone.

A moment later the woman reappeared from out of the waterfall and swam toward her, pushing the water from her face. "That wasn't so frightening."

Together they swam toward the shore. There she accepted a warm blanket from Fiona, and looked down the river. She did not see Niall, but she did not fear for even a moment that he had drowned.

Moments later, downriver, Niall climbed out, water streaming from his body and picked up his tunic from where he'd left it on a stump. His skin was chilled, but he was burning inside . . . and more determined than ever to have Elspeth, and soon. Despite all his warnings to himself to keep his heart closed to her, he could no longer imagine a future that did not include her. She awakened his desire as no other woman ever had. Every moment he had to wait to make love to her—to fully claim her as his own—only made that desire more powerful, more achingly sweet . . . because as much as he wished to deny it, there was more than simple desire between them.

He picked up his boots, carrying them with him, as he proceeded on to the place where Deargh slept.

Only he did not find Deargh in the grass, where he had been before, although their horses and belongings remained in place. Birds lit in the trees, fluttering overhead, peering down at him.

He heard voices, and followed them, wary. Coming into a break in the trees, he found Deargh standing with his back to him, facing a score of fierce-faced bearded men, dressed in leather and fur, and bearing all manner of arms. They all looked at him, scowling and suspicious.

Turning, Deargh looked at him with an odd look in his eyes. He did not smile.

"There ye be."

"Yes?" His muscles tensed with caution.

"It looks like we will not have to search for the Kincaids any longer as they have found us." He turned back to the men, his old *hieland* brogue rolling off his tongue. "Dae ye see heem? Whit ah say is true. Ah hae brooght the Kincaid's eldest son haem tae ye."

Chapter 16

Most of the men were younger than Niall. But there were a few older men among them, with wrinkled and scarred faces. One was missing an eye. Another, an arm. From the look of them, and their rough clothing and hard expressions, they had lived difficult lives since losing their homes and taking to the hills. Perhaps, even, the injuries inflicted upon them had been suffered that night, as they stood with his father.

From out of their midst appeared Murdoch the bard, his hand clenching a long staff, which he used to steady himself.

"I kent that first night it was him," he said. "It was his voice. It is the same as the Kincaid's. Others may not hear it, but withit my sight, I hear things others dinnae."

"Hoo can ye remember a voice for 'at long?" said one of the younger warriors, his gaze cool with skepticism. He wore his dark hair pulled back from his face. Tall and broad shouldered, a faded scar ran from the corner of his mouth, upward, to his cheek.

"He doesnae look a 'hin like the Kincaid," another man scoffed.

"The song you yourself sing says all three sons had *bàn* hair," said the scarred young man, with an air of importance.

"Oh, aye, he did," agreed Deargh brusquely. "But with age, it became *dubh*. As ye see now."

A host of eyes narrowed in suspicion.

The younger man leaned on his sword. "I hae heard of this man's fighting skills. But I walnae follow him as my sworn chief because of the soond of his voice."

Several of the younger heads nodded in agreement.

"Noo 'at ah look upon heem longer, he *diz* look loch the Kincaid," said an old man, squinting and pointing. "See the shape of his head? His nose. Th' way hae holds heemself."

Several of the other older men came closer, squeezing Niall's arms and examining his face, which he suffered patiently, as a tidal wave of emotion moved through him. Joy. Pride. Sadness. Though his recollection was fragmented and altered by time, he . . . remembered some of their faces, though from the perspective of a boy. Aye, he was angry too, to have been denied the company of these men—his clansmen—for the past seventeen years.

The armless man moved to stand beside Deargh, and smiled. "He looks more like his mother's sire, the dark chief they called *Fitheach*, aye, his hair as dark as a raven's wing." He said to the others. "And I min' ye too, Deargh, even underneath all that." He wiggled his fingers at his tattoos. "He was chosen by the Kincaid that night to do exactly what he has done. I trust that he would not present us with an imposter." With his good arm, he clapped a hand on Deargh's shoulder.

Deargh nodded at him in thanks, his eyes damp and bright.

"I am still nae convinced," said the younger warrior. "You are old and sometimes addlepated."

"Addlepated!" The old man pushed toward him. "I'll show you addlepated."

Murdoch shuffled between them, eyes wide and unseeing, and held up his hands.

"There is only one way tae ken for certain. A way only Osgar and I ken."

"And what way would that be?" someone exclaimed.

A hunch-shouldered old man, apparently Osgar, came forward and pointed at Niall. "You must come here, behind the tree, where the others cannot see."

A round of complaints went up.

"Behind the tree?"

"What is it that we cannot all see?"

Niall looked at Deargh and scowled.

Deargh shrugged. "I do not know. But they knew your father. Osgar, there, was on his council. I suggest you go with them."

Behind the tree, Murdoch reached out and touched Niall's chest. Feeling his way to the side, he grasped Niall's right arm and held it aloft.

"Look there. High up, under his arm, nearly tae the shoulder."

Osgar bent, looking underneath. He squinted, and tilted his head.

"Do y' see it?" Murdoch questioned impatiently.

"I see lots of things," Osgar snapped. "The man's got a lot of ink on his skin."

"Well, look harder," insisted the bard.

Osgar grew still. His expression went blank.

Looking up at Niall, he said in a hushed voice, "Aye, it is him." He stepped back, a look of reverence overtaking his aged features. "This man is the true son of our chief. Niall Braewick, the rightful laird of Kincaid."

"What did you see there?" said Niall, lifting his arm.

Murdoch grinned. "When y' were born, your father had a mark put on you—a wolf with a green eye. It matched one he himself was given at the time of his birth, and his father before him. I remember when they took the needle to y'. Ye squalled like a lass."

Niall could not help but smile at that, but his chest ached with grief. Any story from his past held such meaning. Knowing that his father had marked him as his son, in such a way that he would carry the mark with him through life . . . that he held such pride in his sons, touched him deeply, to his soul.

"Did my brothers receive the same mark?"

"Aye." Osgar shouldered between them. "So y' must not tell anyone y' see. There be those who would go out and get the same mark and present themselves here, telling everyone they were the Kincaid's sons. It doesn't mean much now, but if y' do what you say you're going tae do, it will mean quite a lot soon enough."

Niall nodded, knowing they were right.

"Murdoch," he asked. "How is it that the MacClaren allowed you to be his bard?"

"Me?" Murdoch answered. "I am just a blind old man. What threat can I be to him?" He leaned forward, leaning on his staff and grinned. "He does not know how carefully I listen, to learn their weaknesses. That I have waited for a day such as this, and when the time comes I will do my part, just as surely as any Kincaid who wields a sword."

"I know you will," Niall answered.

They emerged from behind the tree.

All the men stood there looking at them.

"Well, wot is it?" one demanded.

"It's his *crom-odhar*, isn't it?" Another chuckled. "Like the rest of us Kincaids, it's ten feet long."

They all laughed heartily.

"No, but it is something just as remarkable," Murdoch answered. "There are reasons why the proof cannot be shared, so you must accept our sworn testimony. This man is true to his word. He is the Kincaid's eldest son, and you must give him your fealty and follow him—and even die for him, if need be—from this moment on."

The men's gazes grew sharper, and they all stood taller.

"As your laird," Niall said in a low voice, meeting each pair of eyes as his gaze moved over them, "I command it of you. What say you, will you share these lands with me again, my Kincaid brothers? My clansmen? Will you share in my vengeance?"

"Aye, laird."

"We will stand with ye."

"We have waited for this day for so long."

"As have I," he answered solemnly . . . before he smiled. "There is so much I wish to know. The MacClarens speak of you as savages, you know."

"Aye, it's a pleasure to harry them, and we do it as often as we can."

"So I heard. One story in particular. Which of you has Donald MacClaren's daughter?"

The scarred young man's eyebrow went up. "That would be me."

"What is your name?" Niall asked, recognizing power and prowess in the young man's shoulders and confident stance, and surmised he would prove a formidable warrior at his side.

"Brochan, laird."

"Does she remain with you by her own will?"

"Oh, aye." He grinned a roguish smile. "She took a wee bit of persuading at first, but . . ."

Laughter sounded all around.

"A *wee* bit," someone said with a chuckle.

"But now she's my wife—"

"Because—" Niall asked.

"Because I asked her, and she said yes," he answered more softly. More seriously. "We'll have our first *bairn* come spring."

A bairn. He thought of Elpeth then, and wondered if they would have children. Daughters and sons.

"Kincaid," said Brochan, looking pensive. "As devoted as we are to our cause, our numbers are small compared to theirs. We have little more than . . . forty able-bodied warriors." He looked around, and others nodded back at him. "Without a doubt our women will take up arms as well, if we should call upon them, but what is our strategy?"

Niall lifted a hand. "I have more men, traveling here even now, and more important, I have allies. I also have a plan. For now, I ask only that you stand ready until I call for you. Make my presence known to any Kincaids in Inverhaven and all surrounding lands, so that they will be ready, but only if you are certain of their loyalty. When the time comes, and it will come soon, I vow to you, my kinsmen, that you will have the greatest place of honor at my side, when the MacClaren is defeated."

"Wot of the Alwyn?" asked Osgar. "He must be held accountable too."

"He will not escape our justice. Once we have taken control here, we will tend to him."

"Very good!" Murdoch exclaimed.

"Aye!" agreed Brochan.

All the men gathered round, placing their hands on his shoulders. Tears shone in some of their eyes—including Deargh's, whom Niall had never once seen in his life, show such emotion. Niall's heart beat with pride, and in anticipation of the long-awaited reckoning to come.

Osgar looked at him steadily. "We have something t' show you now. Can ye come w' us?"

He agreed. But rather than riding into the hills toward

a hidden settlement, as Niall had expected, a boy was left to mind his and Deargh's horses, while they were led on foot straight back across the valley and deep into the shadowed woods behind the castle. Traveling there, he saw firsthand how the Kincaids moved about unseen and unheard, their skill at doing so a disciplined practice, making use of the lay of the land to remain obscured, down to the colors they wore, the grays and greens of stone, lichen, and grass. At last, they arrived at a small clearing.

"Why have you brought me here?" Niall asked.

They all looked at him solemnly.

Osgar stepped forward. "Come with me."

He set off across the grassy field, dotted with patches of fern, and the others followed. When he reached a certain spot, he searched intently, pushing aside the overgrowth with his wrinkled, knobby-knuckled hands.

"Here," he said, resting his hand on a large flat stone. "The Kincaid sword is buried here, with other items of clan importance, waiting to be returned to their rightful place in the castle."

Niall's throat tightened with emotion. "I remember that night, the sword being taken away. I feared it had been destroyed or thrown in a bog, forever lost."

"We just need to know how fast you need us to dig them up."

"Less a fortnight," he answered.

"That soon? You're certain?"

"I am, and you should be too."

They all laughed, but their laughter faded, and they looked at him with peculiar intensity.

"What is it?" he asked, his senses suddenly gone keen.

Osgar's voice took a tone of reverence. "There's something else we must show you now."

"Show me then."

He again followed Osgar to the distant edge of the clearing. Everyone else fell away, trailing behind until only he followed, and Deargh at a short distance.

Osgar bent, and pushed aside a fern, to reveal—

A stone cross laid flat on the ground.

Niall's heart stopped beating, and the earth seemed to disappear from under his feet. He knew what Osgar would say.

"This here"—the old man said softly, stepping back— "is where your father lays. Your mother is there . . ." He pointed. "On that side."

Osgar gestured to the ground beyond, and walking there, pushed aside the groundcover on one side and the other where smaller crosses spread across the earth like stones.

"These are all the others," Osgar said. "Buried together, as well as we could manage. We brought a priest. The ground is consecrated, and he spoke the necessary words over them."

Niall blinked, exhaling. Taken, in an instant, back to that night.

The drums. The fear. The loss.

He had existed ever since with a low, simmering rage ever constant in his thoughts, in his blood—but seeing his parents' graves awakened something blacker and more dangerous inside him. For some reason, in that moment, he thought of Elspeth—saw her face in his mind—as if his soul sought comfort from her. But just as quickly her features blurred, as did his feelings for her . . . all becoming indistinct and obscured by the shadows of hate that filled his mind.

"My brothers . . ." he asked in a hollow voice.

Osgar shook his head. "We never knew what happened to you, nor them. We do not know if they lived or died."

"Do you know who killed my mother and father, and these Kincaids? Who murdered them? Which man— *specifically*, is responsible, all or one?"

"No, Kincaid," Osgar answered quietly. "I was there, but in the melee and darkness, I did not see. They all held the sword, as far as we are concerned. The MacClaren. The Alwyn. And that king, all the way down in his lowland castle, whether he knew what would happen or no, because he emboldened them and then after, looked the other way."

With that, Osgar backed away, and turning, rejoined his companions, who held vigil, watching from a distance in silence.

For the first time in his life, Niall found it difficult to stand. He had lived with the weight of what happened that night on his shoulders for so long, but being here . . . among the graves . . . made his loss infinitely more real. His grief for the loved ones he had lost—and the hatred for the men responsible—eclipsed every other thought. His heart—to whatever degree Elspeth had thawed it—now blackened completely, consumed by ice.

Kneeling, he pressed his hand on the cross that lay between his parents' graves, remembering their faces in his mind.

He whispered, "I am here."

Deargh clasped a hand to his shoulder, and knelt beside him. "Aye, my laird. Do you see? At long last, your son has come home."

That evening, Elspeth dressed carefully, wanting to look especially nice because she knew she would see Niall at the evening meal, and that even if they did not speak, they would at least see each other.

Today had been wonderful. She'd had the joy of her sisters' company, and all the women of the castle and village she adored so much. And then there had been Niall's surprising and passionate kiss underneath the waterfall that she would never, for as long as she lived, forget.

Because of those things, for a brief time the responsibilities her future held had faded to the back of her mind. But the day was over, and it seemed that with each beat of her heart, she was more and more aware of the bittersweet passing of time.

In just two days, the MacClaren caravan would leave Inverhaven for the Cearcal Festival. She had only these few nights left in which to spend time with Niall before she was betrothed, or even married to another man. It was possible she would not even return to Inverhaven from the festival, but be sent straightaway to her new home.

She was torn over what to do. Should she seek him out, for one last, farewell kiss? Should she tell him how much he meant to her? Or would she only be inflicting more pain on herself, and him, when they were forced to part?

In truth, she did not know how she felt about him. Everything had happened so quickly between them, she feared to confess any depth of feeling for him, even to herself. Did she love him? She did not know. How could she even consider the idea, when she was not free to do so?

Elspeth crossed to the window and looked out over the valley. Perhaps it would be better if she stayed away from him completely. Whenever they were alone their attraction got so quickly out of hand, and she had already come so close to losing her virtue to him. But wasn't it more than attraction between them?

As for actual words, he had not declared any feelings for her, other than those spoken in his quarters, which had seemed heartfelt and honest . . . but guarded. He had remained so cool and clearheaded about the forces that kept them apart. On one hand she understood that it must be very difficult for him to share his feelings easily, given the life of solitude he had lived. On the other, it was completely possible he did not feel as deeply for her as she did for him.

She sighed, turning back to the room, her heart aching and heavy. She felt such confusion. She did not know what to do. She only knew she missed him already, and fantasized every other moment about running away with him, promising her love and the rest of her life to him, though in her heart of hearts she knew that even if he asked her to do so, she would never abandon her duty to the family and clan she loved.

At least she told herself that. But what would she do if he told her he loved her? If he asked her to go with him? She did not know, because it had not happened. The difficult truth was that they had run out of time. There was nothing left to do but to say good-bye.

However, that night Niall did not come into the great hall as he normally did, though Deargh was there, sitting shoulder to shoulder among the MacClaren men. Later, alone in bed, she could not sleep, wondering where he had been and knowing his absence left her with just one last day, one night, to say good-bye.

She saw him nowhere the next day. Nor did he appear the next night.

"To be young again!" exclaimed Fiona, who at Elspeth's invitation had come up from the village to spend one last evening together. The meal had long since concluded, and though Elspeth had eaten her meal in the company of her father, Bridget, and the council, she now sat in the shadows along the wall, at a table with Fiona and Ina and her sisters. Nearby, the bard Murdoch sang about a vengeful ghost warrior who took the form of a wolf to slip into the camp of his sleeping enemy.

The old woman smiled, remembering. "I went to the Cearcal myself, to attend to you and your mother. It is an exciting time, with many handsome, very notable young men looking for suitable brides. I know God will lead you to the right choice."

Fiona's hand closed over Elspeth's. The older woman had been kind and discreet enough not to ask her about

Niall, and Elspeth hoped that none of her anxiety over him showed.

"Anyone is better than your original two choices," Ina whispered, eyebrows raised.

They all three laughed—though Elspeth remained almost feverishly distracted by the lateness of the hour, and the understanding that Niall again would not appear.

Had he forgotten that she would leave tomorrow? What if she never saw him again? Was it that he did not care? Or was he too, trying to spare himself the pain of saying good-bye to her? The possibilities were so disparate that they were utterly maddening, when combined with the heartbreak of saying good-bye to her loved ones, including her father, who was ill, and her sisters, who would grow up and go their own ways. Things would never be the same again.

"Speaking of my age," said Fiona. "It is time for me to give you a kiss, and return home."

"I will walk you there," Elspeth insisted, not wanting the woman who had been so much like a mother to her after her own mother's death, to be sent off alone into the night.

Perhaps she would also see Niall out in the courtyard, and be able to say a brief but satisfactory farewell there.

Yet Ina stood as well. "I will go with you."

All the better, so that if she saw him, they would not be alone other than for a few words.

As they meandered through the crowded hall, Elspeth stopped to be kissed on the cheek and embraced by others wishing her the best in finding a match that would make her happy as well as advantage them all as a clan. When they neared the door, a voice called out to her. It was her father, who followed after her. He breathed heavily, as if the walk across the room had fatigued him.

"Child," he looked at her steadily. "I could not help but notice that you were very quiet tonight."

She nodded. "I am sad. I cannot help it. I will miss everyone."

His gaze warmed. "I know this is a time of uncertainty for you. For us all. But I will do everything in my power to make sure you are at peace with your choice. I want you to be happy."

"Thank you, Father." She kissed him on the cheek. "I will return soon. Ina and I are seeing Fiona home."

Conall appeared, strapping on his side arm. "I will accompany the ladies, to be certain everyone returns safely." Looking at Elspeth he said, "If Magnus has heard you are traveling to the Cearcal, he might try to steal you away again. Let us not take any chances."

Elspeth's heart fell. So they were a traveling party now. If she did cross paths with Niall, she would be too closely accompanied to be able to say anything at all to him.

Perhaps . . . perhaps it was all for the best, that things between them ended this way, in a less than spectacular manner.

"Sleep well, Father."

"And you." He bent to kiss her cheek. "We depart tomorrow morning at dawn."

She summoned a smile. "I will be ready."

A servant brought a plaid for her shoulders, and she gathered it around her head and shoulders, just as Fiona and Ina did theirs, while Conall pulled a woolen cap over his head and ears. Outside the air was colder than in days past. Autumn had arrived. In the bailey, the fires were bigger, and the villagers warmly dressed.

Though she searched the light and shadows for Niall, she did not see him. They continued, the three ladies talking and laughing about happy times remembered, as Conall followed behind, and when they reached Fiona's cottage, she and Elspeth made their tearful good-bye. Moments later they returned the same way they had come.

Two MacClaren warriors stood at the gate, talking to the guards there. They fell into step with Conall, talking and laughing boisterously.

The moment Elspeth passed into the bailey, she froze— recognizing Niall in the flickering light of the bonfire, leaning against the castle wall. Only he wasn't alone. In his arms was a pretty, flame-haired young woman, her arms around his shoulders. Smiling, he bent his head for a kiss.

She blinked, disbelieving, going numb from head to toe. Misery spread through her heart, making it fall like a stone in her chest.

It was Isla, a young widow from the village. A beautiful young woman discussed often by the warriors at her father's hearth, who all the unmarried men desperately wished to court. Thus far she had not indicated a choice.

It appeared now, that she had.

Elspeth forced herself to keep walking, although she felt as if she would retch right there on the ground.

His kisses. The things they had done in his quarters. Why would he be with someone else tonight, mere days after he had touched her like that, if he cared for her at all? The answer was obvious to her. Because he did not care. His words . . . his gentle touch, had all been lies, but for what purpose? Merely to seduce her, or in hopes of marrying well himself?

She felt foolish. Naïve. Ashamed. Embarrassed. And furious. Heartbroken? No. She refused to allow herself to feel that.

She was not the only one to notice the couple, who continued to kiss passionately against the wall.

Conall chuckled, looking in their direction. "It appears that Niall and Isla have found one another."

"Poor Isla," she answered in a low voice—yet she shielded her face within the cowl of her plaid, afraid if anyone saw her expression they would see the truth written plainly across it. "She would do well to be more selective with her affections."

"You question his sincerity?" he asked.

She shrugged. "As you yourself once told me, he is a mercenary. It comes as no surprise that he is just as dangerous with a woman's heart as he is with a weapon."

Conall laughed, as did the warriors who walked alongside him.

To think she had feared that she had fallen in love with him.

Now she was *glad* to have seen him for what he truly was. Life would be much easier from this moment on.

Niall watched her go, every muscle in his body tensing, insisting that he go after her, to confess the truth of his actions, and to explain. Instead he remained where he was, holding a woman he cared nothing for, in case she turned back.

That afternoon, as he had knelt on his parents' graves, a powerful bloodlust had overtaken him. Only . . . in the midst of everything, he had seen Elspeth's face. Heard her voice in his head. Calming him. Soothing him.

It was something he could not allow.

In that moment it had become apparent that despite all his caution, despite the hate he carried in his chest, he had come to care too greatly for the pawn in his revenge. Elspeth's gentle nature and joyous spirit calmed the beast in him, so much so that in days prior he had tried to negotiate with his conscience how he could satisfy his need for revenge, while allowing the MacClaren to live, all for her sake.

But surrounded by those graves, filled with his parents and his clanspeople, he knew there could be no absolution granted to the MacClaren. The Kincaid clan's retribution would be brutal and swift, without compassion or remorse, and he as their laird would see that Elspeth's father paid with his life for what he had done.

Niall knew that if Elspeth were present to see the blood and violence he inflicted with his sword—it would destroy her. Kill her, just as certainly as if he cut her down with a sword to her himself.

He had known then what he must do, and that was to get her as far away from here as possible. That meant ensuring she departed tomorrow for the Cearcal, with no feelings for him, to wed someone else.

When he was certain Elspeth had gone inside the castle and would not return, he released Isla, who had pursued him relentlessly the past two nights here beside the bonfire.

"As much as I have enjoyed your company," he said. "I am tired, and I must awaken very early."

She leaned against him, her arms tight around him, refusing to let him go. "I could go with you."

"I don't think so." He smiled, and gently pried free her hands from his plaid. "I have heard more than once that you are looking for a husband, and I could never be that."

She frowned prettily, stepping back. "A pity, that. Oh, go on with you then." She teased, her smile returning. "What good are you to me? You know where I am if you change your mind."

Turning from her, the smile dropped from his lips. With a cold wind sweeping around him, he strode down the darkened path toward his quarters, and once inside, barred the door. Laying back on the bed, he covered his face with his hands. He had never felt so dark inside. So miserable.

He would never forget the look on her face when she had seen him with Isla.

He would never forget, for as long as he lived. Aye, he had wounded her. And aye, he had wounded himself.

But intentionally. He had hurt her now because he cared for her so greatly. Perhaps he even loved her, if he were true to his soul. One day soon he hoped she would realize the gift he had given to her, in sending her away. Even as she despised him for killing her father, and every day during her prayers cursed his name.

Chapter 17

The next morning, as the caravan formed in the bailey, Niall received a summons into the castle, to speak with the MacClaren. He could only assume he would be charged with protecting the borders in the chief's absence—which he would do unless his company of men arrived early, which he prayed they would. Was not the laird's absence a perfect time to seize control of the castle and its surrounding lands? The MacClaren clan defenses would be divided, and easier to disarm — and defeat.

He overheard voices coming from within the laird's council room.

"I will hear no more of this," exclaimed Bridget's voice, high and tremulous. "You are too ill to travel."

Damn. He closed his eyes, and paused outside the door.

The MacClaren would not be departing after all. His first thought was not of new strategy, but of Elspeth . . . would she remain as well?

He did not want her here. He needed her to go.

Entering, he found the room crowded with warriors and council members. The MacClaren reclined on a raised pallet near the fire, his countenance pale and taut and drawn in pain. He wore a loose shift, and blankets covered him. Bridget sat on the floor beside him, her hand on his arm. His physician looked on, his expression grave.

Elspeth stood there too, wearing a simple wheat-colored *lèine*, facing her father, her hands curled at her sides. She wore a single thick braid, over her shoulder, revealing the delicate nape of her neck. His gaze traveled down the proud line of her back, and his chest constricted tight with longing.

Conall shifted stance and lifted a pensive hand to his face, where he rubbed his jaw. "What do you wish to do?"

The MacClaren spoke wearily, but with authority. "You will go without me."

Yes, Elspeth *must* go.

The MacClaren exhaled heavily. "Conall, you and Ennis will also go to the Cearcal, to support Elspeth in making her decision. We have discussed at length what this man must be, and I know any approval you make would be as astute and discerning as mine. Bridget, I know you were eager to attend as well, to reunite with loved ones from your own clan. You go also."

"I will not," she shook her head, scowling. "I will remain here with you."

Her hands seized his, curling tight around them.

Niall had not seen such dedication from her before. But he supposed feelings could change. *Feelings.* Pah. What did he care for their feelings? That he even spent one second of thought on them annoyed him. He did his best to keep a look of irritation from his face.

Conall nodded. "Then all proceeds as planned. However, my laird, if your side warriors remain here with you, someone else must provide the necessary escort."

"Take Niall, then . . ." replied the MacClaren, before coughing heavily into a cloth. "Along with twenty or so others that he chooses." More quietly he said. "I have come to trust him, and I trust him in this." He chuckled. "What man in his right mind would challenge a protector such as that?"

The bottom fell out of Niall's heart.

No. He had already said his good-bye to Elspeth, quick and painful, at least in his mind. He had no wish to do it again. He had no wish to see her courted and wed and sent off to start a life with another man.

"*Anyone* but Niall," Elspeth answered darkly.

Her rejection blasted through him, scaring and painful. And yet her words gave him at least a glimmer of hope that he would be left behind. Would her father respect her wishes?

"Why, daughter?" The chief's gaze flickered to the back of the room where Niall stood, and a smile turned the corner of his lips. "Why would you say that about him?"

"He is arrogant." She crossed her arms over her chest. "I do not like him."

Conall chuckled, as did others.

The MacClaren nodded, his eyebrows going up. "Aye, I had noticed more than once before. His arrogance, which is well earned, I think, and your dislike. So . . . Niall it shall be."

Conall laughed and nodded. "A fine choice."

Niall exhaled through his teeth. *Damn.*

"Father!" Elspeth cried, her arms going straight at her side, fingers spread wide.

He lifted a hand. "What safer escort for my lovely daughter than a man she cannot abide? I will know your virtue is protected. Is that not true, Niall?"

Elspeth's shoulders went rigid as she realized he had been standing behind her all along.

The laird peered at him . . . as did everyone else, turning. Smiling.

Everyone but Elspeth, who stood, holding herself rigidly forward.

What was he to say? He could think of no reasonable excuse to decline this duty.

"Aye," he gritted out. "That is true."

An hour later, he waited at the front of the line of horses and wagons, dressed for travel, holding Fitheach's reins, his muscles drawn with anticipation as he waited with everyone else for Elspeth to emerge.

The doors of the castle opened, and men spilled out. The air changed then. Became charged with energy, and Niall knew a half-second before she appeared, that she would.

She did so, accompanied by the MacClaren, who walked slowly, dressed in long robes, and Bridget. Several women followed, dressed for travel, who would no doubt serve as her attendants in the following days.

But when she walked past him, the air left Niall's lungs. Every time he saw her, he was certain she had never looked lovelier. But truly . . . she had never been more beautiful than this. Aye, she was a warrior's fantasy, laced into a fitted leather jerkin that left no doubt as to the perfection of her waist, hips and breasts. Necklaces formed of leather cording and bronze beads circled her slender neck. She wore her hair in an intricate crown of braids, and the rest loose and falling down her back. She glanced at him as she strode past, from behind kohl-rimmed eyes, her gaze smoky—and dismissive.

His insides burned to cinders.

Deargh looked at him, eyes twinkling.

"Don't look at me like that," he muttered under his breath.

"Like what?" the warrior answered, his bushy brows raised.

"You know like what."

"Aye, lad." He leaned close. "It's called sympathy. You are certain of your decision? It's not too late to keep her for yourself."

"I want her to go."

A litter had been prepared for her travel, painted a dark indigo blue with silver and gold flourishes, with curtains all around for privacy. And yet she shunned that form of lady's travel, and proceeded toward a horse. With some ceremony, she kissed her father good-bye, and even Bridget, before mounting. With Conall and Ennis at either side of her, she proceeded down the road, where well-wishers from the village had gathered, including Fiona who smiling stepped out to offer Elspeth a garland of greenery and colorful streamers, which Elspeth accepted and lay across the shoulders of her horse.

He and Deargh climbed into their saddles, and followed along with the warriors he had selected to accompany them.

They traveled all day at a steady pace until the sky darkened, at which time, the procession halted in a field. Amidst a growing wind, three tents were unpacked. A fire was lit, and a supper of brined herring had by all. Niall did not cross paths with Elspeth. She remained ensconced among her women on the opposite side of the flames, she a tantalizing mystery in the firelight, until she disappeared into her tent, not to be seen again. Soon enough, the council members also retired, leaving only the warriors, who would sleep out of doors.

After seeing to the placement of men for the night watch, Niall wrapped himself in his plaid and reclined against a rounded stone, doing his best to sleep. But as had occurred these past several nights when he found himself alone, memories tormented him, visions of her smile and laugh. Of her skin, slippery and wet underneath the waterfall. Of her in his bed.

He had brought this torment on himself and certainly fate punished him by forcing him to watch as she was given in marriage to another man.

He turned, aching to his bones and buried his face into the wool.

When Elspeth left her tent the next morning, the first person she saw was Niall, standing beside the fire, his legs braced and his arms crossed over his chest, looking distinctly ill-tempered. Wind ruffled his hair, and his cheeks were ruddy with the cold. She knew that if she were to touch him now . . . to embrace him, he would radiate a comforting heat and would smell like wood smoke and earth.

At seeing her—which she assumed he did, although he did not actually *look* at her from what she observed—he set off in the direction of the men, who saddled their horses. No one needed to tell her that he was unhappy at having been pressed into the duty of escorting her. No doubt he wished he was at Inverhaven with Isla, sharing all the same intimacies he had shared with her—and more.

The resulting image that flashed into her mind stole her breath. Why did she torture herself with such thoughts? He was not the man she'd believed him to be. She should not grieve the loss of him, but welcome the opportunity to marry someone more honorable.

And yet a short time later it was he who brought her palfrey forward, looking like a prince and inspiring sighs from her maidservants. A young warrior appeared with a stool for her use, and once she was seated in her saddle, Niall handed her the reins. For a time, he rode behind her, speaking in low tones to Conall, before breaking out of the line to ride some distance ahead with Deargh as they approached their destination.

By early afternoon, they arrived under a clouded sky

at Wyfernloch, a dramatic valley shielded on three sides by steep mountains. She remembered the place from those years ago when she had come with her mother and father, and it made her chest tightened with sudden sadness that the MacClaren could not be here now. Other clans had already arrived and claimed their territory. Dark clouds gathered overhead, and the wind rose. The men went immediately to constructing the dozen or so tents that would house those of the MacClaren clan who had come, centered around a larger rectangular tent where they would feast each night and entertain guests, and she would welcome suitors.

"The Alwyns are here," said Conall, staring across the clearing to another cluster of tents above which a red and white pennant flew. "I will be interested to see if they approach."

She had not seen Magnus since the night he abducted her, but certainly their paths would cross again. When they did, she did not know whether to act angry or conciliatory, but she supposed her heart would tell her what to do if and when she saw him.

The first tent was not yet complete when rain began to pour from the sky. Elspeth raised the hood of her cloak—

Suddenly Niall was there, one hand on her back, another holding the dark canopy of his plaid above her to shield her from the rain. Her heart pounded as he hurried her toward the litter. Pushing aside the curtain, he urged her inside, then turned on his heel, leaving her alone and looking after him.

Only to pause and return, his boots crunching heavily on the earth as he came nearer. Her heart beat faster, knowing he would speak.

With one hand he pushed his hair back from his forehead so that it lay dark and slick against his head, and leaned inward, his other hand gripping the doorframe.

Water ran in rivulets over the strong planes of his cheeks, and spiked the dark lashes that rimmed his eyes. Though the air was cold, she felt the heat of his gaze strike through her.

"I wish you well, Elspeth," he said in a low, controlled voice. "I wish you . . . every happiness. I truly do."

Inside she went numb, realizing this was the closest thing to good-bye they would have—only now spoken with ill feelings between them, at least on her part.

"I wish you happiness as well," she answered. "You and *Isla*."

The words tumbled from her lips, she unable to stop them.

His jaw twitched and his nostrils flared.

Instantly, she knew the taunt had been a weak and childish mistake. They would not wound Niall. They would only reveal the depth of her pain.

"It was but a kiss," he answered in a passionless voice. "Nothing more."

Indeed, he spoke the words as if they meant nothing. As if the pain he had inflicted on her meant nothing. How had she once believed he had a heart, and true feelings for her?

"Only a kiss." She shrugged indifferently, hardening her heart against him, vowing he would not hurt her again. "Just as yours and mine were only kisses. Is that right, Niall?"

He stared at her, his expression a stone wall that concealed any emotion.

She would not play the wounded lover. The one left behind. She had too much pride for that. Nor would she embark upon her new life with only half a heart.

"Go on then," she said, her voice intentionally cool, sinking back against the cushions.

His brows came together, dark and questioning. As if he had never been dismissed.

She pushed the opposite curtain open, and looked out at nothing in particular.

"You are dripping on my skirts."

Three nights later, a large bonfire burned. Niall stood beneath a tree with Deargh, having already watched the revelry unfold for hours. It was the third night—the night before they would travel back to Inverhaven, and all presumed, the night Elspeth would announce her choice of husband, at least to her counselors, so that final negotiations could be entered into.

The previous days had been filled with games for the children as well as the adults, where men and women alike displayed their skills in horsemanship, swords, and fighting. Niall had participated in the war games ferociously, for the sole purpose of expending his growing agitation at being forced to stand by and watch Elspeth compete—and win—in archery . . . ride with heart-stopping skill at the forefront of the hunt . . . and each night laugh and dance in the company of other men. Men who were not the repulsive creatures Keppoch Macpherson and Alan FitzDuff had been, although those two were present as well, campaigning to be recognized as serious choices. But Elspeth had entertained visits from a number of handsome and powerfully connected chiefs and nobles who would honor an alliance with the MacClaren clan and see her ensconced in her new life like a queen, and each night Niall overheard wagers being made on who she would select. If there was a clear favorite, Elspeth gave no sign.

Tonight, each of the clans had prepared separate feasts, putting their hospitality on display, attempting to outdo all the rest, for each feast was open for the enjoyment of all.

The gathered folk walked from one encampment to the next, entering the largest of the tents, drinking mead and ale, dancing and listening to musicians, and hearing stories told—all save for the MacClarens and the Alwyns, who had staked territory on opposite sides of the glen, and made it a point not to intermingle.

A young, dark-haired man in rich robes emerged from the MacClaren tent, accompanied by several companions. He stopped just beyond the threshold and turned to peer back inside, marveling.

"Lord, what a fierce beauty, bright-eyed and fine. I'm in love." He clasped his hands over his heart. "Can you imagine the sons we would have together?" He grinned.

His companion chuckled. "A pity she did not so much as look at you twice."

"True, that," the man agreed, with a slow shake of his head. "But I did not see her look at *anyone* twice, which means I have as good a chance as any." His voice rang with hope. "But I refuse to sit among the others, begging for a glance. It is more important that her counselors fall in love with my father's army and coffers, I think, and that should put me in good stead."

"Come on now," Deargh said in a quiet voice. "Let's go inside. Perhaps it won't be long now, and we can be done with this task and on to more important things."

What else could he do? To stay away while Elspeth made her choice felt too much like cowardice. Niall entered with him, delving into a crush of people, color, and sound. The song of the minstrels lilted bright and cheerful in his ears.

It made good sense to stay close. There had been such heated competition for the Mistress MacClaren's attentions—and her valuable *tocher* lands—he would not be surprised if one or more of her admirers responded to the rejection of their suit with violence. He and Deargh found Conall and Ennis, who sat on stools, taking positions standing behind them.

On the opposite side of the shadowed tent, Elspeth sat on a pallet, resplendent in a scarlet gown, her long skirts spread out around her. She wore her hair parted at the center, in shining thick coils on either side, caught up in fine gold netting that gleamed in the firelight. Three men . . . no, four . . . sat near her, the closest leaning in to whisper in her ear. Elspeth smiled and laughed, her cheeks vivid with color. The other three looked on, scowling and disgruntled.

Niall understood how they felt. The moment he saw her, his stomach muscles had clenched with too many nights of unsatisfied desire, and refused to release.

After the song came to an end, the minstrels paused, before starting up again with a lighthearted trill. Elspeth's handmaidens appeared, all wearing bright ribbons in their hair. They took her up by the hand, bringing her to her feet, and then coaxed the men up as well. At their urging, others from the crowd joined them, making two circles, the ladies within and the men without. In time with the music, they moved in different directions, spinning and laughing and reaching to touch hands as they passed.

Until one of the young men who had been seated beside Elspeth reached out as he passed, and pulled her close—

Swooping down, he kissed her on the mouth. Only Elspeth turned her face, and the kiss met her cheek instead.

Even so, Niall had already taken one step forward—only to be seized and held back by Deargh's fierce grip.

The circles stopped moving. The music fell off . . . and the room grew silent.

Elspeth looked up at the young man, her eyes wide and startled. Looking out at all the onlookers, she laughed.

"What a very nice kiss!" she proclaimed, laughing. "But

how unfair. Should I not now offer a kiss to the others as well?"

The room burst out in laughter—and a pall fell over Niall.

"Someone once told me a kiss is just a kiss." she said, approaching a grinning young man. "Can that be true? Are they all the same?"

Deargh's face turned then, and he looked at Niall hard and steady. Yet Niall looked straight ahead, the words striking a dagger through his heart for it was he that she taunted.

"Nay!" voices shouted, from all around.

"Nay, lady, my kiss is more pleasing." The fellow eagerly welcomed her into his arms—putting a frown on the other man's face. Dramatically dipping her backward, he pressed his lips to hers.

A chaste kiss, all in all, but one that set Niall's blood simmering. He barely heard the cheering of the crowd.

"What in the hell is she doing?" Niall growled to Deargh.

Conall shrugged. "Playing the game."

Elspeth spun free again, smiling, into the arms of another.

"Perhaps you will know your husband by his kiss," called one of her ladies.

"Kiss them all!" another cried, lifting a goblet high.

The musicians resumed their raucous melody, and the room churned with movement, as the dancers resumed their places, more joining in this time. Niall saw Elspeth dancing around the circle of men, quickly kissing one, before moving to the next.

Every muscle in Niall's body seized tight, and he struggled to contain his reaction—an overwhelming impulse to push forward and jerk her away.

Deargh stared at him, *hard*. "If you can't get that look off your face, then you need to go outside and wait there."

"What look?" he growled, his blood simmering in his veins.

Deargh moved closer, and gripped his upper arm. "The one that says you'll flay any man alive who dares touch your woman again."

Niall glared back at him, angry because he knew his companion spoke the truth.

Suddenly, two men broke free from the circle, shoving at one another, their faces contorted with anger.

"This will quickly grow out of hand," Niall muttered, with a jerk of his chin. "I will see to those two. Deargh, secure Elspeth—take her to her tent. Put a stop to this foolishness now."

Ennis stood and joined them. "Yes, that. The time has come that she must choose."

Striding toward the two men, Niall seized them by their tunics and hauled them tripping, dragging, and flailing outside, where they resumed their fight.

He left them, but did not return inside. Instead, he delved into the frigid darkness, allowing it to numb his skin. He wandered, and wandered further, venturing in and out of tents, seeing, but not seeing the faces before again returning to the shadows.

A man crossed his path just then, each of his arms around a laughing woman, making his way toward the bonfire, a wineskin dangling from both hands.

It was Magnus.

"Your heart is inconstant, I see," Niall called out after him.

This snared Magnus's attention. Straightening, he turned, bringing himself—and the two women around. Leaving them behind, he walked toward Niall.

"Is Elspeth, your true love, so quickly forgotten?" Niall sardonically pressed a hand over his heart.

"Nay, my heart is true," Magnus answered, stopping two paces away.

"Then why are you here, with those two, instead of in the MacClaren tent, making an offer to beat out all the others?"

He spoke the words to wound, knowing from all he had heard that Magnus could not compete with the other men who had presented suits.

"Alas, I think you know the answer to that. Not only do our clans hate one another, but I have no lands of my own, no armies to command, making me invisible in the eyes of her father, and sadly love alone will not win in this competition."

"Love . . ." The word struck Niall like a kick to his gut. "You love her, then."

"I do. Very much so." Magnus raised one of the wine-skins, and drank deeply. Lowering it, he wiped his mouth and peered at Niall. "But not in the way you might suppose."

"She said as much. That you were a friend."

Magnus nodded, closing his eyes, looking deeply morose. "And for that reason, I tried to save her."

Niall's ears perked up at that.

"Save her?" Niall's tilted his head and stepped closer. "Save her from what?"

Magnus laughed bitterly.

"What does it matter now?" he said, looking toward the MacClaren tent. "It is already too late."

Chapter 18

Elspeth knew the moment Niall left the tent. Seeing that he did not return, her mood crashed into despair, and suddenly she wanted nothing more than to be alone and away from all this. To avoid the choice she must make for at least a few more hours.

She extricated herself from the amorous embrace of one young man, only to be claimed by another, and brought back into the dance. Through the melee she glimpsed Deurgh coming toward her with judgment in his eyes.

Which made her angry, because he was faithful to Niall and because of that, she would not accept his condemnation. Determined to conduct herself without his intervention, she opened her mouth to command that she be set free—

Only to have her arm seized, and her body pulled away from the circle. She stared into the face of the man looking into hers. Her heart pounded, as she recognized him.

She yanked her arm free, and stepped back from him.

It was the Alwyn—and behind him stood Hugh, his eyes glassy and dull.

The hair on the back of her neck rose in warning, and her mind thundered with one question: Why were they here?

Behind him, the Alwyn's entourage spread out among the crowd, daring to take up goblets of ale and platters of food, as they turned to watch their chief.

"Mistress MacClaren." The chief bowed deeply. He was built like a bull, with a thick neck and muscles everywhere. His hair was brown, with streaks of gray running through.

She stood tall and proud, refusing to shrink beneath his scrutinizing gaze.

She tilted her head in acknowledgment. "Alwyn."

"It has been a long time. Years. Am I right? And how lovely you have grown."

Out of the corner of her eyes, she saw that Deargh and Conall came to stand behind her. Other MacClaren warriors maneuvered closer through the crowd, their gazes alert and wary. She wished . . .

She wished Niall was there.

"It has been years," she answered. "But I know you have not come to flatter me with compliments and to talk of old times. Tell me, why have you come?"

"Dear child, you speak with such authority," he said in a teasing—and altogether dismissive tone.

"Does that offend you?" she answered lightly. "I will not apologize."

His brows came together in offended dismay. "Where . . . is your father?"

He looked all about the room, as if searching for the MacClaren.

"Come now," she replied. "You already know that he did not come."

"A shame." He feigned an expression of sympathy. "He is ill, I hear. Nothing serious, I hope?" He lifted a hand to his chin, covering his mouth for a moment with his fingers, as if in deep thought. "And yet when such things linger on, we must consider the future and how things must change."

His words struck an already sensitive chord inside her heart. Within the long sleeves of her gown, her hands curled into fists. "Do tell me what you mean."

"Is there somewhere private, that you and I can talk?"

"Yes, and my advisors."

"As you wish." He shrugged, his lips taking on a sly smile.

She led them behind a curtain into a small private area—the Alwyn and Hugh, followed by Conall and Ennis. Once inside, the music started again and the merrymaking resumed, but at a more subdued level. Deargh remained at the threshold, to prevent anyone from intruding.

The Alwyn opened his hands and nodded. "It is well known throughout the highlands that your father is seeking a husband for you. And while the Alwyns have not been invited to offer, we wished to present one all the same."

Confusion arose in her mind. An offer . . . on Magnus's behalf? Had he changed his mind, and did he at last intend to formally recognize his bastard son?

If so, where was Magnus?

Magnus was not there, which certainly he would be if that were the Alwyn's plan . . .

So, if not Magnus, then who?

Thank God, the Alwyn himself was married, at least last that she knew, and Hugh was formally betrothed to some other unfortunate girl. Not that it mattered. *Any* offer he made would be refused.

"I can think of no reason why we would not at least hear what you have to say," she said in a magnanimous tone, hoping they would say whatever they had to say, and be gone.

"Ah, what a diplomatic response. Which is more than I could have expected from your father."

"My father has been more than diplomatic in responding to your recent unfounded claims, threats, and aggressions." She tilted her head. "But you are here on another matter. I would invite you to proceed."

His nostrils flared and his chin lowered, and she knew his scowl was a practiced attempt to intimidate. "You are young. I do not know how much you know of the past—the longstanding partnership between your father and me, which has weakened of late, for reasons that are . . . not important here, between you and me."

He continued to patronize her, as if she were a child—because she was a woman, she knew. But she represented her clan, where her father could not, and she must represent them well. That included not holding silent as his slights, however veiled, spilled from his mouth.

"I can think of a number of important reasons they have weakened."

His eyes narrowed on her.

"Whatever the case," he answered, speaking past clenched teeth, and a more apparent edge to his voice. "I would like to see a renewal of good will between our clans. A marriage seems the perfect way to effect this."

"Whom are you proposing that I marry?" It was a question she had to ask, although she had no wish to hear the answer.

"My son Hugh, of course."

The name echoed inside her head. Her gaze glanced aside to alight on the Alwyn's son. Hugh was taller than his father, but in features and coloring, a younger picture of his sire. But there, their similarities ended. She did not know how to explain it . . . but Hugh had always carried shadows within him—a fathomless darkness at the back of his eyes. She avoided looking into his eyes now, because she knew what she would see.

Nothing.

"What say you, Elspeth?" Hugh said, in the same hollow voice that always caught her off guard.

She did not answer. She only took a steadying breath. Just the thought of Hugh touching her made her skin crawl, let alone the prospect of marrying him. But there was another reason for her dismay.

"I apologize for my confusion," she said. "But last I heard Hugh was betrothed to someone else."

"We have decided to forgo that agreement," the Alwyn answered briskly. "As this one deserves precedence. As I will further explain, if you will allow me to do so."

His declaration made no sense. She could imagine no circumstances that would cause him to forgo a marriage agreement made with the ward of his powerful ally, the earl of Buchan. It mattered not what he proposed. She would never marry Hugh. Still, a very real sense of trepidation settled in the pit of her stomach because . . . why would he believe that she would? There was nothing to do but hear what he had to say.

"Well, then." She nodded. "State your terms. I and my council will consider them with all the rest."

He lowered his voice. "Then please listen well, and know that our terms come with a well-intended warning."

"A warning, you say?" Her trepidation increased.

He nodded. "You know of our king. While some of his decisions in the past have benefited all of us, that he is not a . . . *dependable* friend to the northern clans."

Aye, everyone knew the clans tested the king's patience sorely with their independent ways and infighting, and that he had no love of them. He considered them all savages.

Which was why he had recently made his son, Buchan, the Justiciar, to bring the unruliest of factions to heel.

"Go on, please," she said, trying to put the pieces of the growing puzzle together.

He pressed his hands together. "We have heard the king has been, of late, regretful of past decisions made and has undertaken to scrutinizing them, if you can believe that."

"I believe it. But how does that pertain to the Mac-Clarens?"

Because of the council meetings she had attended, she already feared that she knew what he would say.

"Ah . . ." he said. "It was told to me by someone privy to the king's ruminations—"

"The Earl of Buchan, no doubt," she said coolly.

A self-assured smile turned the corner of his lips, and he nodded his head in concurrence. "They told me that your father did not turn out to be as strong an ally in the region as the king had hoped. Because of this, past agreements have been scrutinized. Divisions of property reconsidered. As you know, the castle and the lands the MacClarens now claim as their own were to have been mine."

"That is not true," Elspeth said, shaking her head. Her cheeks burned with annoyance that she must stand and listen to this.

He did not pause in his speech. "As proof, I have the original map, signed by the king's assessor." He gestured with his hand as if to clear the air and to say "no matter." "But that is all in the past, and we are all at the king's mercy, are we not? I only tell you this because I have heard he now wonders if someone else might better serve him, and benefit from holding what are now considered Mac-Claren lands."

"You mean yourself," Elspeth hissed.

Anger crashed like thunder inside her head. She had no doubt who had started the king's ruminations in that direction. The Earl of Buchan—whose feet the Alwyn laid at like a faithful hound.

"I said nothing of the sort," he answered, appearing wounded by her accusation. "The Alwyns do not wish to betray our longstanding friendship with our neighbors, the MacClarens, though that friendship has been sorely strained in recent years. What we *generously* propose, given your father's poor health and the unlikelihood that his current marriage will produce an heir—"

Hugh gave a low, gravelly sounding laugh at this.

"—is that he and the MacClaren council appoint you, my dear, as heretrix of the MacClaren clan lands and *ceann-cinnidh*, the . . . female heir of the chieftaincy upon his death, and that you immediately, after this appointment is made, marry Hugh."

"Why would I do this?" she asked, her eyes flared wide and her pulse racing.

He opened his hands and raised his eyebrows as if it were all obvious. "This will preemptively create a situation the king will find no cause to interfere in, as you see, his justiciar—who has proven to be a loyal friend to the Alwyns, will intervene on our behalf to preserve our interests. This way, the MacClaren lands remain under MacClaren control—as they should be, and the justiciar's wish to reward the Alwyns for their enduring loyalty to him is satisfied."

"If the lands remain under MacClaren control, then what benefit do you get out of this agreement at all?" she asked.

He nodded, pointing a finger at her. "It would be agreed that any male child born of yours and Hugh's union would be named *ceann-cath,* formally recognized by all, at an appropriate age, to one day become chief of both clans."

A child, of course, bearing the clan name of Alwyn.

"This is quite a plan you have presented," she said in a voice devoid of any emotion.

He bowed his head. "In the name of peace and continued prosperity for our peoples."

She nodded, and paced a few steps away.

"I will consider all you have said," she conceded, though concealed within the long sleeves of her gown, her hands trembled.

"Understanding, I hope, that you have no choice." His gaze grew sharp, like a wolf who had cornered a wayward lamb. "It is only a matter of time before the king acts."

"There is always a choice," Elspeth answered. "I will consider all options before making mine."

The Alwyn's eyes darkened, and a look of annoyance flickered across his face. "You do that, child. We will await your answer. Here, if need be."

She shook her head. "It will not be before morning. So you may go."

Behind the Alwyn, Hugh scowled.

"Until morning then," said the Alwyn.

With that, he and Hugh turned and pushed through the curtain. Hugh looked over his shoulder at her, and for the first time their eyes met. Caught in his gaze, Elspeth felt smothered . . . unable to breathe—but then he was gone.

Elspeth turned to Conall, panic pricking her skin. "Is what he says the truth?"

"I do not know," he answered solemnly, his eyes intense.

"Is it possible that he can do what he says?" she demanded.

"Yes," he answered through clenched teeth. "It is much the same way your father came to possess the Kincaid lands. The king can give and take as he pleases."

"What am I to do?"

"I do not know."

"That answer is not good enough," she exclaimed.

She paced the length of the small chamber.

"I will send a message to your father," said Ennis. "I'll send a rider now."

Elspeth nodded. "Yes, inform him of everything. Tell him we will return home the day after tomorrow, and that no decision will be made without him."

She strode past Deargh, toward the curtain threshold.

"Elspeth, where are you going?" called Conall.

If they had no answers for her, she must arrive at them on her own.

"I need time to think. I will not marry Hugh. It must be someone else. One of the others. Someone with as much power as the Alwyn, who will compel him to retreat on his claims. I will have some sort of decision for you in the morning."

As she swept past the curtain, Deargh moved as if to accompany her.

"Deargh," called Ennis.

He stopped in his tracks, and turned around. "Yes?"

"We need a messenger. A fast rider—"

She did not wait to hear the rest, but pushed through the crush of clansmen and guests, making her way to the entry.

"Mistress, what is wrong?" said the youngest of her maids, coming after her.

"I am but tired and will retire to the tent. Stay here and enjoy your last night, all of you." She adored them, each and every one, but she could not suffer their chattering now, not when she needed to think.

Outside, the air was cold, and when she breathed, she saw her breath. Walking through darkness, she took the path between two rows of tents. The wind rippled their sides, and twisted her skirts about her legs.

Something grabbed hold of her roughly—she felt herself yanked to the side.

Shoved into a dark tent, one used as a storeroom—Elspeth could see nothing—only the indistinct shape of a man.

"You say you have choices?" a voice said. A cold, hollow voice she recognized as Hugh's. "I'll make certain you have none."

She tried to dart past him, but he seized her by the arm.

Elspeth screamed—

And in the next moment, she felt the hard strike of his palm against her cheek.

"Where is Elspeth?" Niall said, pushing through the crowd, toward Deargh.

"Gone, I think—a few moments ago."

Niall quickly counted each of her maidservants as still being present.

"With whom as her escort?" he demanded.

"I don't know," Deargh snapped. "Ennis distracted me for but a moment, asking for a messenger to be chosen to ride back to Inverhaven. When I looked back, she was gone. I assume her women went with her—" His gaze froze, fixed across the tent. "Ah damn, there they all are, every one of them."

Niall backed away. "I will go and find her, just to be certain."

He would not rest that night until he knew she was safe.

He turned toward the entrance, but Deargh caught his arm. Turning back, he peered into the man's tattooed face.

"The Alwyn was here and has a plan to force a marriage between her and Hugh. Niall, Buchan is involved somehow. He has made some sort of promise, and emboldened the Alwyn in his claim, that they might obtain, by marriage, not just Elspeth's *tocher* but all of the MacClaren lands." He dipped closer, his teeth gritted together. "Your lands, my laird. The challenge before us just got a little more complicated, and I would say with a certainty the time we have to put our plan into effect has grown much shorter."

Niall jerked his head. "I know. Magnus told me."

"Magnus?" Deargh's brows gathered in question.

"I will tell you later. For now, I must find Elspeth and settle my mind that she is safe."

Outside, he made way toward her tent, but along the way, a sound caught his ear. From inside one of the supply tents, came a man's voice muttering in a threatening tone—and a woman's muffled, but terrified cries, which he immediately recognized as Elspeth's.

His heart seized in his chest, and he knew terror such as he had never known. Pushing inside, lunging into the darkness he perceived the vague outline of a man, crouched on the ground.

Then came the sound of a fist striking flesh. The man's head flew back and he grunted in pain.

"You'll pay dearly for that," he growled, bending down again.

"No, *you* will," growled Niall, tearing him up and onto his feet and spinning him round so that for one brief moment they faced one another in the dark.

Light from the tent's open flap revealed Hugh sneering back at him.

Niall slammed a fist into his face.

"Ooof," Hugh grunted, going down hard on his back.

Rage consumed Niall—more powerful and *personal* than anything he had ever experienced on a battlefield.

Hugh pushed up, but Niall fell atop him, fists beating his face again and again until he felt a *crunch* and Hugh's body went lax beneath him.

Breathing hard, Niall stood. Hugh did not move. Was

he dead? Niall did not know. He did not care. All he cared about was Elspeth, and that Hugh would never touch her again.

Turning, he found her standing against the far wall of the tent in silence. She made not a sound. Not a sniffle or a cry.

"Elspeth?"

She did not answer. He stepped closer.

"I am here," he reached for her. "You are safe now."

But she resisted any comforting embrace, backing away, out of his reach.

"I am *not* safe," she whispered, wrapping her arms around herself. "I will never be safe again."

What had Hugh done to her? He felt half out of his mind with fear that her virtue had been taken in violence.

"Come into the light. I must know if you are all right." Again, he reached for her, but she shifted away. "Let me help you, Elspeth."

"I don't need your help."

And yet she faltered, her legs failing. He lunged, and she fell against his chest. Lifting her into his arms, he held her close.

"I'm taking you away from here."

"I don't want anyone to see me," she murmured against his neck. "Not like this. Please."

"Whatever you wish," he murmured against her temple, inhaling the sweet, familiar fragrance of her hair.

He peered outward, and finding the pathway clear, carried Elspeth the short distance to his tent, where she might be afforded a few more moments of privacy in which to recover. Outside his tent a small lantern hung on an iron hook driven down into earth, left there by the servants who traveled with them. He took his lantern, and carried her inside, behind the inner curtain screen with the intention of lowering her to his pallet. Yet when he set the lantern aside, and knelt, attempting to gently set her down, she refused to release him, her arms clenched around him.

"No," she said thickly, shaking her head.

She was terrified and he hoped he'd killed Hugh for doing this to her.

"I must know if you are hurt," he said softly.

Still holding her, he eased them both down so that they reclined against the cushions, their bodies touching and her still in his arms.

"Let me see you," he urged, coaxing her head back to rest on his shoulder.

In the lamplight he saw a bruise forming on her jaw, and another, high on the opposite cheek. Her gown, and the chemise beneath, gaped, jaggedly torn at the neck. She clasped the destroyed garment against herself, so that her breasts would not be exposed. In her doing so, he saw red marks on her wrist, and dirt on her knuckles. All his senses went numb.

"Elspeth, you must tell me, did Hugh . . ." His throat closed on words so vile he could not even speak them. "Did he—"

"No," she answered, shaking her head. "He would have but you came."

"Thank God," he uttered gutturally, seizing her close, his heart aching with relief.

She quaked in his arms and a single tear rolled down her cheek.

"Don't cry," he murmured, pressing his forehead to hers.

"Don't leave me," she whispered, her hands fisting in his tunic.

"I won't," he murmured, and before he knew it he had pressed his lips to her cheek, wanting to comfort her, to make her pain disappear.

She became still in his arms.

"Kiss me again," she said softly. "Please."

His heart beating faster, he grazed his lips against her bruised jaw.

"Again," she whispered, closing her eyes. "Niall, make me forget."

He kissed the place just under her ear, and then her mouth, gently . . . and just as always occurred when he kissed Elspeth, he was lost. She was his in that moment. Forever.

"I want to be with you, Niall," she murmured in a thick voice. "Now. Tonight. I want you to make love to me."

Chapter 19

Niall closed his eyes, and summoned every fragment of his self-control. As gently as possible, he gripped her arms and separated himself from her person. Standing, he stepped away, putting as much distance between them as possible, because he could not think clearly as long as he held her, as long as her fragrance clouded his mind.

"If only you knew how badly I want to," he said.

"Then why are you over there?" she asked, coming up onto her elbow.

He exhaled through his nose. "Because I care about you, Elspeth. I care about you so much."

She pushed up to sit. "Then why Isla?"

"Isla." He rubbed a hand through his hair, and paced the length of the tent. "She was there, and willing, and I wanted you to see. I wanted you to hate me. To leave me behind, and go on to your new life. I wanted you to forget what happened between us so that you could go away and be happy."

"I care about you too, Niall," she said. "I care about you . . . too much."

Every instinct within him commanded that he go to her. That he take her in his arms and never let go.

Yet he shook his head—and turning from her, gripped the wooden frame of the tent. "How I wish you did not."

He heard her gown rustle in the darkness, and her footsteps approach him. He braced himself for her touch, but still, he flinched when her arms came around his waist and exhaled raggedly as she rested her head against his back.

She spoke in a voice husky with tears. "All I could think while Hugh was . . . was on top of me, was that I wish I had been with you. That I had given myself to you first . . . in love."

His heart staggered heavily in his chest, hearing her speak of love.

She continued, "I feared so desperately in the moment before you arrived that he would be my first, in violence and hate, without my consent. Please, Niall, give me this night. Let me decide for myself. I want it to be you."

Her words—and the soft, womanly press of her body against his, tempted him almost beyond bearing. Not simply because he craved her body, but because he craved *her*.

He turned to her, and cupped her face in his hands.

Bending low, so that his nose almost touched hers, he hissed, "*No*."

He wanted to kiss her. To soothe away the unhappiness he saw on her face. To gather her up in his arms and carry her beyond the curtain and the shadows to his simple bed. But he could not. This was his last chance to force her away, so that she would not witness the beast he would become when he destroyed her father and her clan.

"Niall—" she whispered, pleading, looking into his eyes.

He shook his head, desperate to make her understand.

"Things between us have gone too far. My heart has grown too selfish for that," he said. "Don't you see, Elspeth,

I could *never* make love to you and then let you go. I could not step back and watch as you married another man. If I found out later that you carried my child? I would go mad knowing he or she would never be mine. Don't ask it of me, Elspeth. Let me be an honorable man."

Elspeth could not imagine a more powerful declaration of love than the words Niall had just spoken to her.

"I swear to protect you, Elspeth, and honor you," he said fervently, his gaze intense. His hands moved down to her arms, which he held tightly. "That means defending you, even from myself. Do not let this thing with Hugh, and the Alwyns make you lose hope for happiness. Your heart is good, and you deserve everything I cannot give you. You must be prepared to give your heart—your loyalty—to someone who can."

His words were a balm, soothing her fears and making her whole. The sincerity of his words and his fierce display of honor meant more to her than any touch or kiss ever could.

"You are an honorable man," she said. "The most honorable I have ever known."

He pulled her into his arms, and pressed a kiss to the top of her head. "Would that I were a *different* honorable man. Elspeth, if I could, I would make you mine."

She pressed her face into his tunic, and inhaled his scent, wishing she could stay in his arms forever.

Voices sounded outside the tent. He dropped his hands from her arms and turned, shielding her from any who might burst inside.

"Sir," called a servant softly. "I see that you have taken your lantern. Are you there, inside? We are searching for the Mistress MacClaren."

In the silent shadows, Niall lifted a hand and touched her cheek. She turned her face, pressing a kiss to the palm of his hand. Covering his hand with her own, she squeezed, then gently lowered it away, knowing from this moment she must go on alone.

"I am here," she called, going to the tent opening, and pushing it aside. "Please summon Conall and Ennis, and tell them I must speak with them posthaste."

Firstly, Elspeth saw that the still insensible Hugh was returned to his clan with a formally worded message that the Alwyn heir's unwise attack on the MacClaren's daughter had made any acceptance of his suit impossible.

She then spent the next hour in private counsel with Conall and Ennis, eliminating suitors, narrowing down the list to those who could bolster the MacClaren forces with diplomatic connections and commandable armies of their own. Considering that any candidate would have to be made aware of the rising conflict with the Alwyn clan—and the potential of challenging the king's justiciar, and thereby, the king—the list became even shorter.

Before dawn, before the other clan camps began to stir, before the first tent had been brought down, Elspeth rode out of Wyfernloch in advance of the rest of the MacClaren traveling party, accompanied only by Conall, Ennis, Deargh—and Niall—her intent that no one realize until hours later that she had gone. This would at least delay the inevitable confrontation with the Alwyn, over his rejected suit—and his beaten and humiliated son.

Unencumbered by a caravan of wagons, they covered ground quickly and arrived at Inverhaven just after nightfall.

They rode into the gates of the castle, and were welcomed at the threshold by her father, with Bridget by his side—supporting him, as he leaned against the stones. In the few days they had been gone, the MacClaren appeared to have grown weaker and frailer.

"Daughter," his eyes widened. He touched her bruised cheek, his expression stricken. "What happened to you?"

"Your face," exclaimed Bridget, appearing genuinely horrified.

"It is not as terrible as that," Elspeth assured.

"Much has happened," said Conall, solemnly.

"None of it good," added Elspeth. "You received our missive?"

"I did," he answered. "I am tormented that I was not there to speak on your behalf."

"Your daughter represented our clan well," said Ennis, looking at her in admiration. "She did not wither or retreat in the face of the Alwyn's threats, but challenged him word for word. You would have been proud."

Elspeth kissed her father's hand, and together she and Bridget helped him to his council room. Just before going inside, her eyes met Niall's above her father's head. He nodded, almost imperceptibly, providing silent encouragement, before he accompanied Deargh to the great hall.

Turning to Conall, Elspeth said, "Summon the rest of the council."

He nodded, and quit the room to arrange for summons through servants. In his absence, Elspeth recounted to her father and Bridget all that had occurred, naming the suitors who had offered for her hand, and which might be the most powerful allies among them, in light of the new threat that had been issued from the Alwyn. It was then that Conall returned, and took his place among them.

"Niall's hundred have not yet arrived. Without them, are we strong enough to repel an outright attack?" demanded the MacClaren.

Ennis's gaze narrowed. "If there is an outright war between our clans? If there is no support given to the Alwyn by the justiciar or the king, I think we are closely matched. Once Niall's force of one hundred arrives, I will feel more secure, but even that may be only a provisional solution. Can we afford to pay that many mercenaries and provision them for more than a few months? I do not know. Whatever occurs, any marriage must take place quickly, and our new power must be asserted to the utmost to show that we will not be threatened."

"Whom have you chosen, daughter?" the MacClaren asked, his eyes intent upon her. "Do not say Hugh. It will *never* be Hugh."

She walked several paces. "I will present my choice when all are gathered to hear and respond, and not before."

"Well done, Elspeth," said Bridget admiringly.

Elspeth could not help but notice that a certain peace seemed to have arisen between her father and stepmother. They even looked at each other with what she believed to be guarded affection . . . with Bridget doting on his every need, in a sincerer manner than before.

Within the hour, the council was assembled. Some stood and some sat as Elspeth took the floor at their center, with Conall and Ennis flanking her on either side. Elpeth again repeated all that had occurred at the Cearcal, and shared not only the threat made against their clan by the Alwyn, but Hugh's grievous assault on her person.

When she was done, all faces reflected outrage.

"This must not stand."

"This attack cannot go unanswered."

"We will not bow to their threats—"

"What alternative is there?"

Elspeth nodded, and spoke purposefully, in a voice of authority to men who had watched her grow up from a child.

"The three of us, last night—Conall, Ennis, and I—devised a strategy that we believe will give us the strongest foothold should this conflict indeed become reality."

"Tell us of this strategy," said her father from his chair, his eyes furious.

At a nod from Elspeth, Conall stepped forward. "We propose something very similar to what the Alwyn demanded, that this council will name Elspeth, as the chief's eldest daughter, to be his heir, his *ceann-cinnidh*—"

"We have never had a woman chief—" interrupted one council member.

"Yet it has been done," retorted another, standing from his chair. "And done well."

Ennis interjected, "Elspeth proved herself a worthy match against the Alwyn. Conall and I witnessed it. Though we were both there, prepared to intercede, there was never a need. She handled herself well and good, and put him in his rightful place, which is why Hugh felt the need to force his suit by way of rape. Thank God he was not successful."

"Think hard on this," urged Conall. "This plan keeps the interests of the MacClarens, in the heart and soul of a MacClaren. Married to the right man, she becomes as formidable as any chief."

"So you *will* marry," her father asked.

"I must," answered Elspeth. "For the purpose of elevating our clan's power and status."

Her father leveled his gaze upon her. "Of the candidates described, which have you chosen?" At his side, Bridget watched, riveted.

Elspeth glanced to Conall and Ennis. Both of them nodded, *again* reaffirming their support of her choice.

Though her heart raced, and she took a measured breath, knowing how important it was that she make her announcement calmly, and with confidence.

"I intend to marry Niall."

"*Niall*?" repeated the MacClaren, his voice like thunder.

Bridget's eyes widened with shock.

The room burst out in a jumble of questions and words.

Elspeth raised her hand. "*Be silent*. Hear my reasoning."

All grew quiet.

She walked along the circle formed by the council, looking into each of the men's eyes as she passed. "You have all observed that Niall lives by a strict code of honor. There is no warrior more impressive, or more skilled than he. At the Cearcal, he inspired awe and amazement in all who gathered to watch the competitions. In the end, he was named champion by default because they could muster no more challengers willing to fight him."

"But a mercenary? A man with no people—no loyalties. Could he ever be loyal to us?"

"No loyalties?" countered Elspeth. "That could not be further from the truth. He commands a force of more than a hundred skilled warriors who have sworn to follow him wherever he goes, and who at this very moment approach Inverhaven, awaiting his command to support us in our defense. By marriage to me, they would become our own."

All around, eyes widened, and Conall added, "He inspires loyalty even among our own MacClaren men. They look to him as a leader."

"Aye," said a council member. "I have observed this to be true."

Conall said. "Ennis and I agree with her choice." He turned to the MacClaren. "But not only that my lord. In addition to his qualities as a leader . . . Niall saved Elspeth from Hugh, before her virtue could be had. He has saved her life not one time, but three. Seeing that she is agreeable, should not her hand in marriage, and an invitation to be welcomed into this clan be his reward? His rightful prize?"

Elspeth approached her father, going on her knees before him, and taking his hand in hers.

"Niall has no home. Let *this* be his home. He has no people. Let the MacClarens be his people. He has no sworn loyalties. Let him be loyal to us . . . to *me* . . . I know he will make a good husband, father—and he would defend me and our home unto death."

He looked at her steadily, his eyes shining. "Three days ago you could not even abide his presence."

A smile spread on her lips. "I have changed my mind."

He looked out at the room, over her head. "Who so agrees, that Niall should be given my daughter's hand in marriage?"

"Aye, I agree," came the answer, all around.

"Aye."

"*Aye.*"

"Does he know he is your choice?" the MacClaren asked.

She shook her head, her heart doubling with joy inside her chest. "He does not."

To Conall, he said, "Go and get him. Bring him to me."

"Niall, please come. The MacClaren and his council wish to speak with you."

"And Deargh?"

"Nay, not yet," Conall answered, with one raised hand. "Just you."

Niall stood and turned to Deargh, scowling. In a low voice he said, "If he intends for me to deliver Elspeth to her betrothed, I will refuse."

Deargh nodded, one eyebrow going up. "I understand why you would."

When he entered the room, he was met by silence and stares.

"You summoned me," he said.

"Aye, that I did, Niall," answered the MacClaren, his

gaze intent. "There are some changes of which the council and I wished to inform you."

Changes. Yes—Elspeth would marry and soon be gone from here. Which is precisely what *must* occur. But why had they found it necessary to summon him? As a mercenary, he served his employer. Either they were going to ask him to escort her to her new husband—a task which he would soundly refuse. Or they were going to inform him they did not require his services anymore, which would not trouble him at all. He would almost prefer to separate himself from them before the final assault.

Each smile someone bestowed upon him, each kind word—had begun to feel smothering and strange.

"Go on," he said.

The MacClaren leaned forward in his chair. "You may not be aware, but I have for some time been pressed by this council to name an heir to the chieftaincy."

"I am aware."

He nodded. "After much difficult thought, with consideration to outside challenges—namely, threats made by the Alwyn . . ."

"Yes." Niall nodded.

"It has been decided that I will name Elspeth my *ceann-cinnidh*."

Niall's stomach dropped like a stone. Such a decision would keep Elspeth here, rather than take her away. Not only that, but any aggression toward her father would be an attack against Elspeth as well.

Niall looked to Elspeth.

Her gaze met his steadily.

"Furthermore," the laird continued, his voice husky. "Elspeth has chosen a husband. He is a man worthy of my support, and that of the entire council."

Niall suffered a flare of jealousy, and regret. He did not want to hear the name, although he supposed they would tell him, and he would have to pretend as if he felt nothing.

"What does that have to do with me?" he asked.

"Everything, Niall." The laird smiled. "Elspeth has chosen you."

Chapter 20

The MacClaren's words echoed like cathedral bells inside his head. His blood went hot, and his skin warmed. He exhaled through his nose.

The laird stood, holding on to the chair for support. "Will you, Niall, agree to marry Elspeth, my eldest daughter, future chief of this clan, and in doing so, swear to defend her and these MacClaren lands, even unto death?"

Silence held the room.

"As if they were my very own," he answered solemnly. "Aye, even unto death."

"Very good. You must . . . consider yourself an orphan no more, but a son of this clan. I hope you have no opposition to being married tomorrow."

He looked at Elspeth, feeling as if his soul were on fire, feeling both triumph and pain.

A wild, beautiful blush rose into her cheeks.

"None at all," he answered.

The council members thronged around him then, offering support and congratulations, which he accepted with subdued thanks, before making his way to Elspeth, who had not moved from her place beside her father's chair. She looked up at him, her eyes warm and aglow.

She would not look at him like that if she realized the grave mistake she had made. She would know soon enough, and hate him more than she hated any Alwyn. More, even, than she hated Hugh.

"Elspeth," he said, reaching out his hand, into which she placed her own, without hesitation.

Lifting her hand, he pressed a kiss to the backs of her fingers.

"Until tomorrow then," he said, his eyes burning into hers.

"Until tomorrow," she answered.

Bridget came to stand beside Elspeth. "It looks as if I have a wedding to prepare for. And *quickly*." She laughed. "At least it is not yet midnight. I must go and find the cook, who might otherwise complain at being awakened, but I know she will be more than pleased once she hears she will be preparing Elspeth's wedding day feast."

She left them, making her way to the door.

"Tell her I am sorry," Elspeth called after her.

"I will do no such thing," Bridget replied over her shoulder, turning back. "I will cut cabbages and bake bread myself, to be certain we are ready and prepared."

She disappeared into the corridor.

Conall appeared at Niall's side. "As for the two of you, I know neither of you had any sleep last night. I suggest we all get some now, myself included."

The MacClaren rested a hand on his daughter's shoulder, and looked at Niall. "Your last night in bachelor's quarters. Tomorrow you take residence here in the castle."

Again, Elspeth's cheeks flushed, and this time, everyone noticed and laughed.

Unsettled by their happiness, and knowing he would be

the one to destroy it, Niall backed away. "Good night, then."

He departed the room. Deargh waited for him in the entry hall, his expression curious.

"What has happened?" he questioned. "I heard shouting, but everyone seems very happy about something."

"Come with me," Niall answered. "I will tell you."

When they were halfway across the bailey, Deargh blasted out with a curse. Seizing a hand over his mouth, he looked over his shoulder to be certain no one had overheard.

"You're going to *marry* her?"

"I am, indeed. With the blessing of her father and the council."

"My god." Deargh clenched a fist in the air. "I know you have come to care for her, and for that reason you did everything you could to send her away, but *nothing* could be better than this."

They entered Niall's quarters, where a fire had been lit and a cold supper left for him.

He paced for a moment, before again turning to Deargh. "You must go now and see if the men have arrived in our absence. If they have, tell them they must be ready tomorrow."

"I pray they have," the warrior answered, excitement bright in his eyes.

At the door, he turned back and stared at Niall, with a strange look on his face.

"What is it?" asked Niall.

His expression grew solemn. "I know this is everything we wanted, but I also know this won't be easy for you."

Niall knew he referred to Elspeth, and his feelings for her.

"My loyalties have not been swayed," he replied calmly.

"I am a Kincaid to my soul. Tomorrow, there will be no doubt of that."

"At long last." Deargh nodded and left.

Left alone, the silence rose up around him, along with the memory of his parents' faces. His brothers. His loyalty *had not* been swayed. He remained as devoted to his cause, as he had been every moment and every day since he was a twelve-year-old boy, looking down at hands stained with his father's blood. He felt such satisfaction, knowing at last he would have his revenge against the MacClaren and return his people to their home.

But . . . *Elspeth*.

He neared the fire, and shoved his hands into his hair.

He had never felt so tormented, so eaten alive.

Stripping naked, he bathed at the basin, washing the day's travel from his body and stood by the fire, allowing his skin to dry. He thought of her . . . wishing she was here with him tonight. Wishing he could hold her close, while he slept, so that he could experience that pleasure just *one* time, before everything good between them went to hell.

As if in a dream, the door sounded behind him. Turning, he saw her standing there with her back to the door, breathing fast, her eyes shining and bright, her hair and her body concealed by a cloak.

Every muscle in his body seized with a powerful awareness. Every inch of his skin came alive. She was his every fantasy and she had chosen *him* as her husband, above all the rest. His heart thundering in his chest, he strode toward her and seized her up, lifting her off her feet. He pressed her back against the door, kissing her deeply, claiming her.

Holding her there, suspended, he guided her legs around his waist. She gasped as he kissed her neck, and her hands came up into his hair. He unfastened her cloak and it fell behind her, whispering sensually against the wood.

She wore only a thin chemise, so thin he felt her warmth against his palms, and he could see the golden luminosity of her skin beneath. In a frenzy of pleasure, he kissed her breast through the linen, and her nipple . . . and her rib cage beneath.

"Ah!" She threw her head back in ecstasy.

His body still pressed against hers, he lowered the bar behind her, securing the door. He carried her to the bed, the silken fall of her hair sweeping over his shoulders as she wrapped her arms around his neck and kissed his face. He lay her back, and moved to crouch above her.

"You should have chosen someone else," he said, in a low voice, peering down into her eyes.

"How could I?" she answered, her voice husky with emotion. Her gaze moved over his naked body. "When you are the best choice? My only choice."

His sex reacted to her perusal, jerking against his thigh.

"You'll come to believe that I am a beast," he said tightly.

She met his gaze. "I want that part of you too."

She looked at him with such light in her eyes, certainly imagining that tonight would be the first of a thousand nights together, while he experienced a gravity of heart and jagged fear that it would be the last.

But if she was going to hate him tomorrow, he'd be damned if he would deny himself the pleasure of her body tonight. He was already half out of his mind with wanting her. With needing to be inside her.

"You are not frightened?" he asked.

"Not with you."

"You're like a dream," he said, staring down.

She raised up, and pressed her mouth to the side of his jaw. "You are my dream come true."

He kissed her back, and gently worked her chemise off over her head. He had never been with a virgin. He had never made love to a woman who would be his wife. He looked on her bare skin with reverence, knowing he would forever remember this moment. Firelight painted her body with shadows and light, all curves and secret places. Her breasts mounded high atop her rib cage, their nipples tight and aroused.

The muscles of his shoulders flexed, as he caressed her skin, slowly, worshiping her body, memorizing her and bringing her pleasure. She shifted, and sighed, her gaze moving between his face and his hands as they touched her. When he lowered his head to kiss her breasts, her fingers speared through his hair, holding him tight. Mouth open, he licked and sucked her nipples until she writhed beneath him, feverishly whispering his name.

"You're beautiful," he said, slipping his hands between her legs. "The most beautiful woman I have ever seen. You're mine."

He stroked her there, boldly from the start—yet slowly and gently, eliciting a sharp gasp from her. Bending down, he kissed her deeply, with his tongue, in time with the movement of his hand. Soon, she seized handfuls of the bed linens, hips taking on the same rhythm.

"Niall," she gasped into his mouth, as he slipped one finger, then two, inside her tight, slick heat.

Glancing down, he took in the beautiful display of her passion, her legs spread wide and her arched back. The uninhibited movements she made as she shared his pleasure. With each stroke, with each cry from her mouth, his cock reacted, jerking harder and larger with arousal until need crashed through his veins.

"I will hurt you," he said, his voice sounding thick in his own ears.

"I know," she whispered, her eyes bright and her cheeks flushed and feverish.

Catching her face in his hands, staring into her beautiful

eyes, he lowered his hips between her thighs. Kissing her long and sweetly, he moved his length against her, without entering her, teasing himself—and her—into a pleasing . . . erotic rhythm, capturing her sighs into his mouth.

Reaching the limits of his control, and feeling equal urgency in her movements, he reached between their bodies and gripped himself tight. His arms taut, his shoulders bunched, he grasped her hip and pressed the crown of his cock against soft, wet heat . . . easing slowly, a few torturous . . . blissful inches, into her virgin sheath. He had never known such pleasure. All along, somehow, he had known it would be like this.

She let out a moan—one that sounded half-pleasure and half-pain—and gripped his hips.

"Yes, Niall," she murmured, her hands smoothing over his back. "Make me yours. I want to be yours."

Desire, more consuming than any he had ever known, pricked at the back of his skull. With a low groan, he eased deeper inside her, his sex growing harder and thicker, and more needful the deeper he tested her tight warmth.

Elspeth cried out, her hands seizing Niall's shoulders, widening her legs, shifting to accept his large sex deeper inside her. Yes, there was pain, but also pleasure in making love to him at last, in joining with this warrior who would be her husband.

"Should I go slower?" he murmured against her cheek.

"No," she answered, pressing a kiss to his neck, wanting this. Wanting more than anything to belong to him.

She could not stop looking at him—at his muscles as they flexed against her skin, at his handsome face tight and flushed with pleasure . . . at their bodies where they joined. She had never seen anything more beautiful than the sight of his rigid sex, in firelight, thrusting inside her. Above her, he went still in her arms.

"I want to go deeper, but I don't want to hurt you."

"I'm not afraid of the pain," she murmured. "Don't stop."

Lowering his dark head, he caught her mouth and kissed her long and sweetly, stroking her breasts and nuzzling his face against her neck until she was drunk on him. Kissing her again, he bit her lip, exhaling raggedly, and moved his hips more urgently, thrusting deeper . . . and deeper inside her.

She moved her hips, desperate to accept more of him. Her hands moved over his shoulders and into his hair, seizing handfuls, frantic, her fingertips digging . . . her nails scoring his skin. She felt so unfinished . . . so incomplete and desperate for something more—

He grasped her knee, lifting her leg . . . widening her acceptance. With a hoarse cry, his toes dug into the bed and his hands seized her buttocks. She froze against him as a sharp fissure of *pain* seared through her womb.

"Perfect," he murmured into her hair. "You're so lovely and tight. I can't stop, love. You feel so good, I have to move. Can you move with me?"

Seeking the same pleasure he felt, she moved her hips, matching her thrusts to his, and blessedly . . . amid the pain she found something else.

"Niall!"

"Yes, love."

Yet the absolute fulfilment she sought eluded her, sweet and teasing.

"Now," he urged, his hips moving faster, his hands twining with hers against the sheets. He groaned. "*Ah.* Now, yes."

Pleasure streaked through her in jolts, so intense she screamed his name, and—

The world shifted. Her body disintegrated . . . and she experienced something mysterious and celestial, and so *perfect* she wanted to exist there forever, holding Niall close, and never let him go.

"Ah—*Elspeth*," he cried, his voice deep and ragged, his head going back, his shoulders going hard and tight under her hands. His abdomen went rigid against hers. His sex throbbed powerfully, deep inside her.

He let out another sound, something close to anguish, and after a time of staring down at her, eyes dark and lips parted on his deep and gasping breaths, he slowly . . . eased away.

Falling to the side, he exhaled hard, and gathered her against his chest, so that her head rested on the solid swell of his upper arm. For a long time they lay there, limbs entwined, until at last he lifted his head and gazed down at her, his eyes a dark, unfathomable blue.

"I love you," he murmured, kissing her shoulder, her eyelids, her face. "Remember that," he said with a fierce, fervent intensity. "Remember that always."

He loved her. His declaration reverberated in her ears, warming her through.

"And I love you," she murmured against his skin, inhaling deeply of his scent. She had from that first moment, she thought, but had guarded her heart, afraid to confess the truth, even to herself. She wished she could stay here all night in his arms, until morning, but knew she must not. "You make me so happy."

He sat up, and looked across the room, away from her.

"I will not always make you happy," he answered in a quiet voice.

"And I will not always make *you* happy, I am sure," she answered, charmed by his gravity. She sensed how seriously he took the matter of their impending marriage, and loved him more because of it. "But when we do not make each other happy, we will still love each other."

He looked at her over his shoulder steadily, not speaking. She could only imagine he feared that he could not make her happy as she ought to be. That he was a mercenary, and that she could have chosen a "greater" man.

Couldn't he tell by looking in her eyes, that she not only loved but admired him? That there was no greater man than he in her estimation? Even more so now, seeing him like this. Marrying her . . . being made a leader in the MacClaren clan left him thoughtful, rather than arrogant and boastful. In her heart she knew he would be one of the greatest leaders the MacClarens had ever known.

"Stop worrying," she said, tracing her fingertips over the tattoos of his shoulder, memorizing them, wanting to know them all. Where he had gotten each one, and if they had significance.

"By marrying you, I now have much more to worry about." He bent to kiss her nose. "I have only ever worried for myself."

There was something odd in his voice. Something that sounded of self-reproach.

She peered up at him. "Are you sorry?"

"No."

She smiled. "Neither am I. And all that . . . that we did here, in your bed . . . I want to do that again. Many, many more times." She pulled him down beside her and snuggled against him. "But I must go, else someone will come looking for me. So . . . after the wedding?"

She smiled mischievously, and kissed the underside of his chin, rolling atop him, loving the feel of his muscles flexing against her naked skin, his hardness against her soft. She was surprised to feel his sex jolt hard and ready against her thigh again.

He chuckled—a bit ruefully in tone, to her ears. "We'll see how you feel about that then."

Chapter 21

The next morning, Elspeth was awakened far too early by her sisters.

"You are marrying the mercenary!" cried Mairi. "I still can't believe it."

Her eyes flew open, remembering. *Yes. She was!* She would marry Niall today. She could hardly believe it herself. Her heart swelled—almost painfully—with love and happiness.

Cat planted an elbow in her stomach.

"Today!" And then her brow wrinkled. "Do you even like him?"

"I do!" she exclaimed. She loved his big, honorable heart—and every other virile, muscular inch of him, every scar and tattoo included. Very much so.

"I am *soooooo* envious," moaned Derryth, stretching out beside her, and propping her face on her hand. "Have you kissed him?"

"Aye," Elspeth whispered in a secretive tone. "More than once."

"Bleah!" Cat shouted, wiping her lips.

Mairi, ran toward the window, pushing open the shutter. "You must look outside."

"Why?" Elspeth groaned, wanting to stay beneath the covers a few moments more.

"Just come and see," insisted Cat, following her elder sister and waving her arms.

"I'll stay here," said Derryth, throwing an arm over her eyes. "Seeing it again will just make me more envious than I already am." But her lips smiled.

Elspeth dragged the blanket with her, for the morning was cold, even with the fire Ina had arrived early to light.

She looked outside, over Cat's head. Surprise stole her breath . . . for spread across the valley, just below the castle walls, were men—some mounted, and some standing—all in precise, equally spaced rows. They continued almost as far as the eye could see, and behind them, a vast array of livestock and wagons.

"It is the mercenary's men," Mairi explained.

Elspeth blinked. There were far more than one hundred warriors. By her estimation, there had to be at least three hundred.

"There is Niall!" cried Derryth, who had come to stand at the window after all. She pointed, but Elspeth had already spied him, riding before the first row of warriors, broad-shouldered and commanding, his cloak rippling on the wind behind him. Deargh and several other men she did not recognize followed along behind.

A blush rose to her cheeks, thinking of how passionately he had made love to her the night before, and kissed her so ardently before sending her inside the castle, to sleep alone in her bed, an unmarried woman for the last time.

"It is quite an impressive sight, is it not?" A woman's voice commented from behind them. Turning, Elspeth saw Bridget at the door, with a small chest in her hand. "The MacClaren is pleased, as you can imagine."

At seeing her, the smiles on her sisters' faces faded.

Bridget stepped inside. "Young ladies, your maids are waiting to help you prepare for your sister's wedding. Hurry now, you don't want to keep them waiting."

That left Elspeth alone with their stepmother, who set the chest on the table.

"I hope you don't mind, but I told your maid I would help you prepare for your wedding."

"Of course I don't mind," she answered, secretly wishing for Ina. "I am happy for your help."

"That is very nice of you to say, when I have not always been very nice to you." She smiled, and bit her lower lip. "I want to . . . apologize to you for that."

Elspeth saw the sincerity in Bridget's manner, and it touched her deeply. "I know it was not easy for you to come here. That your marriage to my father was not a love match. That you are young, and he is old."

Bridget closed her eyes. "That is no excuse for how I treated you. For how I treated your father, and your sisters. For the way I . . . behaved with Duncan." She blushed. "I think I believed that if I acted terribly enough, your father might just send me home. However, I am not as wicked as you may suppose. Though it may be difficult to believe, after the way I have carried on with that man . . . I am still a virgin."

Elspeth's eyes widened. "That *is* a surprise."

Bridget shrugged—and made a funny face. "Perhaps I shall be one forever. Your father has been very kind, and patient, more like a father than a husband to me. More than my own father ever was. I regret very much being so cold to him. But we have grown closer, in those days when you were gone to the Cearcal. I realized then . . . I no longer want to go home. That *this* is my home. My family. I want things to be different now. I want to honor the MacClaren, and our marriage vows. I want to be a good wife to him—"

Her voice softened. "If only to give him comfort in his illness."

Tears welled in Elspeth's eyes. She rushed forward, and embraced the young woman, because she looked so alone, and in need of friendship and care.

"Thank you, Bridget."

Bridget returned her embrace, and patted her lightly on the back. Pulling back, she looked at her, her eyes damp as well.

"And while I wish I could be a good mother to you, I really don't know how." She grinned, and winced, biting her lip. "My own mother was not very tender or loving. Indeed, she was not a very nice woman at all. When she died, she was little more than a stranger to me. But perhaps you and I could grow to be something more like sisters."

"I would like that," answered Elspeth.

"I would like that too." Bridget sighed, looking happy and relieved. "Did you see, I have brought something for you?" She tilted her head toward the chest.

"What is it?"

"I thought to bring you my own wedding dress, to see if you might wish to wear it. But then I thought—there might be another dress that would mean something more."

"Another dress?" Elspeth repeated softly.

Bridget nodded. "I persuaded your father to allow me to look in your mother's things."

Emotion struck Elspeth at the center of her chest, stealing her breath. Her eyes widened, and filled with tears. "It is my mother's . . . wedding dress?"

Bridget nodded, blinking shining eyes. "Your father loved her so dearly. As he loves you. I told him it was only right that you should have it, and he agreed."

Elspeth touched a hand to her cheek. "I did not know such a dress even existed. He never said."

"Well . . . what are you waiting for?" Bridget encouraged. "Open it, and see."

"Are you ready?" asked Deargh, looking inward.

"Aye, that I am," Niall said, striding out from his quarters for what would be the last time.

"This is what you've lived your life for."

"And it feels right," he said, his heart tight in his chest.

He had dressed well, in his finest. As a highlander. He had received a small bundle this morning, delivered with his breakfast by a servant woman who he could only assume to be a Kincaid. Inside he had found his father's dagger and a small brooch—his wolf brooch, which he now wore pinned on the linen shirt underneath his plaid, beside his father's larger one. He pressed his hand against the badges and looked to the blue sky above, silently giving tribute to his family, and deceased clansmen, who because of the treachery of the man inside the castle had gone onto heaven before him. He hoped they watched over him now, and held his men safe from harm.

He crossed the bailey, proceeding toward the castle. A hundred of his men lined the path—some forty of their number being Kincaids, secretly blended among the mercenaries. As he passed the men, they fell in behind him, following him through the open doors—leaving behind a hundred of his warriors lining the parapets above—something the MacClaren had agreed to, as a safeguard show of force against a sudden retaliatory Alwyn attack in the midst of the wedding. More men crowded the bailey, and circled the walls outside.

In the great room, candles burned and fragrant herbs scented the air. The crowd grew silent at his appearance on the threshold. He passed through them, his mind filled with thoughts of the woman who he would marry. He had not only made love to her last night, but had spoken true words of love. He hoped she would remember them, in the difficult moments to come. Once married, he hoped that they could find some peaceful accord and have a meaningful life and children together. Yet now, in these moments, he hardened his heart, for he could not allow his concentration to be swayed by concern for her or fear of the shock she would suffer at learning the truth.

He stepped on the dais to stand beside the MacClaren and the priest. Deargh took his position just behind him. Looking outward, he looked into the familiar faces of Kincaids and mercenaries, mingled among the MacClaren people he had come to know. His heart beat strong and steady, even as the minstrels began to play.

Yet the moment Elspeth arrived . . . the world about him stopped.

She entered the room in the company of her sisters, who all wore bright ribbons in their hair, and carried a garland of greenery before her. Even Catrin wore a cream-colored kirtle, and looked like a girl today.

Beneath a circlet of silver, Elspeth's dark hair gleamed, long and shining, over her shoulders and back. She wore a fine, blue-gray gown that shimmered with silver thread and tiny pearls. As she passed through the hall, all eyes turned to her, but her eyes remained focused on him. She shined like a queen. She was *his* queen, and for the briefest moment . . . he forgot all but her.

As she neared, he stepped down from the dais. Extending his hand, she accepted it, and together they returned to stand before the priest, hand in hand.

The import of the moment rippled through him, a powerful wave, yet he held himself steady, listening to the words of the priest, who raised his hands to those gathered behind them.

"Doth anyone know any reason this couple should not be married?"

"Nay," answered many from the crowd—as did the MacClaren, clear and strong.

Looking at both of them, smiling, the priest then asked him and Elspeth the same question.

"Doth either of thee know of any reason why the two of you cannot or should not be joined in holy matrimony?"

His conscience balked, but his course was set. He would not turn back now.

"Nay, there is none," he answered decisively. Elspeth answered the same, and squeezed his hand. Glancing up at him, she smiled, glowing with love.

"Niall, wilt thou have this woman to thy wedded wife? Wilt thou love her . . . and honor her . . . keep and guard her . . . in health and in sickness . . . as a husband should a wife, forsaking all others on account of her, keep thee only unto her, so long as ye both shall live?"

"Aye," he answered, listening carefully to the words, to be certain he made no false vows.

He *would* love and honor and keep and guard her through all the days and trials of their life. Even if she cursed and hated him, and withheld from him the pleasure of her love and her body. He would also forsake all others . . . *except* for his murdered family and kinsmen, for which he would exact revenge against her father, just moments from now—an exceptional circumstance he felt quite certain he had agreeably worked out with the Lord on a rainy hillside, many years ago.

"I will."

More words were spoken, words he pondered and ruminated over, and accepted wholeheartedly, not the least of which when Elspeth looked up at him eyes shining and warm, and said, "And therefore I plight thee my troth."

"The rings," said the priest, presenting his open hand.

Niall removed them from a pouch secured at the belt

of his tunic—two silver rings, one large and one small, which he himself had fashioned early that morning over a fire in the distant field, with his personal blacksmith assisting. Made from one of the daggers he had carried that night, seventeen winters ago, each ring bore designs that matched several that could also be found etched onto his skin, but most importantly, the wolf's eye that identified him, and now Elspeth, as a Kincaid.

After blessing the rings, the priest returned them to their hands. He looked into Elspeth's eyes as he slid the ring onto her finger, hoping one day she could look back on this moment and feel something less than hate for him.

Side by side, they knelt and received the church's blessing.

He exhaled through his nose, steadying himself for the moment to come. Standing, turning they accepted a cheer from the crowd and the MacClaren, smiling proudly, stepped forward, holding a gleaming longsword in his hand.

His heartbeat slowed . . . the way it always did in the penultimate moment before battle. Every sensation clarified so that he heard every sound, smelled every scent, felt even the brush of the air against his skin.

"Niall, please kneel and accept the MacClaren oath of fealty."

His muscles drew tight within his limbs, and he stood ready.

Beside him, Elspeth sighed. Of course she did. She loved him, and believed that by marrying him, she had given him a family, and a home. He took no joy in hurting her. A clash of emotions swept through his veins, painful and sweet.

"Nay, MacClaren . . ." he answered, looking straight into the man's eyes. "I cannot."

The room grew hushed. Out of the corner of his eye, he saw Elspeth's shoulders go rigid.

"I will never take the MacClaren vow of fealty." He turned to the crowd, and heard Deargh's boots as he stepped closer, the hiss of steel as his sword left its scabbard. "Because this is *my* home. Not yours. I am Niall Braewick, the eldest son of the betrayed and murdered Laird Kincaid and his lady wife. By my right, as his *ceanncath*—

He heard Elspeth gasp, but turned his head and looked past her, to level a fierce glare at the MacClaren, whose face had gone stricken and pale. A number of Kincaid men pushed forward, seizing Conall and Ennis and the other members of the council. Elspeth's sisters looked at him in bewilderment and fear, and rushed to stand with Bridget behind their father, where they too were circled by Kincaids swarming the dais. The crowed moved, in sudden tumult. Voices shouted.

He continued, his voice growing louder. "—I reclaim my birthright . . . this castle and the wrongfully stolen Kincaid lands . . . as my own."

He turned back to the hall, and drew his sword—the Kincaid longsword—and held it high.

"*Tha sinn Kincaids*," he shouted, feeling the power of the words thunder through him and the blood of his ancestors course through his veins. "*Tha sinn braithrean*."

A chorus of voices joined his, powerful and clear, coming not only from the Kincaids, men and women, young and old, but the fighting men who had sworn their loyalty to him. The air echoed with the hum of swords being drawn, as they moved through the crowd, pushing forward, spreading out, subduing any who appeared as if they might intercede.

"*Tha sinn seo talamh*."

He turned toward the MacClaren—but Elspeth stepped

into his path, her eyes agleam with tears, her expression somewhere between outrage and pain.

"Niall!" she said sharply, and for a brief moment his heart faltered.

She held out shaking hands, as if she would touch him—but she did not, fisting them instead.

He shielded his heart from her tears.

He looked into her eyes. "Do you remember when I told you that you should have chosen someone else?" he asked quietly, but not without feeling, for he did feel sympathy for her in this moment. He loved her truly, and knew full well that he broke her heart. "You should have listened."

Conall shouted, "Priest, there is no marriage. It must be annulled."

"This man misrepresented himself," Ennis added to that petition. "And no consummation has taken place."

Niall paused by the priest. "There has been no misrepresentation. I identified myself plainly from the start." More quietly he said. "And the marriage was duly consummated, after we both pledged our troth."

Elspeth let out a sound of outrage.

"Is this true?" asked the priest, his face florid with fear and excitement.

With a cry, Elspeth covered her face with her hands.

The priest, nodded, backing away. "The bride confirms . . . the marriage is valid in the eyes of God."

Niall felt a moment's fleeting regret for the shame he had just brought her, but set it aside, as regrets had no place in what he was about to do.

He proceeded toward her father, who stepped backward, stumbling, weakly raising his sword.

Behind the MacClaren, Bridget cried, "*Please, no.*"

She shielded his daughters.

Niall felt Elspeth's hand seize his arm—but heard Deargh's footsteps behind him, and a scuffle as he subdued

Elspeth. She let out a strangled sob. The warrior muttered a few fierce, but calming words.

"What say you to this, MacClaren?" He extended his sword, pointing the tip at his enemy's chest. "Know that your response will determine how the rest will go."

Chapter 22

It seemed as if the MacClaren stood frozen for an eternity, but at last he spoke.

"I would ask for mercy for my family and my clan," he said in a hollow voice. "And none for myself. Slay me now if you wish. I have confessed all to God and am prepared to forfeit my life as recompense for my sins."

"What are you saying?" Conall shouted, his eyes wild. "We don't even know who this man is. He has not proven that his claim is true."

"He is son of the Kincaid," shouted several of the Kincaid men.

"True and verified, by those who served his father."

"I require no further proof," the MacClaren answered, in a voice of tremulous certainty. "I see his father in his eyes, looking back at me. I do not know how I did not see it all along."

He lowered the sword. "I . . . surrender to Niall Braewick, the true Kincaid, all that which is rightfully his—excepting my daughter's *tocher* lands where I hope he will allow my family and my clanspeople to go, in peace, as they had no part in this. It was I, and I alone, who agreed to the treachery against his father and clan."

Niall stared at him, almost too startled by the words to believe. The man all but confessed to the murder of his father. Triumph reverberated through his soul.

Conall surged forward, pushing against the arms of the warriors who held him back. "Not without the agreement of the council."

"The MacClaren's surrender is sufficient," Niall said. Given the MacClaren's outright surrender, he could not find it in himself to slay the man here on the dais, as his family watched. Niall nodded to his men. "Secure them for the night."

With that, they were led to chambers upstairs and any MacClaren clanspeople present and every servant, herded to the bailey, where they would be watched over for the night.

With rapid efficiency, planned from the moment he had stepped foot across the threshold little more than two fortnights ago, the gates were closed and the castle secured under his command. All about them, as Niall had instructed, Kincaid warriors removed MacClaren shields and weapons, tapestries, and pennants from the wall.

Elspeth, her eyes aflame and her cheeks bright, glared at him accusingly before moving in the direction her family was being taken.

"No," said Niall, his voice firm, and Elspeth froze. "She is my wife and does not go with the others. Secure the Lady Kincaid in my tower chambers. Any vacant chambers will do."

"I want to go with my family," she said, her angry eyes streaming tears.

"You will not."

Her eyes flashed brighter than before, and yanking her

arm free from Deargh's grasp, she proceeded on her own to the tower stairs, with the warrior following.

The next few hours were spent in the lord's council chamber, meeting with his chosen council, men he had selected from among the surviving Kincaid men and his own warriors. Plans for the holding of the castle and surrounding lands were further discussed. Documents were drawn, which would be sent to Edinburgh where the next Parliament and General Council would meet, asserting his rightful claim. If Niall had learned anything during his time at court, it was that the king appreciated formality, and saw documents presented for his approval as an acknowledgement of his sovereignty.

Though Niall could not guarantee his claim would be formalized, it was likely given the history of what had occurred at Inverhaven—and the growing influence of *his* allies, the king's two oldest son's—that the monarch would decline to interfere, at least for the time being and that was all Niall needed for now.

Every moment of his life, since leaving *An Caisteal Niaul,* seventeen years ago, had been in preparation for this. He had grown strong and cunning, living the life of a mercenary abroad, but in recent years he had returned to the court of Scotland for one purpose only. To watch and listen. To make allies of his own, that he might call upon to support him in a time of conflict, such as now. He had not curried favor with the king, who grew old and sick, and who of late kept mostly to his castle at Dundonald— but rather his sons. It was true—he had acted for some time as Buchan's personal guard, but he had done so at the clandestine behest of the king's eldest sons, the Earls of Carrick and Fife, so that he might report upon their younger brother's activities, as they knew his behavior grew out of hand. The secret alliance had earned him their respect and friendship, and although he had never confessed his true identity to either, he hoped the bond he'd forged with them would serve him well now.

Everything had gone better than planned. He had no regrets . . . save for Elspeth.

Elspeth stood at the window, looking out into the night. Below, Kincaids and mercenaries celebrated, while the MacClarens remained secured in the bailey. She touched the cold stones, peering down, wondering what it would feel like to throw herself to earth below. Did she not deserve to die a terrible death for falling in love with Niall Braewick? For giving him the means to soundly and terribly defeat her father and her clan?

But she pulled back, sickened by her own cowardice. She did not want to die. She wanted more than everything, for this to be a terrible dream that she could awaken from.

It couldn't be true. Her father, a murderer? And yet he had denied nothing. He who had prepared to battle the Alwyn to keep these lands, had surrendered them to the Kincaid without argument.

Where was her father? What was he thinking? Her sisters and Bridget . . . they must all be so afraid and as confused as she was over what had occurred. And the MacClaren people. Would they be forced from their homes? Would they die, attempting to defend their families?

One thing she knew to be true . . . her heart was shattered. She trembled with anger and hurt. Niall had kissed her. Seduced her. Made her believe that he loved her. Worst of all, he had married her, all for this.

She collapsed into the chair, heartsick with grief over losing him. Not him, but the man she'd believed him to be. A man she now knew had never existed.

Hours later, as night and silence fell over the castle, she heard the sound of the door. Heart racing, and legs unsteady, she stood from the chair where she had waited all that time.

He stood in silence, looking at her, a tall shadow in the darkness, his face inscrutable.

"Do you *want* to catch your death?" he demanded, his voice low and tight.

She did not answer. All the angry words and accusations that had crowded her mind in the hours that she'd sat alone in silence seemed to have abandoned her.

He strode past her, so close she felt his warmth and continued on to close the shutter she'd left open. Only then did she realize how cold the room was and that she shivered, her skin numb from the chill. He knelt, his back to her, and built a fire.

For a long time, he remained there, looking into the flames. At last, standing, he turned to her, eclipsing the light. She stepped back.

His jaw twitched. "Do you truly think I would hurt you?"

"You already have," she whispered.

And yet she hadn't stepped away because she was frightened of him. Rather, she was frightened of herself with him. Because already, after just a moment in his presence, she found herself searching his face for the Niall she had known before.

He shook his head, looking down at the floor between them.

"Ask me anything," he said, opening his palms to her. "Anything you wish."

"How could you have done this to me?" she asked in a choked voice.

He closed his eyes for a moment, before lifting his gaze to stare at her unwaveringly. "I tried to send you away. I told you that you would come to despise me."

"You were right." She did despise him. He had taken

everything from her. Her family. Her clan. Even her virtue.

"This was my home, Elspeth," he answered fiercely. "He killed my father. My mother. My brothers too, though I have not found their graves. He would have killed me as well if I had not escaped."

She shook her head, and wrapped her arms around her waist. "I can't believe it of him. My father would not do such a thing. He is not a murderer! You speak of a man I do not know."

He shifted his stance, covering his mouth with his hand for a moment before answering quietly. "I do not know if his hand held the sword, but he conspired with the Alwyn, and commanded his men in an attack and as a result, my family and many with them are dead. These lands were wrongly taken. My people displaced." He came closer, but did not touch her. "Elspeth, I speak only the truth. I have always only ever spoken the truth to you."

His blue eyes pierced into her soul, demanding that she believe and understand. But no matter what had occurred those many years ago, she could not allow herself to forget that she had been grievously used by him in the present. The man she had trusted above all others. He had taken her trust, and manipulated her and deceived her.

"But it is also the *truth*," she choked out, her voice rising in accusation, "that you seduced me, then married me, and now possess me, all as part of your revenge plot against him."

Agony stole her breath. Once she had allowed herself to love him, she had loved him powerfully, with all of her heart. Tears blurred her vision, and she turned away, covering her face with her hands, unable to look at him, not wanting him to see the depth of her pain, so powerful it silenced her voice and weakened her legs—

He was there behind her, catching her against his chest. She gasped, shocked by the power of his touch.

"Yes, that is true," he murmured, his breath warm against her cheek. "But also because from the first moment I saw you, I wanted you. *I want you*, Elspeth, *for me*, in a way that has nothing to do with any of this."

She struggled, straining to be free. *Wanting nothing more than this, his arms around her. His strength and comfort.* She shook her head, too afraid to believe that he meant the words he said. "If my father murdered yours, how can you feel anything true for me?"

"I don't know," he answered in a guttural voice, pressing his face to her hair, kissing her there. "But damn me to hell, I do."

He spoke with such passion. Her heart ached to respond in kind. But she could not be the fool she had been before. She would not allow herself to be used again.

"All lies," she answered, wrenching free, whirling to stare at him. "Our marriage is based on lies."

"That's not true." His lips thinned and his eyes flashed with temper. "I would have been within my right to slay your father for what he has done. For the life he has lived all these years, in my father's stead. And yet I did not. *Because of you*," he thundered. "Can you not see, Elspeth, that it is you who possesses me?"

Her heart reacted, and her eyes flooded with tears. "No."

He came toward her, and although she backed away he moved quickly—capturing her by the arms, easily overpowering her, imprisoning her in his embrace, yet gently, his hands on her body, his shadow all around. "Stop fighting me."

Her hands fisted in his tunic, she sagged against him and would have fallen if not for the support of his arms.

"Just let me go," she whispered, her cheek against his chest.

"Never," he said, gathering her more closely against him. Bringing his hand up beneath her chin, he tenderly lifted her gaze to his. She saw then, the dark shadows under his eyes. The tension of the moment, stricken on his face. Could it be true, that he was as tormented as she? "You are my wife, Elspeth, and I am your husband."

"I hate you for what you've done," she blurted.

"But you don't . . . hate . . . me," he answered between gritted teeth, but without arrogance. Rather, the words sounded to her ears like a gruff plea that she care for him as she had before.

When he slowly bent . . . and dared to kiss the corner of her lips, her heart expanded in her chest. She went utterly still as his mouth closed on hers, her entire being focused on him and the way she felt complete in his arms.

Feeling her resolve slip away, she closed her eyes. "I *can't* forgive you—"

"I can live with that," he murmured, tilting her back in his arms so that her head rested on his shoulder, kissing her cheek. Her forehead. Her eyelids.

Her limbs went soft and languid, as desire overtook her, silken and warm. Of their own power, her hands came up to touch his face. Her lips opened to his, and she inhaled his familiar breath, gasping from the power of the need that rose up within her.

Arms going round his neck, she let out a sound of desperation from deep in her throat. "Niall."

The line between right and wrong, loyal and disloyal blurred. She knew only need for him, too powerful and overwhelming to deny. Lifting her from the floor, he carried her into the shadows of the room, to the bed. There, as if abandoning herself to fantasy, she surrendered to the deeper darkness inside the curtains of the bed, desperate to forget the grief and sadness, and to be with him.

Her hands pulled at his tunic, lifting. With abandon, she

kissed him . . . touched . . . tasted his bare skin just as he
with his hands and mouth, worshiped hers. Desire blinded
her to all but sensation and satisfaction, and within
moments they were both naked, and he inside her, both
thrusting, the canopy filled with their moans and cries
of ecstasy.

Afterward, he held her tight, and kissed away her tears.
"You're mine forever, Elspeth. I am yours. Nothing will
ever change that."

Niall arose before dawn. After washing in darkness, he
looked down on Elspeth in the bed, her beautiful, naked
body tangled in the linens. At last, after hours of making
love in the shadows of their dark bed she had slept, but fit-
fully. She painted a poignant picture, her skin pale and
shadows under her eyes. The sight pained his heart—but
what was he to do?

He had expected yesterday to be difficult. He was not
the sort to gloat or boast over triumphs. He had known that
people would be hurt. Innocent people, caught up in a conflict between two men. He took no pleasure in that. But he
had not expected to feel so gutted by the sight of Elspeth's
tears, and knew that although they had taken comfort in
one another the night before, the coming days would not
be easy between them.

He left her sleeping, and at the door informed the guard
he was not needed further there. Elspeth was his wife,
not his prisoner. He would have her move freely, and without restriction. Downstairs, the kitchens radiated warmth,
and the scent of baked bread, baked by Kincaid women,
who had arrived sometime in the night. It pleased him to
hear laughter and lighthearted conversation in the air.
The sounds of hope and talk of the past—and the future.

Taking aside a young woman, he instructed her to go
out into the bailey and find whoever had been Elspeth's

maid, and see that her clothes and belongings were collected and installed in their marital chamber. With thoughts of her weighing heavy on his heart and mind, he did as he knew he must do. He went to the council room and commanded that the MacClaren be brought to him.

He appeared a short time later, dressed in the same garments as the night before, his expression solemn and haggard.

Niall could not look at him without thinking of Elspeth . . . his wife, laying upstairs, brokenhearted. How different this moment would be if not for her. Indeed, it was remarkable the man stood alive in front of him at all, and not lay on the cold earth, awaiting burial while wrapped in a shroud.

"What have you done with my daughter?" he asked roughly.

"She is asleep upstairs."

He frowned, morose. "I would hear a promise that you will not hurt her."

"She is my wife." Niall took a chair, and looked at the man steadily. "I will honor her as such. Sit." He indicated the chair beside him.

At first the MacClaren looked as if he would refuse, but then he sat. "I . . . imagine that you have many questions to ask me."

"Yes."

He nodded. "You know that I am ill . . ."

"Yes."

"I have often wondered if I have given myself this sickness. Inflicted it upon myself by carrying this heavy burden of guilt on my soul for so long. It eats at a man." He pressed at his torso. "Inside."

"Did you kill them? My father? My . . . mother? My brothers?"

He shook his head. "Not with my sword—" He looked

down at his hands. "But, aye. I killed them no less. With my ambition and my greed."

"What happened that night?"

"Of course, you deserve to know," he answered gravely. "Perhaps I should start before that."

Niall leaned back, crossing his arms over his chest. "Whatever you wish."

The older man looked at him steadily. "I married far better than myself when I married Elspeth's mother. My Rosemary. She is the only woman I ever loved, and I loved her . . . madly." His gaze became distant. "Do you know we met at the Cearcal?" He nodded. "We eloped from there, and in doing so nearly started a war between our clans."

Niall remained silent, listening, but not understanding why the MacClaren wanted to tell him a sentimental love story. Yet . . . the story would mean something to Elspeth, and might help him better know her, so he did not interrupt.

The MacClaren tilted his head. "Rosemary's circumstances changed, married to me. They had been much finer with her family. She never once complained, and always told me she was content, but I always wanted to give her better. So after a number of difficult years, when the Alwyn came to me talking of the king's wishes and wrongs that needed to be righted, I . . . listened. Promises were made, that I felt at that time I could not refuse. Clans were being displaced at the time, and others elevated to new status. I was determined that whatever happened was providence and that I would do whatever I could to ensure the MacClarens would emerge better from the unrest."

"And that mine should fall."

"Yes." He nodded. He held silent a long moment before continuing. "That night, we frightened a lot of people and made a lot of terrible threats. . . . but no one was supposed to die. Certainly not your family. You must know, I had the Alwyn's agreement on that. Your father's surrender, and his imprisonment, was to bring about change, and intervention from the crown that would benefit the MacClarens but I had no part in any plot to murder him."

"Then what happened?" Niall asked, breathing deeply.

"I still don't know to this day." The MacClaren shook his head. "We received your father's surrender, and he and his men emerged from the castle. . . . Then, it was as if hell unleashed an army of demons. Men came from everywhere, and killed them all. These men came down from the hills, as if they had been waiting there and . . . it was over in a matter of moments. The men were gone."

Hearing this, Niall leaned forward in his chair, a black rage filling his soul.

"Were they Alwyn's men?"

"I cannot say. He withheld all from me, but I know and I swear to you he was not surprised by their appearance. I suspect they were mercenaries, but at whose behest they acted, I do not know though the Alwyn told me they were necessary because I could not be depended on to complete the task at hand. I will tell you now, I have always suspected the men were sent by Buchan, though there is nothing I can do to prove it. Of course he was no earl then, but David the Second's nephew, and hungry for power and land. After a time of imprisonment for rebellion, along with his father and brothers, he'd sworn himself loyal to the king . . . but you know men like him. They are only ever loyal to themselves."

Buchan. Niall rested his elbows on his knees, sickened by what he heard, but knowing of the man's propensity for cruelty. "Then what?"

"Afterward, some months later, I received a royal emissary from Edinburgh who granted me possession of this castle and these lands, with words to the effect that they had been . . . *vacated* by their prior owner. This angered the Alywn greatly, because he received a lesser portion of land. He has always claimed that I was given what was due to him. Discord has grown between us ever since."

Niall closed his eyes.

"I do not ask for your forgiveness," the MacClaren said. "I would not forgive me. I mutely accepted the prize of your father's lands, because I wanted Rosemary and my children to see me as a great man. And I will have you know, I paid a terrible price for it. My wife . . . she had been childhood friends with your mother. Did you know? And though I kept the truth of what happened that night from her, I know she knew I had somehow taken part and that our clan benefited from an unjust betrayal of the Kincaids. She . . . never forgave me. After that she looked at me with different eyes. She died not long after, I suspect because she could not live with the knowledge of what I had done. So you see, I bear responsibility not only for the deaths of your family and your clanspeople, but of my one true love as well."

Niall stood, and went to the window, his mind dark with hate and questions that only the Alwyn could answer now. Outside, his men encamped along the castle walls, upon the hillside.

He was satisfied with all that had taken place in the past hours . . . but his vengeance was not yet complete.

Turning back, he looked at his wife's father. "Don't you want to know your fate? Whether I have decided to execute you, or will allow you to live?"

The MacClaren stood. "Whatever you decide, I am at peace. I only pray you will look kindly on my girls, Bridget included."

Niall summoned his council, who would be present

when his judgment was rendered. Some half hour later, a woman's voice came from outside the door.

Deargh, who was only just arriving in the company of others, called to him. "Kincaid."

Niall turned from where he stood, looking into the fire. "What is it?"

"There are women here who say they must speak to you."

It was the Kincaid clanswoman he had sent to attend to Elspeth, with another anxious-looking young woman, whom he assumed to be her MacClaren maid.

"We went to Lady Kincaid's room, and Ina here observed that a number of things were missing. She was a bit angered by it, thinking her mistress's belongings had been absconded with when the castle was overtaken yesterday. We all know how things go missing. But then we went to your chambers that you are to share with the lady, and it . . . well, it appears she has gone missing as well."

Chapter 23

Elspeth urged the palfrey into a run, and looked over her shoulder again, certain that any moment she would see Niall thundering after her on his black destrier. When she had emerged from their chamber to find no guard at watch, she had not made the immediate decision to escape. Instead, she had gone to the council chamber and overheard her father's confession.

The torment of the day before returned with smothering force. Her father was a murderer. Her husband had married her for revenge. She had been weak to forget that for even a moment last night in Niall's arms. Is that why he had kissed her? Made love to her? To silence her. To force her to choose?

She could not choose. She only knew she had to flee. To get away so she could think and decide what was right, without either of their eyes on her, making demands for loyalty and love. How much time did she have before her absence was noticed? Not long, as she had marched out of the castle as plain as day to the stables, and calmly instructed Niall's own men to saddle her horse.

Now with each gallop of the animal beneath her, she felt more desperate to get as far away as she could. Taking a less-traveled path that led around a soaring stone crag—she came face-to-face with a group of five men standing beside as many horses. She jerked the reins, startled, not knowing who they were and knowing she must avoid them at all costs.

But Magnus broke away from them, waving his arms and shouting for her to stop.

Seeing him, all her emotions broke free. In that moment, she did not care that he had tried to abduct her, and marry her, or that he had burned down her father's granary.

"Elspeth, what is wrong?"

She dismounted and ran into his arms, breaking into tears against his shoulder.

"Why are you crying?" He grasped her by the arms, his gaze moving over her. "What has happened? *Did someone hurt you*?" He exhaled, and touched her face where faint bruises still showed on her skin.

With a wave of his hand, the men drew aside, giving them privacy so they could talk.

"Who did this to you?"

She pulled her face away. "Hugh did that to me."

"*What*?" he demanded, his face flushing with anger.

"Your father did not tell you?"

"Hugh was returned to us beaten, along with your refusal to marry him. He was enraged. He still is. That is all I know."

She backed away from him. "So much has happened since then."

"Tell me what," he demanded, following her as she retreated, his eyes dark with concern. "I know that there is an army encamped outside Inverhaven."

"Yes—it is Niall's," she blurted, wiping her eyes with her sleeve.

"Niall? The mercenary?"

"He is not only a mercenary, Magnus, but the dead Kincaid's eldest son."

Magnus shook his head in disbelief, his gaze growing intense. "That cannot be. All of the Kincaid's sons are dead. They died along with him."

"Do you know anything about what happened that night? Was the Kincaid indeed a traitor?"

"I do not know. The Alwyn does not discuss it."

"Well, believe me in this, Niall Braewick did not die, Magnus, he lived, and . . . and"—tears flooded her eyes— "he says my father had a hand in murdering his father, as did yours. It is something my father did not deny." Her lip trembled. Her hands trembled. *Heaven help her she could not stop trembling.* "I don't know how to feel. But he was here existing among us, waiting to have his revenge all along. To take back his castle and his lands, but that is not all—"

"What else is there?" he said, covering his mouth with his hand, looking shocked.

"*I married him.*"

"What?" His eyes flew wide. "Before or after you knew?"

"Before! And that is not even the worst."

"I don't think I want to hear," he muttered. "But tell me."

"I love him." Again, she fell against his shoulder, burying her face. "I love him and I don't know what to do."

She felt better just confessing the burden on her heart. She felt miserable too.

He held her tight, and looked down at her. "Tell me what you want to do. I will help you."

"I don't know," she said into his tunic, and looked up through tears. "What kind of a daughter would I be to love the man who has taken everything from my father and my clan? And if my father is guilty, how can I love him still, knowing he has taken so much from my husband?"

"I don't know, Elspeth." He held her in silence for a long moment. "But I will protect you while you decide."

Hours later, as night fell, Niall still searched the lands around Inverhaven for any sign of Elspeth. After the castle had been searched, he had found Fiona—a kindly old woman he had upset terribly with his questions, but who claimed to know nothing. He had insisted to Deargh that he alone would find her and return her home, but thus far he had found no trace of her.

Elspeth had run away from him, and he had never felt more helpless . . . more *heartsick* . . . or more uncertain of what to do.

His greatest fear was that she was alone, cold and afraid, believing she had no home to return to, and that her husband was a monster. Was that not what he had revealed himself to be on the dais, in those moments after they were married? A man without compassion for others? For Elspeth's young sisters, who had no doubt been terrified, seeing him threaten and humiliate their father. For the scores of innocent MacClarens who now feared for their lives, and their homes. For a young bride with love in her eyes, who saw the man she loved become something else, dark and vengeful—the beast he had tried so desperately to hide from her.

All for revenge. Nay—all for pride. And now she was gone.

He could have claimed justice without inflicting the same terror that had been inflicted on him and his people those years ago.

Inside his chest, his heart felt crushed. He did not consider returning to the castle for even one moment. He had to find her. He had to keep searching, until he did. Lingering in the back of his mind was a terrible guilt that she had only submitted to his lovemaking the night before, out of fear that otherwise he would harm her. No, he had not forced her, but he should have given her more time. He should have waited until the conflicts between them were better resolved.

Just then he saw a rider coming toward him at a fast canter, a man unfamiliar to him. He rested his hand on the hilt of his sword, prepared to respond to any aggression if required. Yet the man continued past him—only to circle back around.

"Kincaid?" he called, grinning.

"Who is asking?"

"I bring a message from Magnus," the man said.

"What message is that?" he asked, his mood gone instantly suspicious.

"He told me to tell you, he has your wife."

The man circled again, racing off in a southwesterly direction. Niall followed him all the way to the Alwyn border, where Magnus waited on foot, leaning against a solitary tree. He dismounted, and strode toward him, exerting every ounce of self-discipline not to also reach out and seize the man by his tunic, for if Elspeth had gone to Magnus for protection he must know why, because in this moment he felt jealous and furious and betrayed. Yet he had the sanity of mind to know he had no right to feel those emotions, when it had been his actions that had compelled her to run away.

"You say you have Elspeth," he uttered. "Where is she?"

Magnus nodded. "I do have her . . . in a way."

"*What* way is that?" he demanded.

"I know where she is, which is more than you can say,

and you're her husband." He spoke in a taunting tone. "Supposedly."

Niall's eyes narrowed on him. "What do you mean, *supposedly*?"

Magnus crossed his arms over his chest, and peered upward as if in thought. "Is a marriage even valid, if one party misrepresents who they were, at the time they took the vows?"

"I never misrepresented myself," Niall countered.

"How could you *not* have misrepresented yourself?" Magnus narrowed his gaze on him. "No one knew who you were."

"No one ever asked the right questions, that's why." He tilted his head, strode close, and narrowed his eyes. He growled, "Now tell me where she is."

Magnus sauntered away a few steps before turning. "Make me understand why you want her back so badly?"

"She is my wife."

"Hmmm, yes. And she is my friend. I must know, what do you intend to do with her?" He shrugged, his manner easy. "Beat her? Throw her in your dungeon? Confine her to the tower?"

Niall retorted, "I don't know what is going on over at the Alwyn stronghold—but that is not how Kincaid men treat their wives."

"Try harder," he exhaled, feigning disappointment, and sat on a rock. "I'm still not convinced."

He lost all patience. He would not play games where Elspeth was involved.

Now he did move forward and seize Magnus up by the tunic. "She is gone, Magnus. She is gone and I love her, and without her . . . until I find her . . . *I cannot breathe*."

Magnus stared at him, then jerked away, straightening his garment.

"She loves you too," he answered quietly. "And she's afraid and miserable, and there's nothing I can do to help her. That's the only reason I'm going to tell you where she is." He extricated himself from Niall's grasp. "Well, not the *only* reason."

"What other reason is there?" Niall demanded impatiently.

"If I do you this favor, will you see that I get my horse back?"

Elspeth sat in a chair, looking into the fire. Magnus had been very kind, allowing her to stay in the cottage where his mother had, until recently, lived before marrying her new husband and moving into the village. Tucked into an earthen hillside, its thatched roof and stone chimney were barely visible to any passerby, especially now that night had fallen.

For hours, she had done nothing but think and agonize over those she loved, and how she might continue loving them all as fiercely as she had before. But all her agonizing had produced no clear answers about what to do. She could not shake the feeling of shock and disappointment, that her father had a part in taking Niall's family's lives. That he had been the one to set a young boy's life on a course of homelessness, loneliness, and rage. How, knowing this, could she love him still? Yet   she did. Certainly her father deserved punishment for what he had done. Yet each time she pondered the thought, tears fell and her heart rejected the possibility of his death.

And . . . Niall. How could she blame him for what *he* had done?

She had thought back on their every moment together, and could find no hate, no lack of care in the way he had treated her. It was true, what he'd said the night before—he'd tried to push her away, so she would marry someone else and not be forced to bear witness to her father's defeat. Why had he done that? Was it too much to believe that he loved her as she loved him? Yet how could they ever be happy together, with all the pain between them? How could she live with him each day if he exacted his revenge against her father? She could not simply stand by and accept him with open arms.

It was late, and from the sound of the gale rising outside, she feared that a storm might be upon her. She had already undressed for bed, and wore only her chemise. But best she fetch a bit more peat for the fire, to see her through until morning. Taking up a large basket, she unbarred the door and peered into the black darkness. Cold inched up her legs, creeping under her thin garment, causing her to shiver. Pulling her plaid around her shoulders, she made her way to the peat pile at the side of the house. The wind rose in a roar, and pulled at her garments, pitching them about her legs. The basket filled, she hurried back inside, and secured the door. She turned.

And gasped, seeing a tall, dark shadow beside the fire—a man whose face she could not see for the shadows. But she recognized him just the same.

"Forgive me," said a voice—Niall's, and he strode toward her. Her heart felt as if it burst inside her chest.

She dropped the basket, a moment before finding herself wrapped up in his strong embrace, so passionate and fierce she could hardly breathe.

"Forgive me," he said again softly. "Not for what I have done, but for bringing you pain."

"There is nothing to forgive," she cried, seizing him tight, afraid to believe he was truly there. That he had come for her. She meant the words, but hearing his plea opened her heart to him completely.

Now that he was there, she never wanted to let him go.

His hands came up to touch her face, and he peered down. "Listen to me, my love. Your father and I have come to terms—"

"Terms," she whispered, almost afraid to hear, almost afraid to hope.

He nodded, smiling guardedly.

"I love you, Elspeth," he said solemnly. "Without you, it all means nothing. You are my wife, and I want you beside me. For you, I will accept justice without death or vengeance. For you, I will try my utmost to forgive." His lips fell upon her cheeks, and her mouth, and her forehead, worshipful and hotly urgent, lighting a fire inside her heart. "Please, Elspeth, I beg you, just come home."

"Yes, I will," she agreed, gasping as he kissed her.

His hands caught in her plaid, pushing it from her shoulders, leaving her standing only in her shift.

"I need you," he said in a low rumbling voice, from deep in his throat. His mouth found hers again, his hands finding her waist, clenching her there, fisting in the linen. "I need you so badly. I need you *now*."

Elspeth could not even respond for the passion rising inside her, so strong and overwhelming, she could only kiss him back, and touch him *everywhere*, his shoulders, his back, his face, unshaven and so pleasingly rough against her fingertips. She pushed his plaid from his shoulders, his belt from his waist—until with a groan he wrenched his tunic up and over his shoulders, throwing it to the ground, leaving him naked before her.

His movements urgent . . . *impatient*, he seized her beneath her buttocks, lifted her, bracing her against the wall, shoving her garment high up her waist, his hips coming hard against hers as she clung to his shoulders, his arousal hard and apparent against her thigh. She moved—and his hand came between them—

"Niall!" she cried, her mind blurred with pleasure as he entered her.

His body went rigid for a moment, then he moved again, thrusting deeper, and then again.

Oh, the pleasures of a capable and muscular man. A warrior. Her beast.

He held her easily there, impaling her body against the wall, one hand supporting her, the other cupping and squeezing her breast with his calloused palm. In the golden firelight, his dark head bent, and he took her nipple into his mouth, all the while moving against her, unleashing on her an unrelenting pleasure inside her, such as she had never imagined in her wildest, most wicked dreams of him.

"I can't get deep enough inside you," he gasped and turning, carried her to the bed, each step bringing her pleasure as his sex jolted deep inside her. He lay her on the coverlet and spread her knees wide, and after thrusting several times, held her thighs at his hips, and rolled, bringing her atop him.

She moaned, sinking onto him, savoring the pleasure of being on top.

"Move, darling. Like this." His hands gripped her hips and he showed her the rhythm, which she eagerly took to, taking her pleasure, her palms planted against his chest, and in doing so giving him pleasure as well, the evidence of which she saw on his face, painted in firelight, as he looked up at her, his eyes dark with passion, his chest rising and falling, and his gasping, groaning breaths.

The bed creaked and groaned beneath them, as their urgency increased.

"Now," he urged, lifting up onto his elbows and giving a powerful thrust of his hips, lifting her, stunning her—

And hurtling her into a dazzling paradise, an explosion of pleasure intermingled with the purest sensation of love, so intense she wanted to feel it forever.

And yet it subsided . . . to be replaced by his arms, his body, wrapping around her. "Elspeth. *My love.*"

Chapter 24

"Come," Niall said, extending his hand. "Let us go out, and walk among our people."

Our people. It was the first time in the two days since they had returned together from the cottage, that he'd said the words. Elspeth's heart brimmed with happiness and pride she had not known could be possible. At last it seemed real that she and Niall were married, and they would build a life together, here in this place that they both loved.

As part of the agreement between Niall and her father, the MacClaren, Bridget and her sisters had departed earlier that morning to take residence some distance away in what had been Elspeth's home when she was a child—the castle that had been part of her *tocher*. They had taken many of their servants and warriors with them, as well as all items of importance to the MacClaren clan. However, a good number had remained, making it known they wished to swear fealty to the laird of Kincaid and to be part of a new future with him as their leader. Conall, however, never wavered in his loyalty to the MacClaren, and followed his chief.

Even so, Elspeth knew the loss of the others' allegiance had pained her father. But he was firm in his assertion that Niall was the rightful lord of Inverhaven and its surrounding lands. And so it had been a bittersweet good-bye, with many tears from Elspeth and her sisters, but not all unhappy ones as her family was not so far that she would not see them again soon, and she would, as she remained concerned for her father's health.

But hours had passed, and with them any vestige of sadness. She felt at peace. With Niall at her side, she had received the Kincaid people into the castle, and walked with many through the halls where she listened as they talked of memories. Others came bearing meaningful Kincaid relics, ancient weaponry and tapestries and carvings that had once hung in honor on the walls of the castle. Elspeth had seen that they were returned to their rightful places, and was rewarded by the gratitude and love she saw reflected in Niall's eyes. He had pulled her aside for more than a few ardent kisses.

With the falling of night, bonfires burned, and a celebration unfolded. They meandered through, talking to Kincaids and MacClarens alike, letting it be known that in the coming days, everyone would have an audience with the chief and his lady, and that all would soon be settled on a parcel of land.

It was then that Elspeth saw the face of someone surprising, in the light of a distant fire. It was Magnus.

She looked to Niall, afraid he would be angry by the presence of an Alwyn clansmen, so close to their home, especially when she knew Niall's pursuit of justice was not yet complete and there was still conflict with the Alwyn to come. But he looked steadily back at her.

"Go on, just this once. But tell him not to return. Our clans remain enemies, and I cannot have him here."

She nodded. "Yes, I understand, and I will."

She crossed the earth to stand beside Magnus and smiled at him.

"Is he angry I am here?" he asked. "Is he insisting that I go?"

"No." She moved closer, peering into his eyes. "Well, yes. But you understand, don't you?"

He nodded. "I do. But I went to the cottage and you were gone, I had to make sure you were all right."

"I am well, Magnus. He is everything to me, and I am very happy."

"Then I am happy for you."

Elspeth's heart expanded with joy and fondness at hearing his admission.

She reached to touch his arm. "Niall told me why you tried to force me to elope that night. Because you were trying to save me from a marriage to Hugh. Is that true?"

He nodded. "Buchan's ward refused to marry him, and he turned his sights on you."

"Thank you, my friend."

He smiled, and nodded toward Niall. "It appears that you saved yourself. You have a devoted beast to protect you now."

She clasped her hands together, and a different emotion rose up inside her chest. "And he will stop at nothing to learn the truth of that night. Who was responsible for the deaths of his family. You know he will come for the Alwyn, eventually. And you, if you stand with him."

"I know."

"You would be welcome here."

"I know that too." He looked at the fire. Crossing his arms over his chest, he said, "But this is not my home.

Even so, you must tell Niall that the Alwyn has sent a messenger to Edinburgh, formally challenging his claim on these lands."

"On what basis?" she demanded, drawing her plaid around her shoulders against a sudden gust of wind.

He glanced sideways at her. "On the basis he is an imposter, and not the true son of the Kincaid."

Her heart flared with anger. "But he *is* the true son of the Kincaid."

Magnus shook his head, and stood, straightening. "I know you believe that, but the Alwyn has a powerful ally and unless there is a way to prove his identity beyond a shadow of a doubt . . ."

"Niall has his own allies, Magnus," she said, feeling the heat of anger rise in her cheeks, hating the danger that even now threatened her and Niall's happiness. "And there *is* proof of his birth."

"What proof?" he demanded quietly. "Truly, I wish to know. I need to know, so I know what to believe."

Had she said too much? She drew back, turning from him. "I can't tell you," she answered softly. "It's a secret, and I have promised not to tell."

She would never betray Niall's trust, and part of that meant protecting his secrets. He wanted so desperately to find his brothers. To know they were alive. If there was any hope of that, she must do all she could to help him.

"Then by all means," Magnus replied sardonically. "I won't beg you to tell."

But if there was a way, through Magnus, to make the Alwyn back down . . .

She took several steps toward him. "He bears a secret mark, known only by those few who survive from his father's council. He, himself, did not even know the importance of the mark until they told him. More than that, I cannot say."

Magnus's brows gathered. "What sort of mark?"

"A very distinctive tattoo," she answered in a confidential tone. "But I won't tell you where and you mustn't tell anyone what I've said. If you are my friend, Magnus, you'll promise that you won't."

He blinked slowly, and swallowed hard.

"Where is this tattoo?" he asked in a low voice.

"I already told you, I won't tell you where," she retorted. "To do so would be disloyal to my husband. It's a secret that only a few Kincaid men know, and would swear to, that identifies the ancient line of the Kincaid."

His shoulders straightened, and he searched the darkness, as if for Niall. "Take me to him."

His voice was strange . . . intense.

"Why?" she asked

"I'll only tell you both."

She led him over the stony earth, to a smaller fire a distance away, where Niall sat with the Kincaid council, three old men who elbowed each other and smiled when she came near. Only for their smiles to fall away when they realized it was an Alwyn who accompanied her.

Her husband stood, looking sternly at Magnus.

"Niall," she announced. "Magnus wishes to speak to you."

"Yes?" he asked, his eyebrow going up dismissively.

"I would speak to you alone," Magnus said, glancing at the men sitting there. "You and Elspeth."

Niall set off across the grass, but did not go far, only a brief span of paces. Magnus and Elspeth followed.

"This is far enough," said Niall.

"Whatever," snapped Magnus. "Have them all hear, if you wish."

He covered his mouth with his hand, and looking at Niall warily, he said, "Elspeth says you bear a distinctive tattoo, identifying you as a son of the Kincaid."

Niall glanced darkly at Elspeth. Instantly, she was filled with enormous guilt. Why had she even mentioned it?

"I did not describe it," she said defensively, lifting a hand. "I would not do that."

"You must tell me what it looks like," Magnus demanded.

"I will not," answered Niall sharply, his eyes flashing a warning.

Magnus closed the distance between them, and the two men stood looking eye to eye.

"It's very important. I need to know."

Elspeth looked at Magnus in confusion.

"I can't imagine why," Niall answered, looking angry now—so angry Elspeth feared he would tell Magnus he had to leave, and that they would part as enemies.

"Curse you, Kincaid." Magnus tore at his own tunic sleeve, wrenching the loose linen high to reveal his muscular arm. Lifting his elbow over his head, he stepped closer. "Does the damned thing look anything like this?"

Niall stared at his arm, his eyes widening.

"Good god," her husband uttered hoarsely, lifting a hand to his mouth, his eyes shining.

"Oh, Niall." Elspeth whispered, her heart pounding. "Magnus?"

At a distance, the Kincaid men rose to their feet.

Hours later, Niall pulled Elspeth into their chambers, which were dark save for the fire. Stopping there, at the door, he kissed her before leaving her to go to the window, where he pushed open the shutter and looked out on the night landscape of his lands.

Elspeth joined him there, wrapping her arms around his waist.

"My *brother*," Niall said, holding her, his voice hushed. "I still can't believe it. Magnus . . . *Faelan*, is alive."

So many questions remained unanswered, such as how Faelan came to be living among the Alwyns, and known as their laird's bastard son. They were answers even Faelan did not know.

"I'm so happy for you," Elspeth whispered. "And him. My friend, all these years. What a wonderful shock."

"Indeed."

Though their reunion had been a happy and emotional one, Faelan had been understandably shocked and had insisted on secrecy for now. He had left Inverhaven in the night, just as he had come. But he and Niall would soon meet again, as brothers, to decide what must be done.

"If he is alive, then perhaps Cullen is as well," she said, looking up at him.

He kissed her head, and stroked her hair. "I fear it is almost too much to hope for."

"But hope, we must," she answered, going up on her toes to kiss him.

He bent, and the smile left his face. He drew his thumb along the underside of her jaw.

"There is something I want to give to you," he said. He took something that had been tucked into his belt. Holding her hand in his, he closed something hard and smooth inside her palm.

Opening her hand, she saw that she held a Kincaid badge. A smaller version of the one he wore. The wolf's emerald eye glimmered in the night.

"It is the badge I wore as a boy. I want you to wear it, if you will."

"Of course I will," she said, smiling.

"Even though you are a MacClaren," he teased.

"Nay, Niall," she answered. "I am a Kincaid."

He helped her fasten the brooch to the bodice of her gown, his touch slow and lingering, transforming into a caress against the upper swell of her breast . . . her throat . . . her cheek. Going up on her toes, she kissed his jaw.

"I love you," he said, his hand touching her hair. "More than myself. Because of you . . . everything seems possible. I still don't know what will happen. What our future will bring. But for now, this is all that matters. This life we are beginning together, you and me, and our people. Our daughters and sons. I will do everything within my power to protect and defend it."

"As will I." Bringing her hand up beneath his, she pressed a kiss to his palm. "I love you, Niall."

He let out a low growl of pleasure, and bent to kiss her. She sensed the arousal growing up between them, and as proof, he urged her gently . . . seductively . . . backward toward the bed.

"I can't get enough of you," he murmured huskily. Catching her waist, he kissed her lips, more urgently. "I will never have enough of you."

"Nor I of you," she answered, her body and soul responding. "Take me to bed, husband."

She gasped as he lifted her off the ground and carried her the rest of the way. There, in deeper shadows, he kissed her gently . . . sweetly, and she sighed, feeling blissful and utterly complete.

"I love all of your kisses," she murmured, her eyes aglow with love.

"All of them, you say?" he teased, pressing her back against the pillows.

"Every . . . single . . . one." She pulled him close and kissing his face, pressed her lips near his ear and whispered. "But truth be told, I like it best when you kiss me like a beast."

Read on for an excerpt from

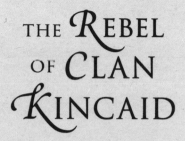

THE REBEL
OF CLAN
KINCAID

Coming soon from St. Martin's Paperbacks

prologue

Magnus stared back into the face of the man, who until this moment he had considered to be the most arrogant, most self-important, son-of-a-sow he had ever had the misfortune to encounter.

His scalp tightened and the night around him seemed to convulse as he tried to make sense of the words he had just heard.

"Did you hear what I said?" said Niall Braewick stepping closer, his features blackened by shadows, the bonfire blazing behind him. "That mark on your arm proves you are not the Alwyn's bastard, as you have been led for all these years to believe . . . but that like me you are the son of the murdered Laird Kincaid."

Magnus' pulse ramped again, hearing the words repeated.

He lifted a hand to the back of his neck . . . to his mouth . . . and shifted stance, rendered unsteady by the tangled snarl of emotions blasting up from his soul.

The Laird Kincaid. A legendary Highlander who years before had voiced opposition to the crown—and afterward died violently, under the most mysterious of circumstances, along with his wife, his warriors . . .

And his three young sons.

He had heard the ghost stories. The songs the bards sang. All were dead. Slain. Buried in some secret haunted grove in the forest known only to those Kincaids who had survived the slaughter that fateful night, and who afterward had taken to the hills beyond Inverhaven, living life like savages rather than submit to another clan or laird.

Lairds such as his father—*not his father?*—the Alwyn, and their neighbor, the MacClaren. Men to whom the Crown had granted the "forfeited" Kincaid lands in the aftermath of the massacre.

And yet the Kincaids had come down from those hills. All around him, in the present, the "savages" celebrated their victory against the defeated MacClaren, in the orange glow of the bonfire and the shadow of Inverhaven's castle walls, which in a day, they had shockingly reclaimed, with the backing of Niall's mercenary army.

And they promised vengeance against the Alwyn next.

"We are not enemies, you and I." Niall—now installed at Inverhaven as the laird of Kincaid—grasped his shoulders, hard. "*You are my brother.*"

Magnus's childhood friend, Elspeth MacClaren, who only two days before had been tricked into marrying the Kincaid and who now claimed to love the warrior with all of her heart, moved to stand at her husband's side, her eyes wide.

"The mark on Magnus' arm matches yours?" she asked in hushed amazement.

The secret mark, a wolf's head located on the underside of his arm, tucked high under his shoulder, seemed to burn on Magnus's skin. He stood rigid and silent, almost wishing he could take the moment that he had revealed it back. He had only come to see if Elspeth was safe and well after her father's defeat. Instead, in a blink, the world had turned upside down.

Him, a son of the Kincaid?

A birthmark, his mother . . . or the woman who had called herself his mother for all these years, a one-time mistress of the Alwyn, had whispered. *A devil's mark* that he must never show to anyone.

But later, when he was older, he'd known that wasn't true.

He'd realized that the mark etched on his skin—the one he could barely see himself for its peculiar location—had been placed there not by the Devil, or even by God, but by man.

Others moved close, their faces wavering in the light of the bonfire. Old men, young men. All Kincaids, all enemies of his clan.

Not his clan? Not . . . his enemies?

"The secret mark!" exclaimed a one-eyed old man, his bushy gray eyebrows going up in amazement.

"Is it true?" demanded another, pressing close, shoulder to shoulder with others doing the same.

Magnus broke free of the Kincaid's hold and stepped back, turning away from the smothering weight of their collective curiosity and expectations, away from the light of the fire and into deeper shadows where they would not see the bewilderment on his face.

"Aye, it is true," Niall said behind him, nodding. "Look for yourselves. He is one of three sons—the second son, if I judge correctly. His name is *not* Magnus." He spat the name, as if it were an offense. "But Faelan. Faelan, my brother. Do you remember nothing of our childhood?"

Faelan . . . it was an ancient Irish name, meaning little wolf. A saint's name.

My little wolf, the man in his dreams had said with warmth and affection. A man whose face he could never recall upon awakening, but whose spirit even in waking times seemed to reside in his soul.

"None of this makes sense," Magnus uttered beneath his breath.

All of it made sense.

He rubbed his palm between his eyes because suddenly he *hurt* there from thinking so hard, from trying to understand how his life, just like that, could fall away and be replaced by another.

A life. A family. A proud ancient legacy.

Having lived all his life, as he could recall it, as the unrecognized and unwelcome bastard son of the Alwyn, should he not feel satisfaction? A sense of belonging, at long last?

But he did not.

Because it was a *lost* life. An *unknown* family and clan. An ancient legacy lost to violence, treachery and blood. His family, taken from him. A lifetime of memories, stolen.

A gentle hand touched his shoulder, and he flinched.

Elspeth said, "Magnus . . . Faelan? Oh, I don't know what to call you! I can only imagine how you must feel."

He turned, looking down into her pale face, before looking beyond and higher, directly to her husband, who remained fixed to the same spot, arms crossed over his chest, his mouth tight, looking at him guardedly, perhaps even with suspicion, as if he did not understand his response or lack thereof.

"I have questions," Magnus answered, in a guttural growl. "And I would ask that you give me time, so that I might have answers."

Elspeth nodded, her eyes soft with sympathy. "But it makes sense, don't you see? You must have suffered some injury that night or soon after, and that is why you remained mute for all that time, for years after, not speaking. That is why you don't remember."

Yes, that. There had always been missing time. Missing memories. A blurry, indistinct blot at the center of his existence. A blot that even now remained.

"I do remember . . . some things," he murmured.

Drums beating. Fear. The flash of swords. And blood. For years his "mother" told him they weren't memories at all, just nightmares that lingered in his mind. Nightmares that he must forget.

"The memories never made sense before," he said. "Now they do."

The Kincaid, his . . . *brother*—approached, his blue eyes vibrant with emotion.

"Then stay and join me against the Alwyn. He bears responsibility for the deaths of our parents and our clansmen. Our father was no traitor, and 'twas no honorable battle in which he and the others died. The MacClaren confessed his part, and in doing so, confessed the Alwyn's as well. It was murder, plain and clear, inspired by greed to take our clan's land and power."

Eyes wide with sadness, Elspeth whispered, "It is true."

The Kincaid clenched his fist between them. "There were others also, warriors with unseen faces and unknown loyalties, who came down that night from the hills— belonging neither to the MacClaren nor the Alwyn—who carried out the massacre. We must learn their identities." His tone became more urgent. "Faelan, the Alwyn knows who they are."

It was too much. The thoughts crowding his mind. He needed time to think, to be alone, and decide what to do.

One hand staving through his hair, he backed away, muttering, "I must go. I . . . I will . . . return when I can."

His boots crunched upon the path, as he stalked away from them, delving further into darkness.

"That's it?" the Kincaid called after him, his voice

hollow with dismay and accusation. "You're just going to leave?"

Magnus stopped, and looked down at the earth. At the stones and dirt and grass beneath his leather boot. Kincaid land.

His land. *His legacy.*

Turning, he found them all gathered in a line, shoulder to shoulder, looking at him.

He took several steps toward them, until he was close enough to look into his brother's eyes.

"I don't know you." Looking aside, his gaze swept across the faces of the others. "I don't know any of you. You are strangers to me—and I'm angry about that."

Anger. Yes. That was what he felt. He wanted to rage. He wanted to punch a stone wall. He wanted to bellow until he was hoarse from it.

"Then stay," said the Kincaid, stepping forward out of the line. "Take your place here."

"Yes, stay," Elspeth pleaded.

He shook his head and exhaled through his nose, commanding self-control as a fury such as he had never known reverberated through his veins.

"A brother. A mother and father. A clan." He lifted his hands, as the fire in his soul burned hotter. "It is all I ever wanted."

He paused, and clenched his hands into fists.

"But it was stolen from me." His heart thundered in his chest. "I have been *grievously* deceived. Because of that deceit, all these years I have lived at that lecher's feet, a cast off. His bastard. His second best." He again met Niall's gaze, and slowly nodded. "Aye, there is revenge to be had against the Alwyn, brother—but know this. It is I who will take it."

Chapter 1

"Awaken, child," said a woman's voice, low with urgency. The dim light of a lantern washed over the stone walls of Tara Iverach's small chamber. "Your guardian sends word that he travels near and wishes an audience."

Tara pushed up on the narrow bed. The drab blanket fell away, exposing her skin to the chill. She shivered and seized the wool back against her neck and shoulders. Sister Agnes' words echoed in her ears.

Her guardian . . . Alexander Stewart, the powerful earl of Buchan . . . *here*, in this humble place?

To see her?

"You must be mistaken," she said, her voice thick with sleep.

She had never even met him. He had shown no interest in her in the five years since her parents' deaths, when he had become responsible for her and her older sister, Arabel. Almost immediately he had summoned Arabel to be presented at court, while she had been delivered to Duncroft Priory where she had remained ever since, with only a rare letter from Arabel—once, perhaps twice a year—to remind her she had not been completely forgotten.

"I wish that I were mistaken," Sister Agnes replied with a peevish lift of her brows. "I would much rather be sleeping than tending to you. Now hurry. You must be ready before sixth hour prayers."

So it was true.

Tara's heart jumped, beating faster. What did Buchan's visit mean? Would she be taken away from Duncroft? Would her life change somehow, from this day on?

Sister Agnes took hold of her braid. Deftly unfastening it, she combed out Tara's hair with quick, brusque strokes.

Tara gasped, wincing, and rubbing at her temple.

Others entered then, two sleepy-eyed sisters carrying a small hip tub and servants with steaming buckets of water. Oh . . . a *real* bath—a rare luxury here. Most certainly she would be rushed through, and not allowed to enjoy it.

That much proved true. In less than an hour, she stood in the chapel along with the other inhabitants of the priory reciting prayers, her skin scrubbed pink and her hair tightly braided into circlets on either side of her head—but covered, as it was *always* covered with a veil. She dutifully murmured the words, but her thoughts wandered elsewhere.

Might this be the last time she stood here? The last time she would wear this shapeless gray gown? It was almost too much to hope for. After years of the cloister's quiet, uneventful existence, she had come to believe she would be confined here forevermore, forgotten by all, her life unlived—her heart never having loved.

Not that the other women who resided at the priory served an unimportant or unfulfilled purpose. They had chosen to devote themselves to the Lord, striving each day to center their thoughts and energies on Him.

Well, *most* of them had chosen to be here. Some were

here, not precisely by choice. There was Lady Mary, a lively and intriguing gentlewoman who had been deposited here around the same time as Tara, but by a husband who claimed she was mad in order to repudiate her so that he could marry her prettier and much younger cousin.

Lady Mary was not the only "mad" wife at Duncroft Priory. Indeed, there was a row of rooms, just beside Tara's, each one occupied by a raving lunatic who never raved, never lunaticked. Scattered among them were a few accused adulteresses.

Some of the sequestered ladies seemed completely content to exist in the peace and quiet, away from the turmoil that had committed them here. Indeed, some only left their chambers for prayers.

Others ached to return to at least some aspects of the life they had left behind—as did Tara. She remembered happy scenes of life as it had been when her parents were alive. Now, no longer a child, she wanted to attend festivals and tournaments, as her sister described in her letters. She wanted to gossip with friends, and dance and laugh, and be introduced to—and flirt—with young men, the sort of creature she'd not caught a single glimpse of in her five long years here. Her chest tightened with wistful hope.

She wanted to *live*.

And now Buchan was coming, which gave her hope. Perhaps now that she was twenty, he would present her at court, as he had Arabel, and she and her sister could spend their days together in happy coexistence, as they had when they were younger. Maybe not every day, because Arabel would be married soon, if she was not already, as the last letter she'd written several months before had shared the news the earl had betrothed her to the eldest son of a powerful ally.

Just as the prayers came to an end, from behind Tara there came a sudden, excited whispering of female voices.

Glancing over her shoulder, she saw two dark haired, angular-jawed young men in the doorway wearing fine leather hauberks belted with silver studded scabbards. They peered inside, their cheeks ruddy, their hair ruffled as if from travel, smiling arrogantly, at least to her unpracticed eye, though she could not claim to be an expert on male expressions. Several of the younger ladies from the Mad and Adulterous Wives corridor smiled back at them.

An older man with a close trimmed dark beard and imperious bearing joined them, shouldering between them, his features drawn with impatience. All three men had similar prominent noses and dark eyes that identified them as kin to one another. Tara's pulse tripped. It had to be Buchan. She had imagined someone older, and gray haired.

"Where is my ward?" he demanded testily, causing her heartbeat to ramp higher. "Come now, my time is important. Please don't waste it."

Sister Agnes approached him quickly, nodding and extended an arm toward Tara. "Mistress Iverach, this way."

Tara moved quickly as well, not wishing to be barked at for tarrying overlong. All along her way, the ladies stood back, watching the moment unfold. As she drew near, three pairs of male eyes latched onto her. It had been years since she had drawn the attention of anyone besides that of her fellow ladies. Her cheeks betrayed her self-consciousness, filling with heat.

Her gaze met the earl's for the briefest moment—and they struck her through with their intensity.

"My lord," she murmured, bowing her head and curtsying as her mother had taught her to do so many years before, arms slightly extended.

"Mistress Iverach," he said in a low voice. "How . . . lovely you are."

"This way," said Sister Agnes.

Tara held back, waiting for the men to follow, but they only stared at her in darkly amused silence.

The earl gestured that she should go before them. "I insist."

She lowered her gaze and followed Sister Agnes. The heavy fall of their boots sounded on the stones close behind her and she felt their stares on her back. Perhaps it was only her lack of familiarity with men, but there was something distinctly unnerving about the earl and his sons. Though handsome and clearly schooled in all manner of noble manners, they cast an intimidating . . . *predatory* energy that put her on her guard.

Once inside the room, in which a large table had been laid out with an extensive breakfast, Sister Agnes remained near the door, silent and watching, while Tara moved toward the hearth, turning to face her visitors. The earl approached her, all elegance and good graces.

He smiled. "Most certainly by now you have surmised that I am Buchan, your guardian. These are my sons . . . Duncan Stewart, my eldest—" He gestured to one, with a wider face and a lock of hair that fell across his forehead, who nodded solemnly—and then to the other, who boldly held her gaze like a sharp eyed, overconfident wolf. "And that is Robert."

Tara acknowledged each with a nod.

"And you, Mistress Iverach . . . you are . . . a child no more, a woman full grown." The earl moved closer to her, so close she could feel the heat of his body through the leather he wore. Lifting a hand, he pulled the veil from her hair, and grasped her by the shoulders.

She tensed, every fragment of her body going aware at the strength in his touch.

His eyebrows rose as he stared at her hair, which was tightly braided and fastened demurely in coils at her nape.

"How very . . . uncommon," he breathed, nostrils flaring. "The shade . . . so unlike your sister's."

It was often remarked upon that she and Arabel looked nothing alike, but that wasn't true. Their features were very similar. It was only that her hair was red, while her sister's was brown. Red hair was common enough, but she had been told more than once by one sister or another that her particular shade—

The earl's voice grew husky. "Hair like that puts wicked thoughts into a man's mind."

The sisters had expressed similarly mortifying opinions.

Tara's cheeks flamed, and she wanted nothing more than to tear her veil from his hands and return it to her head. Instead, she held still, chin raised as the earl's gaze raked over her with more interest than she felt proper, given that he was her guardian, and last she knew, a married man.

His gaze shifted over her shoulder, to Sister Agnes. "Could you . . . leave us alone, please? So that we might speak privately?"

Tara rarely prayed outside of morning, midday and evening prayers, but she prayed now, and fervently.

Sister Agnes responded, "Forgive me, but I cannot. It is not convent practice to leave a young lady alone with any man who is not her father or her husband."

Tara held in her sigh of relief.

A sour expression flickered across the earl's face.

"I am her guardian," he answered in an imperious tone.

"*Not* . . . her father or her husband," said the nun, with all composure.

He squinted his eyes, and scowled. "Must I remind you of the generous support I provide to the sisters of this abbey?"

The hair along the back of Tara's neck rose in alarm that

he continued to insist. She did not know why, precisely, but she knew she did not wish to be left alone with him and his wolfish sons. Had her sister felt the same instinctive caution?

"No, my lord," Sister Agnes replied, her expression unchanged. "You need not."

The earl smirked. "Then—"

Sister Agnes stood straight, her slender hands clasped at the waist of her nun's habit. Her eyes gleamed with challenge. "As I said, it is *not* . . . convent practice . . . to leave a young lady alone . . . with any man who is not her father or her husband."

Buchan rolled his eyes and let out a condescending *huff*. Duncan chuckled, amused, and strode to the table, where he poured himself a goblet of ale, and lowered himself, sprawling, into a chair. Robert joined him, sliding a goblet for his brother to fill. Behind them, the window shutters rattled, harried by a strong gust of autumn wind.

Releasing Tara, the earl brusquely returned her veil, dismissively thrusting the crumpled mass into her hands. In the next moment he pronounced, "I have come to see you because it is time that you are wed."

"Wed," she repeated softly.

The ground shifted beneath her feet—or very well seemed to. Did he speak generally or had an agreement already been made? She had hoped to be presented at court and to enjoy life away from the abbey and its restrictions for a time, not be married straightaway—

But she realized that she could not make demands of the earl. Her father, for whatever reason, had left her and her sister's futures in this man's hands. To question him, or argue against his decisions would show disrespect to her father's memory. At least that was what Arabel had written to her when Tara had complained of being left at the abbey overly long.

"Yes, sire." She nodded, even as her heart sank in her chest.

One corner of his lips turned upward, offering half a smile. Lifting a hand, he grazed a knuckle down her cheek.

"Good, obedient child."

Turning toward the fire, he extended his hands and rubbed them together, warming them.

"A beneficial betrothal has already been arranged," he said, speaking toward the mantel. Her heart constricted, at having her answer. "You will be conveyed to your new home posthaste, and married to the son of the Laird Alwyn."

The Laird Alwyn.

Her heart filled with sudden brightness at hearing that familiar name—one mentioned in her sister's last letter, as the name of her own betrothed.

"To a younger son of the Laird Alwyn?" She nodded happily. "And so my sister will be there as well, with her husband, the Alwyn's elder son?"

"No," he answered abruptly.

He moved toward the table where his sons devoured their meal like ravenous wolves. He perused the repast that had been laid out.

"No?" she questioned softly.

Glancing at her over his shoulder, he shook his head, looking distracted. More interested in the food now than her. He took up Duncan's goblet and drank from it, and reached toward a platter. "It is you who will be fortunate enough to marry the eldest son. His name is . . . Howard or—" He waved a hand. "—Hugh." He pointed a finger and nodded. "Yes, that is it. Hugh."

Hugh. It was the name of her *sister's* betrothed. Her chest went tight.

Tara drew closer. "Was not Arabel to have married Hugh?"

Buchan turned to her, a capon leg held in his hand.

"She can't very well do that now, can she?" he said quietly.

The earl took a bite, and chewed slowly, his lips shining with juices, as his gaze hardened . . . and narrowed on her. Tara's heart skipped a beat, stumbling over some unknown warning, some instinctive fear.

"I don't understand what you are saying," she whispered.

His sons paused, glancing at their father, and at each other.

The earl swallowed, and his eyes grew dark as a crow's. "What I'm saying is that your sister is dead. And that you will take her place."